"Karen E. Olson has lau[...] *The Missing Ink*, featuri[...] is proud that she make[...] grown women laugh. I look forward to more adventures for this Las Vegas needle artist."

—Elaine Viets, author of *Killer Cuts*

Praise for Karen E. Olson's Annie Seymour Mysteries

Shot Girl

"Olson excels at plotting—with liberal doses of humor— and Annie grows more fascinating, and more human, with each novel. This one's a winner from page one."

—*Richmond Times-Dispatch*

"Even though the case looks to be fairly straightforward, it turns out Annie isn't quite as forthcoming as some readers might like her to be. So we get multiple investigations of what really happened and how much Annie can be trusted. It makes for greater depth to add that frisson of doubt and allows Olson to step up to a new storytelling level."

—*The Baltimore Sun*

"Olson continues a winning streak with her latest Annie Seymour outing.... This first-rate mystery will not only keep you guessing, it will provide fun and laughter along the way."

—*Romantic Times* (4 stars)

"[*Shot Girl*] features the same clever plotting, great local color, and terrific personal touches that have been a hall-mark of the series since it began."

—*Connecticut Post*

Dead of the Day

"Karen E. Olson knows this beat like the back of her hand. I really enjoyed *Dead of the Day*."

—Michael Connelly

continued ...

"Humor enlivens this first-person account. . . . This remains a series with considerable potential." —*Booklist*

"Olson's characters are her own, and her fast-paced plot and great ending make it a perfect read for patrons who like a bit of humor in their mysteries." —*Library Journal*

"Olson knows exactly how to blend an appealing heroine, an intricate plot, and inventive humor. Annie's is a story worth pursuing and a story well worth reading."
—*Richmond Times-Dispatch*

"Humor, plenty of motives, and strong character development make this a fast, fun read." —*Monsters and Critics*

"Olson's second mystery hits the mark with setting, plot, and character. . . . Her lovably imperfect heroine charms, and the antics of her coworkers and the residents of 'da neighborhood' will keep you intrigued and amused."
—*Romantic Times* (4 stars)

Sacred Cows

"A sharply written and beautifully plotted story."
—*Chicago Tribune*

"Olson writes with a light touch that is the perfect complement for this charming mystery." —*Chicago Sun-Times*

"In this just-the-facts-ma'am journalism procedural, Karen E. Olson plunges readers into the salty-tongued world of cynical reporter sleuth Annie Seymour. . . . [The story] spins from sinister to slapstick and back in the breadth of a page. Engaging."
—Denise Hamilton, bestselling author of *Savage Garden*

"A boilermaker of a first novel. . . . Olson writes with great good humor, but *Sacred Cows* is also a roughhouse tale. Her appealing and intrepid protagonist and well-constructed plot make this book one of the best debut novels of the year." —*The Cleveland Plain Dealer*

Also by Karen E. Olson

Sacred Cows
Secondhand Smoke
Dead of the Day
Shot Girl

The Missing Ink

A TATTOO SHOP MYSTERY

Karen E. Olson

AN OBSIDIAN MYSTERY

OBSIDIAN
Published by New American Library, a division of
Penguin Group (USA) Inc., 375 Hudson Street,
New York, New York 10014, USA
Penguin Group (Canada), 90 Eglinton Avenue East, Suite 700, Toronto,
Ontario M4P 2Y3, Canada (a division of Pearson Penguin Canada Inc.)
Penguin Books Ltd., 80 Strand, London WC2R 0RL, England
Penguin Ireland, 25 St. Stephen's Green, Dublin 2,
Ireland (a division of Penguin Books Ltd.)
Penguin Group (Australia), 250 Camberwell Road, Camberwell, Victoria 3124,
Australia (a division of Pearson Australia Group Pty. Ltd.)
Penguin Books India Pvt. Ltd., 11 Community Centre, Panchsheel Park,
New Delhi - 110 017, India
Penguin Group (NZ), 67 Apollo Drive, Rosedale, North Shore 0632,
New Zealand (a division of Pearson New Zealand Ltd.)
Penguin Books (South Africa) (Pty.) Ltd., 24 Sturdee Avenue,
Rosebank, Johannesburg 2196, South Africa

Penguin Books Ltd., Registered Offices:
80 Strand, London WC2R 0RL, England

First published by Obsidian, an imprint of New American Library,
a division of Penguin Group (USA) Inc.

First Printing, July 2009
10 9 8 7 6 5 4 3 2 1

To Ernest and Edith Hoffman

ACKNOWLEDGMENTS

The author wishes to thank Alison Gaylin, Clair Lamb, Louise Ure, Jeff Shelby, Lori Armstrong, Eleanor Kohlsaat, Cheryl Violante, and Carissa Violante for their help in the early stages of the manuscript; Mary Stella and Chris Hoffman for coming up with the title; Julio Rodriguez at Hope Gallery; Sharon and Joe at Cheesecake and Crime in Henderson, Nevada; Lee Lofland for his police expertise; Rita and Chris Kompst for myriad e-mails with information about Las Vegas; and Bonnie and Jonathan Rothburg and Robbin Seipold for their generosity. Agent Jack Scovil again offered his sage advice and humor. Editor Kristen Weber planted the idea, and her support and enthusiasm were, as usual, inspiring and validating. The book *Bodies of Subversion: A Secret History of Women and Tattoo* by Margot Mifflin was invaluable. And finally, the author is indebted to Chris and Julia Hoffman for their patience and support during the writing process, and she didn't even have to twist their arms when she said, "Hey, let's go to Vegas."

Chapter 1

I've made grown men cry.

It's not a crime.

I wasn't sure exactly what the cop was doing, hovering outside the shop. Was he expecting a robbery? Was he just giving us a little free security?

I pulled the door open and stepped outside.

"Can I help you, Officer?" I politely asked his profile. I knew how to talk to cops: Keep it cordial, no sudden moves.

He was studying the frosted letters on the window, his hands on his hips. He didn't look ready to grab the gun or the nightstick that flanked his stocky frame. He turned his head slowly, his mouth set in a grim line, eyes narrowed as they settled on my face.

It unsettled me. Usually people stared at the ink on my left arm—a detailed replica of Monet's water lily garden, complete with a weeping willow and footbridge—or the dragon that creeps up over my right breast under my tank top.

"You work here?" he finally asked, his voice as deep as I'd expected.

"I'm the owner. Brett Kavanaugh."

A twitch in his left cheek told me he didn't expect that, even though the name of the shop is The Painted Lady and he'd obviously known that, since he'd been staring at the letters long enough. Or maybe he recognized my last name.

"What can I do for you?" I asked again, when he didn't say anything.

"I'm looking for a girl."

I chuckled. "This is Vegas; a lot of guys are looking for girls. But this is a tattoo shop, not a brothel."

He didn't even crack a smile.

Okay, so the name of the shop might not have been a great idea, and occasionally we did get calls asking for girls. But this was the first time a cop had come around.

I folded my arms across my chest. "You can't stay outside my shop. We've got clients. It's not exactly good for business." I had another thought. "Unless, of course, you want to come in?"

He ignored my question, reached over, and pulled a photograph out of his breast pocket. He held it up so I could see it.

"Recognize her?"

I stepped closer to see it better.

"Why are you looking for her?" I asked.

The cop, whose nameplate dubbed him Willis, shook his head. "Do you recognize her?"

"Is she dead?"

"No."

That narrowed it down.

"What's up with her, then?"

Willis took a deep breath, obviously irritated. I didn't much care. I was curious; I had a half hour until my next client, so I had some time to kill.

"You haven't seen her?" It was a new tack for him, and he made the transition smoothly.

"Are you checking at every shop?"

"Yes."

At least we weren't being discriminated against. I wondered how long it took him to go into Shooz. Those stiletto heels could be even more intimidating than my tats.

The Venetian Grand Canal Shoppes are what da Vinci would've designed if he were a capitalist. Besides Shooz—my favorite store—there was Ann Taylor, Ca'd'Oro, Kenneth Cole, Gandini, and Davidoff, among others.

Then there's The Painted Lady.

At first, I figured some palms got greased for the shop to get this location. It's sandwiched between Barneys New York and Jack Gallery. But I found out that Flip Armstrong, the guy I bought the business from, apparently had tattooed a prominent city politician's name in a very private place on a local hooker. It's amazing what a little blackmail will do for you.

The only prerequisite was that we had to look respectable. No street-shop flash in the windows. No sign advertising tattoos. Anyone walking by would think we were an art gallery; through the glass windows, passersby could see the long mahogany table that served as our front desk, a spray of orchids perched on its edge. Paintings hung on the cream-colored walls on either side that hid the four private rooms behind them. The blond laminate flooring was sleek, sophisticated. What the public couldn't see was the staff room behind the second room on the right, and the small waiting area with a long black leather sofa and glass coffee table covered with tat magazines behind the room on the left. A large, vertical, comic-book version of one of Degas's ballerinas adorned the back wall.

"Got a big job ahead of you. You working alone?" I wasn't answering Willis's questions, and his irritation was growing.

"Just yes or no: Did you see her or not?"

I shrugged. I may know how to talk to cops, but I also knew not to say anything that might incriminate me—or anyone else.

He shoved the picture back in his pocket and brushed past me in long strides, his face flushed red. Another uniformed cop was coming out of Godiva across the way—maybe he needed a chocolate-covered strawberry to get him through the rest of his canvass—but I turned my attention back to Willis when I heard a shout. He'd collided with a family of four as he crossed the footbridge over the canal that ran past St. Mark's Square. A gondola sailed under the bridge, the gondolier never missing a stroke.

I could never be fooled into thinking this was really Venice, but the tourists liked to believe the illusion.

Las Vegas is one big illusion.

I went back into the shop, thinking about that picture. It hadn't fooled me, either.

There was no mistaking it: That girl had been in the shop two days ago. She had wanted a devotion tattoo.

Chapter 2

Bitsy was getting on my nerves. She was dragging her stool around the staff room as if it were a puppy on a leash, and the scraping against the floor echoed through the shop like fingernails on a blackboard.

"Do you *have* to do that?" I asked, wishing the sound of my machine would drown it out, but it was merely a soft whine butting up against a cyclone.

She poked her head into the room where I was trying to finish up the portrait of Jesus on a guy's back, her face level with mine, even though I was sitting. Bitsy is a little person. The stool is her way of compensating. I was ready to compensate her just to get rid of the thing.

"I will pretend that you did not ask me that," she said, tossing her blond curls back over her shoulder.

We were both a little on edge.

The guy draped over the chair in front of me ignored us. He'd been here before, actually a couple of times. A portrait of his daughter was on his upper arm, and his mother, who'd died the year before, was on his chest. Jesus was new to the party. It was his version of the Holy Trinity, and I was enabling him by permanently embedding it in ink on his body.

If Sister Mary Eucharista at Our Lady of Perpetual

Mercy School could see me now, she'd rap my hands five times with a ruler.

"Are you going to tell Tim?" Bitsy asked.

"Tell him what?"

"About the girl. What else?" Bitsy and Willis would tie in an irritation contest. I might come in a close second.

"I'll tell him when I get home."

"You could've told that cop about Tim."

Bitsy didn't get it. If I'd told Willis that Detective Tim Kavanaugh was my brother, it would seem like I was going over his head. Which was what I planned to do. However, he didn't have to know that. We'd already established a tense relationship.

Anyway, he may have put two and two together when he'd heard my last name. How many Kavanaughs were there in Vegas anyway? That plus the fact that Tim and I were relative carbon copies of each other would've been even more of a clue. And clues were his business.

Bitsy and I had been over and over the girl's visit the other night. She'd seemed a little skittish, but we'd chalked that up to it being her first time. She didn't even get the ink. She just made an appointment and then never showed.

"You're sure it was her in the picture?" Bitsy asked for the umpteenth time.

"Yes." I felt like a broken record. It was a recent picture—I could tell that even though it was a photocopy. She was in her late twenties, the long dark hair pulled into a fashionably tousled knot, a pair of big, black Jackie O sunglasses outlined in rhinestones on top of her head, her face white and narrow with brilliant blue eyes that indicated colored contact lenses. I couldn't tell what she wore for the snapshot, but when she showed up here, she was wearing a thin white lace baby-doll top with spaghetti straps, a black bra peeking through, and skinny jeans with strappy red sandals. At first glance, she could have been one of those rich girls partying in Vegas for the weekend—or a working girl. It was hard to tell, since the wardrobes were similar these days.

She said her name was Kelly Masters. She said the concierge at the Bellagio had recommended us.

She said she wanted to surprise her fiancé on their wedding night. So much for the working-girl theory. The diamond on her hand could've been listed as one of the wonders of the world, the way it flashed like a strobe across the walls when the light hit it.

From the small bag over her shoulder, Kelly took a rather rudimentary drawing of a heart with what I supposed were two hands clasped underneath it.

"I want his name—Matthew—too," she said.

I'm not big on devotion tats. Relationships might start out great, but statistics were against most people. And relationships that had any foothold in Vegas were dubious, in my opinion. What happens in Vegas may stay here, but tattoos didn't have that option. They went home with you.

That said, a client is a client, and as David St. Hubbins of *Spinal Tap* noted, it's a fine line between stupid and clever.

I was used to straddling that line myself, so I cut her a break.

We made an appointment for the next day. I told her I'd make a proper sketch, she could take a look, and I could make changes, if she wanted.

Then she left.

I carried out my part of the bargain—my sketch was much more elaborate than the simple one she'd handed me—but Bitsy doubted she'd come back. We'd even bet on it. My wallet was a hundred dollars lighter. They don't say Vegas is for suckers for nothing.

"Wonder where she is," Bitsy said thoughtfully.

"Maybe she and Matthew had a fight," I suggested. I gave Jesus' nose a little more shadow before lifting my foot off the pedal. The machine stopped whirring, and I assessed the Son of God before me.

Not bad, if I did say so myself.

"Cops don't come looking for you unless something awful's happened," Bitsy said.

"You're done," I told the young man, handing him a small mirror so he could take a look at himself in the full-length one on the staff room door. As he went to see my handiwork, I shook my head at Bitsy. "He said she wasn't dead."

"He could've been lying."

I mulled that over for a second. Willis didn't seem like the type to lie. Then again, I didn't know him well.

The young man came back and handed me the mirror. "It's *awesome*," he said.

Sister Mary Eucharista felt the same way, although she had her own descriptive adjectives.

I covered the ink with Saran Wrap, taping it down and going through the laundry list of how to take care of the tattoo. The skin was the color of bubble gum right now, but after it healed and peeled like sunburn, it would begin to look like his other tats. Not that he'd notice much, since it was on his back.

He paid Bitsy at the front table, the cash and credit card machine discreetly hidden in a drawer, and I went into the staff room. Joel and Ace had gone home at ten o'clock. It was eleven now, and Bitsy and I were going to call it a day. I could hear Bitsy's stool sliding across the floor in the room I'd just vacated. She'd already taken care of the books for the day—usually my job, as boss, but she was capable and knew I'd be toast after hours with Jesus—and she was trashing the disposable needles, leftover ink, ink cups, and gloves. The needle bar would be put in the autoclave for sterilization.

I started sketching a design for the next day on the light table. Bitsy had turned off the sound system, and it was too quiet. I grabbed the remote for the small TV set in the corner.

I should've called Tim to tell him about Kelly right away, after Willis left.

Because her face was plastered across the screen on the local news.

But the anchor didn't call her Kelly Masters.

Apparently, her real name was Elise Lyon.

Chapter 3

Tim waited until after he got off the phone with his people at the police department before interrogating me. "You didn't think to call?"

I knew Tim would be upset. We were standing in the kitchen; I still had my messenger bag over my shoulder, but Tim had been home for a while and was wearing a pair of sweats and a T-shirt touting the Mets.

"I got busy. I spent four hours on this Jesus tat. There wasn't time to call. I figured I'd tell you when I got home."

It was a lame excuse. I'd had twenty minutes before the kid showed, and I spent the time gossiping about Kelly Masters with everyone in the shop.

"I didn't know why the cops were looking for her," I said when he didn't say anything. The TV reporter hadn't said much either, except that anyone who'd seen her should call the police. "That cop didn't tell me anything. Just wanted to know if I recognized her. I'm not clairvoyant."

I was babbling over my guilt. I knew something was amiss the minute he showed me the picture. It didn't matter how much I tried to talk myself out of it, with Bitsy or with Tim. Kelly, or Elise, was in trouble, and Bitsy and I *had* seen her. But being a tattooist is sort of like being a psychiatrist. Some people come to us discreetly, and they expect discretion in return. I had to tread that line carefully.

Tim reached into the fridge, grabbed the milk, and poured himself a glass. He was drawing this out.

"So what's her story?" I tried to sound nonchalant, shrugging the bag over my head and slinging it on one of the chairs at the table.

"Nothing you need to worry about, as long as you're telling me everything." He took a long drink, leaving a milk mustache. He didn't wipe it away.

"I am."

"We'll need to talk to Bitsy, too."

"Of course." Bitsy was already anticipating that. She'd come up with more possibilities as we locked up the shop: rape, domestic violence, maybe Kelly was a terrorist. A little extreme, but I had to admit it might not be out of the realm of possibility. Especially since Tim was being just as closemouthed about it as Willis had been. I thought I'd have been a shoo-in to find out the whole story once I got home. Should've known better.

Tim and I had been living together for two years now. He'd left our childhood home in northern New Jersey and moved to Vegas ten years ago, getting a job as a blackjack dealer. A year of that was enough, and he ended up at the police academy, training to be a cop like our father. It's in the DNA.

He bought the house in Henderson three years ago, when he and his ex-girlfriend, Shawna, had toyed with the idea of getting married. Well, he'd been toying with the idea, but she was dead serious. After a year, when she finally realized there was no diamond in her future, she moved out and he was stuck with the mortgage, so he got on the phone, trying to convince me that living in the desert would be heaven compared to scraping ice off my windshield in Jersey.

No kidding.

He also had a friend, Flip, who was selling his business. I had some money saved up, and Mickey said it was time for me to move on. I'd worked at the Ink Spot for eight years, starting as a trainee right out of college. Mickey taught me everything he could, and I was getting too comfortable. I needed a challenge. Buying Flip's shop seemed like a plan.

So here I was, a woman who owned her own business, and I was about to start whining like a kid on the playground because my brother wouldn't share information with me.

Contradictions are what make people interesting.

"Can't you give me a little hint? Did she do something? Is she hiding? Is she like that crazy runaway bride?" The moment I said it, I wondered if that was it. She'd been wearing that huge rock, she wanted devotion ink, but she never came back. Trouble in paradise.

From the flush that crawled up Tim's neck, I knew I was right. He could be as stoic as the next cop among his own and with real criminals, but with his sister, he caved every time.

I grinned. "That's it, isn't it? She was supposed to get married, but she took off. Couldn't handle it or something, right?"

Tim put his glass in the sink and wiped his mouth with the back of his hand, which he then wiped on his sweats. "You can think what you like," he said. "I'm going to bed. I have to get up early." He brushed past me, his eyes on the floor.

He paused before turning toward his room. "Oh, Willis asked a lot of questions about you."

Willis? "That cop?" I asked. "You're kidding, right?"

Tim chuckled. "He couldn't understand why you would do what you do."

"Did you enlighten him?"

"Not my place."

I thought a second. "I never mentioned that you were my brother."

"Brett, you're almost as tall as I am, you've got red hair like me, and our faces look almost exactly the same except I shave and you don't have my freckles. When he heard your last name, he put it together. Good night." He disappeared into his bedroom.

Willis wasn't the first to express curiosity about my career choice. My mother still grabbed for the smelling salts when someone put the word "tattoo" in front of "artist" to describe me.

Granted, I'd started out as a painter, but I liked to eat, earn money. Tattoos were profitable. Profitable enough to buy a business.

People should just mind their own business.

I rummaged through the fridge and found some leftover fried rice and a small bottle of Pellegrino. Taking them over to the long brown leather couch in the living room, I picked up the remote and turned on the fifty-two-inch flat-screen TV that hung on the far wall—Tim had done some serious electronics shopping after Shawna left; besides the TV, a surround-sound audio system had been wired throughout the house. I dropped a few grains of rice on the leather and wiped them up with my finger before starting to channel surf.

I couldn't decide what I wanted to watch, so I ended up on CNN. The volume was low, so I wouldn't bother Tim, and Lou Dobbs was going on about illegal immigration for the umpteenth time. It was white noise while I ate.

I was about to bring my empty dish to the sink when the top news stories of the day flashed on the screen.

One of them caught my eye.

Missing woman traced to Las Vegas.

I put my plate back on the coffee table and turned the sound up as the two anchors began their reports. I had to wait until after a story about a tornado somewhere in Arkansas and another about the housing crisis.

Finally: "A woman reported missing three days ago by her fiancé was spotted in a Las Vegas casino. Elise Lyon of Philadelphia had an airline ticket to Los Angeles on Tuesday, but she never boarded the plane. Her car was found in long-term parking at Dulles International Airport in Washington, D.C."

Somehow she'd gotten to Las Vegas, and if she flew any sort of commercial airline it was likely she used the same name she'd given me—Kelly Masters—rather than her own; otherwise they would've tracked her down by now.

It was hard these days to get through airport security, however. They checked photo IDs against boarding passes. I wondered about fake IDs. With technology available today to anyone, it wouldn't be hard to produce something passable.

Or maybe she chartered a flight. Or took the train. Or a bus. Scratch that. The chartered flight, maybe, but totally not a bus. She didn't have that look about her.

Tim's call to the department about her name obviously wasn't on the media's radar yet.

"The wedding is scheduled for tomorrow in Philadelphia at her parents' estate, but it looks as if the bride will leave the groom at the altar."

That was harsh. I felt for Matthew—I could only be on a first-name basis with him, because that was all I knew of him.

"Elise Lyon's parents are not speaking to the media, but we have her future father-in-law, developer Bruce Manning, via satellite."

Bruce Manning? Wow. Now that was a household name. He made Donald Trump look like a bag person. Manning owned properties all over the country, and he'd just opened a swanky new resort and casino on the Strip. He called it Versailles, and having been to the real one, I could vouch for how authentic it looked. It was that Vegas illusion again.

"What do you think happened to your future daughter-in-law, Mr. Manning?"

"We just want to make sure she's safe." Manning's bright white hair was perfectly coiffed, his tie perfectly knotted. He looked directly at the camera as he spoke, his words measured and firm.

I leaned forward in my seat as if I'd miss something if I didn't.

"My son has been devastated by Elise's disappearance. None of us believes she would leave of her own accord."

"Do you believe foul play is involved?"

"You have to talk to the police about that."

"But you believe she was taken to Las Vegas against her will?"

This was better than the soaps. Although my encounter with Kelly, or Elise, or whatever she was calling herself today, didn't indicate she was someone who'd been kidnapped. She'd been a little nervous, but no one else was hovering around. She was alone. And if someone had kidnapped her, why would she be allowed to go to a tattoo parlor for devotion ink? She'd said it was a surprise for her fiancé.

Maybe she just took a quick trip here before the wedding to unwind, get the tat, go home, and get hitched. She could easily turn up tomorrow in Philadelphia in her white dress and pearls.

I wondered why her parents weren't going public. Did they think that having Bruce Manning on the air would be enough to generate interest and, thus, lead police to their daughter? And what about the groom? Where was he?

I'd been so engrossed in my own thoughts that I didn't hear the rest of the interview with Bruce Manning. But I was paying attention when the two anchors grimly discussed the report afterward:

"Bruce Manning has just opened Versailles, the newest, most extravagant Las Vegas resort. His son, Bruce Manning Jr., who goes by the nickname Chip, is dividing his time between his father's New York City development offices and the new resort. He and Elise Lyon have planned to move into a penthouse in one of his father's buildings on the Upper West Side in Manhattan after their wedding. We can only hope Elise Lyon is found safe. Anyone with any information about her should contact the local police department immediately."

I saw right through the picture of Kelly/Elise as it popped up on the screen. My brain was a few sentences back.

Kelly/Elise had wanted her devotion tat to say "Matthew."

Her fiancé's name was Chip, or Bruce.

Who was Matthew?

Chapter 4

Tim was gone when I got up, but the note I'd left him saying Kelly wanted her ink to say "Matthew" was no longer on the kitchen table. As I fired up the engine in my Mustang Bullitt—I've got a thing for Steve McQueen; what woman doesn't?—I was a little resentful that I was doing his job for him and he still wouldn't tell me anything.

I was getting obsessed with Kelly/Elise. It was the most interesting thing that had happened for a while.

I slipped on my sunglasses and pulled out of the driveway.

Henderson to the Strip isn't too far, just a straight shot on 215. But there's traffic. Always traffic. Vegas has grown even in the short time I've been here, and between the residential population and the tourists and gas prices, well, it made me start thinking seriously about public transportation. The only thing I didn't like was that I worked until midnight most nights, and taking a bus that late meant dealing with a lot more than just greenhouse gases.

Anyway, if I took the bus, I wouldn't be able to crank Springsteen, who was singing about the Badlands.

I wasn't putting the top down today, though. The desert in June is like an oven, and don't get me started on that "it's a dry heat" crap. Heat is heat, whether it's wet or dry. The sun is searing, and even after only three years, the red tile roof on our house had faded to a pale pink.

In the distance, the mountains beckoned me. A hike at Red Rock Canyon, just outside the city and a world away, would balance my chi, but with the temperature hovering above a hundred, I'd risk more than just a bad mood. I didn't much believe in Chinese hocus-pocus—the sisters had instilled a lifetime of the fear of God in me—but I knew when I was feeling a little off.

I had a cheap pass for the Henderson outdoor competition pool—that was my summer exercise. It didn't have the same powers as Red Rock, but gliding through the water, the rhythmic breathing, the emptying of my mind as I counted each stroke, each lap, centered me in a different way. Sometimes Tim came with me, arriving at the pool at six a.m., and we'd swim side by side. We've been mistaken for synchronized swimmers because we look so much alike. We were both on our high school team, but he's five years older.

As I approached, I saw the Strip's lights were off, the glitz diminished by the glare of the sun. The magic just wasn't there in the daytime. From a distance, it looked like a kid had dropped a bunch of toys in one spot and hadn't bothered to straighten them out: a castle, the Statue of Liberty, a golden lion, the Eiffel Tower, an Egyptian pyramid, a Space Needle. A playground for adults, where no one can really win, but the illusion puts blinders on.

Instead of driving up Las Vegas Boulevard, I veered off onto Koval Lane, which runs parallel and behind the MGM, Flamingo, Paris, and the Venetian. Strip traffic isn't so bad in the mornings, but the lights are too long and I get too frustrated.

While prices in Vegas have gone up—impossible to get that $2.99 breakfast buffet, unless you're far off the Strip— parking can still be free. I turned left into the Venetian's driveway and then right into the self-parking garage. I drove up to the sixth level and eased the Mustang into a spot. I slung my black messenger bag over my shoulder, adjusting it so the strap crossed over my chest. I wore my usual tank top—fuchsia, today—and a billowy cotton hippie skirt with an Indian print. My Tevas kept me from towering too tall, but I still topped out at five-nine.

Getting out of the car, I felt like I'd stepped into the center of a volcano; the heat was trapped in the garage, and it closed in around me. I hightailed it to the elevator, hitting the button too many times, like that would make the doors open faster. Once it got to the third level, where the Venetian Grand Canal Shoppes were, I went back out into the heat and looped around up to the walkway. The automatic doors slid open, the cold, air-conditioned breeze washing over me. I sighed with relief.

Springsteen warbled "Born to Run" in my bag. I reached in for my cell phone.

You can take the girl out of Jersey, but you can't take Jersey out of the girl.

The caller ID said, *Restricted*. I flipped the cover, asked a tentative, "Hello?"

"Brett?"

It was Tim. "Yeah?"

"Couple of quick questions. When Elise Lyon came into your shop, what was she wearing?"

I described her outfit. "Why do you need to know that?"

He ignored me. "Did she seem frightened?"

He'd asked me that last night. "No." My voice echoed through the phone. "Hey, am I on speaker?"

A woman brushed past me, glaring at the phone in my ear. I made a face at her and leaned against the wall.

"Was she with anyone?"

"I told you, she was alone. She didn't seem afraid, except maybe a little nervous about the idea of a tat."

"How nervous?"

"As nervous as someone who's never gotten one before." I paused. "It hurts. And it's permanent. People know that coming in."

"But she still wanted to go through with it?"

"We might never know, will we?" Immediately I was sorry I'd been so flip, but sometimes I speak without thinking.

"I'll probably be over there in an hour or so to talk to Bitsy. See if she noticed anything else."

"She'll be at the shop all day," I said. "Anytime."

"Okay, see you in a bit." He ended the call.

I closed the phone and stared at it a second. Maybe Bitsy and I *were* the last ones to speak to Kelly/Elise.

A quick stop at the kiosk for a bottle of water, and I contemplated the two paths I could take to my shop.

The right one went past Kenneth Cole, so I took that one, stopping to check out a great pair of black patent-leather pumps with peep toes rimmed in red. I'd been eyeing them for days now. I could see myself in those shoes, already had an outfit picked out in my head.

As I was daydreaming, I suddenly had the feeling I was being watched. I didn't turn around, but tried to see in the reflection in the store window if anyone was behind me. It was still early; the mall crowd was sparse.

I spotted him a few yards away, across the canal, the light hitting him just right so I could see him clearly.

He was taller than me—I put him at about six-four—and well built. The tattoos that bled down his face and under his T-shirt and onto his arms might have been considered uncomfortably excessive by someone not in the business. They didn't bother me.

What bothered me was the way he was staring at me.

He saw me staring back. He raised his hand, making the sign of a gun with his thumb and forefinger. With a small *pop* movement of his lips, he moved his hand to make it look as though he shot at me.

And then he nodded and walked away.

Chapter 5

For a few seconds I was frozen as if my feet had grown roots, my Tevas clutching the mall floor so tightly I couldn't let go.

He walked into St. Mark's Square, along the other side of the canal.

I noticed little things, like how he was wearing a jean jacket with the sleeves cut off, a Harley logo on the back. His legs were slightly bowed, and he had an exaggerated cowboy saunter. He wasn't in a hurry; his stride was slow, methodical. Like he was giving me a chance to come after him.

But truth be told, I didn't really want to.

I waited until he passed the footbridge before I finally took my first step, gradually speeding up and power walking in the same direction he'd gone. By now, however, I was too far behind and I'd lost sight of him as he turned the corner.

Joel Sloane, one of my tattooists, was coming toward me. He was carrying a big soft pretzel and a coffee. Breakfast of champions.

I waved, a frantic, *I'm a little crazy* kind of wave. I was still creeped out, even though the guy had disappeared.

Joel saw me, grinned, and stopped, raising the pretzel in a greeting.

The woman walking behind Joel crashed into him. Not

difficult, since Joel weighs about three hundred pounds and could stop a freight train, and the woman probably weighed ninety pounds wet.

I was close enough now to hear the woman telling Joel how rude he was, how could he just stop in the middle of a walkway? Joel's face was red with embarrassment as he apologized profusely. When I reached him, I touched his arm in support, and he nodded at me.

The woman must have been in her sixties, according to the skin on her neck, chest, and hands, but her face was smooth as silk. Either exceptional Botox or a fantastic face-lift. Maybe both. Her hands clutched several shopping bags, and she flipped her hair back over her shoulder as she stared at my arm, taking in the whole garden scene, her expression showing disgust. She looked from me to Joel, noticing now the Betty Boop intertwined with a black-and-red geometric design on his left arm, the skeleton and hatchet prominent in the sleeve on his right, and the barbed-wire tat around his neck.

"Be more careful next time," she said to Joel, flouncing past.

Joel chuckled. "She needs to loosen up," he said when she was out of earshot.

"Maybe we should give her some tats on the house," I suggested. "Hey, did you notice that big guy with all the ink? He was across the canal." The canal wasn't that wide; it was a mini-illusion. How else would it fit in a mall?

Joel frowned. "Yeah, I saw him."

"Look familiar?"

"It's not my work, but that eagle that wrapped around his neck was pretty cool."

Now that he mentioned it, my memory flashed on it. It *was* cool, but that didn't mean the overall package wasn't creepy.

Joel started walking toward the shop, and I fell into step beside him. "So, who is he?" he asked.

"I don't know. But he was watching me, and it was uncomfortable."

Joel immediately looked concerned. "In what way?"

I told him about how he aimed his finger at me and pretended to shoot.

His concern deepened. "I can call a couple of people and see if they know who he is. It was enough ink so someone should be able to identify him just on a description."

Joel knew everyone in the tattoo business in Las Vegas.

"That would be great. I don't want to run into him again." Major understatement.

Joel started to breathe a little more heavily. All that weight was a chore to carry around.

"Pretzel for breakfast?" I asked.

Joel took a bite. "I'm going to start Weight Watchers next week."

I nodded, like he really would this time, instead of going out after a couple hours and sneaking some Häagen-Dazs or gelato or Godiva chocolate on his break. It wasn't my place to say anything.

"That woman was pretty rude," I said to change the subject.

"I shouldn't have stopped short."

"So what? She didn't have to talk to you that way."

"You're right, but she'd had some *fabulous* work done. And she'd been shopping at Privilege. They've got gorgeous stuff."

Joel's tats belied his nature. The ink, his size, the blond braid that hung down his back, and the hoop earring—as well as the long chain looped into his jeans pocket that kept him from losing his keys—indicated a brawny, tough guy. His tone told a whole different story. He'd never talked about a boyfriend, but he never talked about women, either, unless it was to comment on their clothes or shoes or plastic surgery. It made Ace uncomfortable, but Ace had his own problems, so he kept his mouth shut.

"So, what are you going to do about that guy?" Joel asked as we reached the shop.

I pushed the door open. I tried to be nonchalant. "Unless I see him again, nothing. I mean, I could've been overreacting." I knew I wasn't, and Joel was onto me.

He shook his head. "Don't underestimate it. You *knew* he was watching you, and you don't know why."

Bitsy was standing on her stool, helping Ace straighten a new painting over the front desk. Ace's most recent artwork was a rip-off of Ingres's *Odalisque*—he'd taken to doing his own comic-book versions of classic paintings that also included da Vinci's Mona Lisa, Vincent van Gogh's *Starry Night* (although it could invariably be argued that it's already a cartoon), and Botticelli's *Birth of Venus* (which I dubbed *Venus on a Half Shell*). The Degas on the far wall was one of his. Because we looked like a gallery, he actually sold some of his work on a fairly regular basis.

The people who wandered in here by mistake were relieved they could buy something other than a tat.

Generally, we were by appointment only, no walk-ins, and we got a lot of referrals from the hotel concierges.

"Bitsy says that missing woman was here." Ace ran his hands through his abundantly thick dark hair, which fell gracefully just above his shoulders. It was a gesture meant to draw attention to himself; Ace was all about attention. He had those chiseled good looks that indicated possible plastic surgery—because what man could be so striking without it?—and clear blue eyes that seemed somehow reflective, like a pool. Even his tats were perfectly aligned on either arm, dipping ever so slightly onto the backs of his hands into fleurs-de-lis. He was a true artiste, lamenting his plight as a tattooist, unable to pursue his art as he wished, frustrated—but not enough to cut off an ear for anyone.

It was enough to make us all roll our eyes in unison.

"Tim needs to talk to you," I told Bitsy.

The stool still didn't take her to eye level with me, but it was close. I noticed she had on a new pair of khaki trousers and a white eyelet blouse. Bitsy was rather conservative in her style, wearing no makeup except for a little mascara, but she didn't really need any. She had flawless skin any woman would kill for. She was the only one in the shop without ink. I'd asked her once why she didn't have a tat, and she said she just didn't want one. I'm not into peer pressure, so I let it alone.

"He called. He should be here soon."

I knew he was doing his job, but wasn't it enough that he'd already told me he'd be by? Like he didn't trust that I'd relay his message to Bitsy. Sometimes he still treated me like his little sister. If the rent weren't so good, I'd move out and get my own place.

I put my bag in the staff room. I'd left a design only partly done on the light table the night before. An older woman wanted "something special" to cover her mastectomy scar, something that indicated emotional growth and physical strength. I'd started drawing an oak tree, delicate leaves at the ends of thin branches that gradually grew thicker into the trunk and ended in a mass of roots.

I took the pencil and sketched it out further, adding more details. When I was in school at the University of the Arts in Philadelphia, I'd dreamed of going to Paris and putting up an easel next to the Seine, painting on a stiff white canvas.

Instead, my canvas was alive, soft and moving, and my brush had turned into a machine with a needle on the end of it.

The first time I'd touched that needle to my own skin, I knew this was what I wanted to do.

My mother, who moved with my father to a retirement community in Port St. Lucie, Florida, right after I left for Vegas, said a Hail Mary for me every day.

I heard some sort of commotion out in the front of the shop. I pushed the sketch aside, put my pencil down, and got up. As I moved toward the door, I heard Bitsy arguing with a man.

"She's busy. I can help you," Bitsy said.

"I want to talk to the owner!"

For a second, I froze, wondering if it was the big tattooed guy who'd been watching me. I shrugged off the apprehension, telling myself that if it were, I'd at least know what he wanted now. Still, I tentatively pushed the door open.

The man Bitsy was arguing with didn't have one tat. At least none that I could see. He was in his late twenties, early thirties maybe, as clean-cut as he could be, with a short, military-like haircut, nicely pressed button-down shirt, and jeans that looked like they'd been ironed.

I took another look at his face.

He was the spitting image of his father.

It was Chip Manning, jilted groom.

Chapter 6

He saw me peeking out the staff room door, and within two strides he was standing in front of me. I had no choice but to stand tall and face him.

"Are you the owner?"

I nodded.

He held out his hand. "I'm Chip Manning."

I took it, noting that his grip was a little slack. "Brett Kavanaugh. What can I help you with?"

"I understand you saw Elise. Elise Lyon. My fiancée." His expression told me he expected something from me, but I wasn't sure just what.

"She didn't say much," I tried.

"But you saw her." His grief was etched across his face. "What did she say? How did she act?"

He obviously cared for the girl. Maybe she *had* been kidnapped. Or maybe she just left him because he smothered her.

Ace had stopped hanging his paintings and was blatantly listening to the conversation. Joel hovered near the front desk, fingering the orchid that didn't look very healthy. I made a mental note to tell Bitsy to get us a new one.

"She was fine," I said. I didn't want to tell him about Matthew. "How did you find out about us? That she came in here? Only the police know."

Chip gazed at me. "My father knows a lot of people in the police department."

I didn't doubt that. He probably got a call last night after Tim relayed the news that I'd seen Kelly/Elise. "Does he know you're here?"

He got a deer-in-the-headlights look about him. "No. He wanted me to stay out of it; he'd take care of it."

"So you sneaked out to come talk to us yourself?"

"Of course not." He became defiant. "I've got my driver."

His driver. Might have known. Bitsy rolled her eyes at me.

Chip noticed.

"He's my best friend," he said.

Sadly, that was probably true. Sounded like his father kept him on a pretty short leash. But I gave him credit for making an effort to do something on his own.

"Did she say why she was here?" Chip looked from me to Bitsy to Joel to Ace.

"She wanted a tattoo," Bitsy said, her tone indicating that it was a stupid question. It *was* a tattoo shop.

Chip shoved his hands in his pockets, his eyes landing on me again after a second of assessing Bitsy. It was as if he'd just noticed she was a little person, and he wasn't quite sure how to deal with that.

"Why?" he asked me.

"Why what?" I could play stupid. And I didn't like it that he'd glossed over Bitsy so easily.

"Didn't she say why she wanted the tattoo? I mean, it wasn't exactly something I thought Elise would ever do. She wasn't like that." He didn't seem to realize that he was talking to people who were "like that."

He also didn't think Elise would leave him at the altar, either, but who was I to mention it?

"We don't always know if there's a specific reason a person wants a tattoo," I said slowly, as if explaining something to a toddler. "It's not our place to ask. Sometimes someone will volunteer the information, sometimes not."

"So she didn't say?"

"She said she wanted to surprise her fiancé on her wedding night." Bitsy had a habit of just blurting things out.

Chip seemed startled that she spoke again, but I gave him extra credit when he directed his next question to her. "Why would she come to Vegas, then, for a tattoo? She could've gotten one at home."

It was a rhetorical question, one that didn't need an answer, but Bitsy could not be stopped.

"Maybe she just wanted one last fling before getting married," she suggested.

Not the right thing to say.

Chip raised his head, and the confusion was replaced by anger. "She said it was over!" he muttered.

"What was over?" Joel asked.

Chip looked at Joel in a sort of male-solidarity way, like Joel would understand.

"She cheated on me. Three months ago. She tried to break off the engagement, but I knew she didn't really mean it. Things were better after that."

The groom was always the last to know.

"Maybe she needed a little more space," Joel said. "So she came out here, was going to be a little wild, and then go home and marry you."

His words hung in the air. I could see the little gears in Chip's brain working overtime.

"Well, then, where is she, if that's what she was going to do?" He stared down Joel, as if Joel had all the answers.

Joel just had a little pretzel salt on his chin. He wasn't Dr. Phil.

I had to stop this.

"I'm sorry, Chip," I said, "but we can't really shed any more light on what happened to your fiancée than we already have. She came in here, she made an appointment for the next day, she left. She never came back. We didn't know anything until we saw it on the news last night."

His hands were back out of his pockets, and they dangled

loosely by his sides. The hangdog look was back. He swung more wildly through emotions than a woman going through menopause.

"I'm sorry; I only wanted to know," he said.

Joel walked around me and patted him on the back. "That's all right; don't worry about it." He started steering him toward the door.

Chip stopped in the doorway. He looked at each of us and nodded. "Thanks for everything," he said. "Thanks for telling the police that she was here. At least I know something."

I wanted to throw him another bone. "She said she was staying at the Bellagio."

He frowned. "No, no, she wasn't."

I tried to remember what she'd said. About being referred by the concierge there. I told Chip as much.

He still wore the frown. "No, we've checked all the hotels. There was no Elise Lyon registered anywhere."

"She told us her name was Kelly Masters."

He pursed his lips a little, his brows knit into a frown, and he blinked a few times. I was afraid he was going to cry. "No Kelly Masters, either," he finally said, his voice catching on the name, like it was going down the wrong way.

I was about to ask how he knew about Kelly Masters, but then thought twice about it. He'd already indicated that his father had friends in high places and had information as it developed. At this point, I didn't want to prolong the visit. I just wanted him out of my shop.

Despite my first impression that he was devoted to Elise, it now seemed that Chip was more like a spoiled little boy who was just trying to get a possession back. He was more petulant than passionate about trying to find Elise. That affair she had still bothered him; that was clear.

The door was wide open now. I willed him to walk through it.

"Thank you, everyone," he said, but stopped short of leaving.

"Is there something else?" I asked, trying to keep impatience out of my voice.

He looked up and down the walkway, shaking his head. "He's not here."

"Who?"

"My driver."

For being his "best friend," Chip didn't seem to be on a first-name basis with the guy.

"Maybe he's window-shopping," Ace suggested.

Chip pulled a cell phone off his belt and punched in some numbers. "Where are you?" he asked, still half in, half out of the shop.

I shrugged at Bitsy and was about to go finish my sketch when Chip ended his call.

"He's at the food court. How do I find that?"

He was helpless.

"Which one?" Joel asked. "There are two."

Chip sighed. He punched numbers into his phone. "Matt? Which food court?" He waited a few seconds, stuck his phone in his pocket, and said, "Wherever the Nathan's hot dogs is."

Joel gave him directions, but I wasn't paying attention. My brain was buzzing.

His driver's name was Matt?

Chapter 7

"Matt?" I said when Chip finally left, the door shutting behind him. "Matthew? Don't you get it?"

"You think his driver is the guy from the devotion ink?" Bitsy asked.

"Why not?"

I wanted to ask him myself and started for the door. Joel beat me to it. "I'm coming with you," he said.

I didn't have the heart to tell him he'd slow me down, but he knew.

"You had that guy watching you," he reminded me.

"So you're going to be my personal bodyguard?"

"What's going on?" Bitsy didn't know about the tattooed guy.

I shook my head. "Tell you later. Hold down the fort." I looked at Joel. "Okay, come on."

As we speed-walked, Joel asked, "Do you think this Matt's the one she had the affair with three months ago?"

"Seems likely," I said. "It probably wasn't really over."

"But then why agree to go through with the marriage?"

Joel didn't understand. Wedding plans are made, and sometimes it seems like it would just be easier to go through with it than to cancel and suffer the embarrassment and the questions.

I didn't have a problem with the latter.

I just moved across the country.

Paul hadn't even tried to come after me. At least Chip was trying to find Elise.

My family—with the exception of Tim—thought I was running away. Maybe I was, but not in the way they thought. I was running to a new life, a place where I'd have my own identity again. It was so easy with the wrong person to lose that.

I didn't even need therapy to figure all that out.

I couldn't walk down memory lane now. I wanted to find Matt and have a little private word with him. Getting Chip out of the way might be challenging, but between me and Joel, we could probably do it.

We passed the Lime Ice Frozen Bar, glanced around at the Häagen-Dazs, Rice & Noodle Works, New York Pretzel, and finally Nathan's. Joel's mouth started watering at the sight of the ice cream, but I tugged on his arm and scanned the crowd.

We didn't see Chip anywhere.

"Maybe Matt met up with him and they took off already," Joel said.

"You just want to go get some ice cream." I sighed. "Okay, go, but get me something, too." Nothing like ice cream before lunch. "I'm going to keep looking."

Joel scurried off as fast as a heavy man could.

I ventured beyond the food court and went back out toward the Palazzo shops that extended just beyond the end of the Venetian's canal. I took the escalator down, feeling the coolness from the waterfall that splashed into a large circular area at the bottom. I scanned the customers at the gelato place—there weren't many, since it was still early, but a couple diehards were scooping the creamy Italian ice cream out of cups. I had issues with five-dollar scoops of gelato. Just like I had issues with that waterfall.

I didn't have time to get on my environmental soapbox. I looped around the back of the escalators to where the box office for the Blue Man Group squatted in the corner. Not a soul back here. A full circle later and I was going back up the escalator, conceding defeat.

I felt deflated. I'd missed my chance to find out if Chip's driver was the subject of Elise's devotion ink.

A nudge at my elbow, and I saw Joel's extended hand offering me a mint-chip cone.

"Thanks," I said, absently licking it.

"Did you see them?"

"No."

My eyes skirted around the tourists as we went back toward the shop, but everyone just blended into everyone else and it became a blur.

Bitsy was scribbling in the appointment book, the phone tucked against her cheek. Ace was in with Jonathan Rothberg, a client who was in the middle of getting a complicated Harry Potter sleeve—the entire cast with the Death Eater tat from the fifth movie at its center. Because there was so much to it, this was Jonathan's second visit for the same ink. He had told us he was a rocket scientist, and we couldn't tell if he was joking. Probably not. Everyone was getting tats these days.

Joel and I went into the staff room.

"What was she like?" Joel asked. He leaned against the wall next to me, slurping the ice cream out from the bottom of his cone. I knew he was asking about Kelly, or rather, Elise.

"Rich girl," I said simply. "You know the type." They came to Vegas in droves, the twentysomethings who partied all night and brought their cocktails into the pool with them the next day after a few hours' sleep. Hair of the dog and all that. But Elise wasn't drunk; I wouldn't have made the appointment with her if she had been. And she didn't have the usual girl pack hanging around outside to see if she'd really go through with it. No, Elise was different. I think she really *was* going to surprise Matthew. Instead, the tables got turned somehow, and Chip was the one who was surprised.

"What if she's dead?" Joel asked too loudly, interrupting my thoughts.

I put a finger to my lips. "Sssh," I whispered.

He leaned toward me, folding his arms across his chest. "So what if she's dead?" he repeated in a stage whisper.

"The cop yesterday told me she wasn't."

"How does he know?"

How *did* he know? She could be dead, or she could be in Los Angeles or Hawaii or New York now.

Another thought made me pause.

"She could be married to Matthew by now," I said.

"What?"

"Maybe after she left here, she and Matthew got married."

"But you said she wanted the tat for her wedding night."

"Maybe she couldn't wait. Maybe she found out Chip had found her here, and she and Matthew took off."

It was all speculation. And if Chip's driver Matt was Kelly's Matthew, it seemed unlikely, since Matt was with Chip. I had no clue what happened to Elise. I just hoped that wherever she was, she was alive and happy. She obviously had her reasons to leave Chip at the altar, and it wasn't for me to make judgments about that.

Voices echoed from the front of the shop, and Joel and I instinctively both reached for the door at the same time. Bitsy pushed it open and peered around it, blinking a couple of times before focusing on me.

"Brett? You might want to come out here."

I'd had enough disruptions for one day and it was still early. But it might be Tim.

Bitsy's face was animated. Not in a good way.

"Who is it?" I asked as I took a step.

She didn't answer, just let me go past her.

A light blinded me, and the lens of a TV camera was shoved in front of my face.

Chapter 8

Someone had alerted the media.

"Miss Kavanaugh, can you tell us about Elise Lyon's state of mind when she was here the other day?" She wasn't as tall as I was, blond, with that fake, stiff smile worn by every TV reporter.

"How do you—"

"She has no comment." Tim had arrived simultaneously, coming in behind them, holding his hand up in front of the camera lens.

"Detective—"

"No one has any comment," Tim said firmly, now attempting to steer them backward and out the door.

"But, Detective, Elise Lyon was last seen here, at your sister's shop." The reporter wouldn't give up. I recognized her now as Leigh Holmes, Channel Six. "We'd like to get her impression of the missing woman." For the noon news, no doubt.

"And I said, no one has any comment." Tim's voice echoed through the shop.

Joel and Bitsy stood staring, their mouths half-open.

With one more push, Tim got the camera guy out the door, and he held it for Leigh Holmes as she walked through, tossing him a dirty look.

They had a one-night stand a while back. She sings opera

during her orgasms. I called Joel in desperation during an aria from *Tosca* because I couldn't take it anymore, and he was kind enough to let me sleep on his couch. I'm not sure she knows we live together, because I hadn't been home when she arrived or when she left.

Tim was asking Bitsy if they could talk in the staff room for more privacy. As they walked by me, he said, "You're next."

"What? Didn't I answer all your questions?"

"I need to get an official statement from you. I need to get all the information I can." He lowered his voice and leaned toward me. "As you can tell by the media, the fact that this is Bruce Manning's future daughter-in-law is putting a lot of pressure on the department to find the girl. And there's a lot of pressure on me, because you're my sister, and because you and Bitsy probably were the last two people to speak to her the other night. No one else has come forward. We can't trace her steps any further."

"How did Leigh Holmes find out about us, anyway? Aren't you policemen supposed to keep some things secret or something?"

Annoyance crossed his face, but I couldn't tell whether it was at me or at Leigh Holmes.

"I don't know how she found out," he said.

Maybe she'd exchanged a little aria for some information from one of Tim's colleagues.

I parked myself at the front desk until Melinda Butterfield walked in a few minutes later. My oak tree. I sent her into my room, and I grabbed the sketch off the light table. She loved it.

I flattened the chair so she could lie down and be more comfortable before putting the design stencil on her chest, pulling the tracing paper back carefully to see the outline on her skin. I'd done three or four tats over scars like this already. The first time had played with my head a little, because I knew that the woman underneath my fingers had had cancer and had to have a breast removed. Each of the women I'd worked on had expressed eloquently their desire not to have plastic surgery but something beautiful to illustrate their survival.

It made me take pause about how it was so easy to take life for granted.

Many people who came into the shop had a story, a deeply personal story.

But then there were the morons.

Can't have one without the other. It's what keeps the world balanced.

After Melinda approved of the placement, I dipped the machine's needle into the cap of black ink and began to draw.

I hadn't been at it too long when a knock came at the door. I peeled off my gloves and told Melinda I'd just be a minute.

"When will you be done?" Tim asked.

"It could be three hours or so."

He glanced at his watch. "Can I come back? Let's say six o'clock."

"Only if you bring something to eat."

"What do you want?"

That was too easy, but I wasn't going to argue.

"In-N-Out Burger. Double-Double with fries and a chocolate shake." They didn't have In-N-Out back east. It was one of the perks of living here.

"Okay." He gave me a peck on the cheek—highly unprofessional, but my mother would approve—and left.

I'd been working on Melinda's ink for an hour when I heard Bitsy squealing outside. It sounded like good squealing, not bad. My hand was a little crampy, so I turned off the machine.

"Do you want to take a short break?" I asked Melinda.

She nodded. I put a piece of plastic wrap over the tat so she could put on a robe and go to the bathroom. I followed her out into the hall, turning to see Bitsy's grin spread from ear to ear as she spoke on the phone. When she saw me watching her, she put her hand over the receiver and whispered, "It's Diane Sawyer's people."

"Who?"

Bitsy rolled her eyes. "*Good Morning America*? *Prime-Time*? *20/20*? You *are* familiar with those, right?" She picked up a pen and started scribbling. "Yes, that's fine, yes, thank you." And she hung up, her face glowing.

It was like she'd finally found the Emerald City.

I, on the other hand, was trying out for the part of the Wicked Witch of the West.

"You didn't set up some sort of interview, did you?" I asked, visions of Leigh Holmes on a national stage dancing in my head.

Bitsy couldn't wipe the smile off her face, even in the face of my obvious displeasure.

"Bitsy, this is like all those other awful missing-women stories. The media's playing on everyone's grief."

Bitsy shook her head. "I don't care. All I know is, I have to figure out what to wear tomorrow."

"Tomorrow? They're coming tomorrow?"

"Diane is in L.A. doing something about something," Bitsy said, now on a first-name basis with someone she'd never met. "They'll be here around noon. They want it for *20/20* tomorrow night."

"It's not so bad, is it?" Joel asked as he came out of his room, having overheard. I could see Bitsy's enthusiasm was rubbing off on him.

I could only hope Ace would be on my side.

He wasn't.

He took one look in the mirror and immediately made a hair appointment for first thing in the morning. He asked Bitsy if she could move a couple of his paintings to the waiting area at the back of the shop, which they figured was the best place for the interview.

"We need some more flowers," Joel said. "More orchids."

Bitsy canceled the next day's morning and early afternoon appointments. We couldn't possibly work with a camera crew and Diane Sawyer in the shop. Bitsy ran around, dragging that stool along with her, cleaning like I'd never seen her clean before. She took the almost-dead orchid into the staff room, planning to take it home with her and nurse it back to health. She had a sunroom at her house that doubled as a greenhouse for wayward orchids. She frequently rotated the flowers out, claiming our indoor lights weren't conducive to keeping orchids "happy."

Bitsy said she'd bring a new orchid from home in the morning so it would be "fresh," like one she'd get today would be too old by then. Right.

I went back to Melinda, my head swirling as I drew that oak tree.

I had time to kill after Melinda left, happy with her new tat. I was happy with the money that went into the till. I was still thinking about those Kenneth Cole peep-toe shoes. Tim didn't show at six with my Double Double as promised, and when I tried to call him, I just got voice mail.

Joel brought me a Johnny Rockets burger—not as good as In-N-Out—but I think it was less an act of kindness than a desire for one himself. It wasn't that I didn't appreciate it, but he'd already had the pretzel and the ice cream, gone out for lunch and then some sort of snack after that—no one knew what—and now the burgers.

Weight Watchers would make a load off him.

He knew what I was thinking and batted his eyes at me, his mouth curled in a Cheshire-cat grin.

"I don't start counting points until next week."

"I didn't say anything."

"You didn't have to."

Joel and I had a weird sort of connection that usually only people who'd known each other for a lifetime had.

"Sorry," I said into my burger.

Joel clicked on the TV.

We were coming into the news late, halfway in, so we

found out what the weather was going to be like for the next week—sunny and hot, more of the same—and that the Dodgers were preparing for their next game with the Diamondbacks.

The pet of the week was a dog named Sasha.

Just as I was about to shut it off, Leigh Holmes's face filled the screen. The lights from the police cars behind her flashed red and white, and an airplane took off behind her. The "Breaking News" logo flashed at the bottom of the screen.

"Police are investigating the body of a woman found in a car here at McCarran airport," she said. "Sources tell us it could be Elise Lyon, the missing woman from Philadelphia."

Chapter 9

"They couldn't come up with some sort of 'runaway bride' name for her?" Joel asked as he wadded up the empty burger wrapper and tossed it in the trash can. "They're so lame."

I shushed him.

"The car was rented by a Kelly Masters, our sources tell us, which is the name Elise Lyon used when she went to a local tattoo parlor two days ago."

What had happened to Elise Lyon after she left the shop the other night? But I barely had time to think about that because the picture changed, and now, instead of Leigh Holmes's, it was my face that flashed on the screen. I recognized it from when I walked out of the staff room this morning into their assault on me.

"You look fabulous on TV!" Joel said. "The light picked up all the highlights you just got. And your red hair against the silver in your ears, well, it looks great."

I studied my face, trying to see what Joel did, but all I saw was what I imagined everyone else would: the short, chopped haircut, hoops that ran the length of my earlobes, the dragon on my chest, the water lilies on my arm.

"Brett Kavanaugh, owner of The Painted Lady at the

Venetian Grand Canal Shoppes, may have been one of the last people to have seen Elise Lyon alive."

Joel slapped my arm playfully. "That's the best free advertising we could get!"

I wasn't sure it was a good thing. Between this and *20/20*, we would undoubtedly attract some new clients, but for all the wrong reasons. They'd see what they would expect: the tattooed lady, the dwarf, and the fat man. Ace, with his movie-star good looks, would be the only "normal"-looking one among us. Wasn't that a joke.

"Brett Kavanaugh is the sister of Detective Tim Kavanaugh, who is in charge of the investigation."

They showed Tim come in the shop and make them turn off the camera.

"Detective Kavanaugh was questioning his sister and her employees earlier today, but he had no comment for the record."

"Oh, don't look so sad," Joel said, his arm snaking over my shoulder. "You really do look great on TV. And we'll get some business out of this."

I shrugged off his arm and, as I was about to turn off the TV, I saw something that made me stop short.

I pointed. "There, do you see him?"

Joel was too late; the picture had already changed back to Leigh Holmes at the airport.

"What did you see?" he asked.

"It was that guy, the bald, tattooed guy who was watching me this morning in the mall. He was outside the shop. I saw him in the window behind Tim." My heart was pounding. Who *was* that guy?

I turned off the TV.

"Hey, she might have had more."

"She doesn't have anything. Otherwise she would've said it right away. Anyway, I can't concentrate on that now."

"Do you really think the guy is stalking you or something?"

I shook my head. "I don't know. It's really creeping me out."

Joel took his cell phone out of his breast pocket. "I'm going to call around, see if I can find out who he is, okay?"

I nodded.

He stood up and pecked my cheek. "I'll take a walk outside."

While he tried to track down that ink, I punched Tim's number into my cell phone.

"Listen, I'm tied up right now," he said without even saying "hello."

"Are you at the airport?"

Heavy sigh. "You saw it on TV."

"Just now. Was the car really rented by Kelly Masters? Is it Kelly—I mean Elise Lyon—in the car?"

"I can't say anything right now. I'll see you when I see you." And he hung up.

I hated it when he did that.

And I hated it that I couldn't just drive over to the airport and see what was going on.

I had to ink four shoulders—four women who each wanted the same image of a book to commemorate their friendship and the fact that they'd met in a book club. They were in Vegas for a long weekend to celebrate twenty years together and didn't want everything that happened in Vegas to stay here. I'd sketched a small red book with golden tassels and four blue stars, and they loved it.

They brought a bottle of champagne, and while we didn't exactly condone that, Bitsy conceded it was a special occasion, and between the four of them, they probably wouldn't get drunk on one bottle.

They cheered one another on as I worked, and I found myself thinking about Mickey and the rest of the gang at the Ink Spot, back home. I missed that camaraderie, and even though I was forming bonds here in Vegas, it wasn't the same yet.

When I was done, they insisted I share a glass with them.

After they left, I went into the staff room. The light table was a mess of tracing papers and stencils. Bitsy would file everything at the end of the day, but I started to help by making piles. As I shuffled the bits around, I spotted the crude drawing Kelly Masters—or, rather, Elise Lyon—had handed me just a couple of nights ago.

I ignored the rest and picked it up, studying it as if it would give me some sort of clue as to what her story really was.

She couldn't draw, that was for sure.

I traced the outline with my finger, but the light from the table illuminated the paper, and I could see something was written on the back. I flipped it over to see an address written in pencil.

It was a familiar address, a lot farther up on Las Vegas Boulevard. Near Fremont Street.

It was Murder Ink.

A tattoo shop. Our competition.

Chapter 10

Elise might have just gotten the names of other tattoo shops in Vegas and then picked one. The hole in that story, however, was that there was only one address written on the slip of paper. Unless she'd been there and decided not to stay.

Not out of the realm of possibility. I knew Jeff Coleman, the shop owner. He specialized in flash, the stock designs that lined the walls of his shop. No originality to his work; his street shop located next to Goodfellas Bail Bonds catered to walk-ins, and he stayed open until four a.m. so anyone out partying who wanted a tattoo on the spur of the moment would wake up the next morning with one. He didn't have a conscience about who or what he tattooed, as long as he put money in the till.

He was everything I didn't want our shop to become. So far, we'd succeeded.

All bets were off once we were splashed all over *20/20*.

I put the drawing in my bag.

"You okay?" Joel stuck his head through the door.

I shrugged. "Yeah, I guess so." Not very convincing. "Any luck with the eagle tat?"

"Seems like it's pretty common flash. But I'll keep asking around. And your nine o'clock is here."

I rummaged through the piles I'd just made and found the

stencils of the matching derringers that would adorn the inside upper arms of a young woman who'd also recently gotten a boob job. Charlotte Sampson had just graduated from college with a degree in accounting, but I wasn't convinced she really meant to actually work as an accountant. She'd given herself a rather bad tattoo of a heart on the inside of her wrist, and when she saw my work, she insisted that I fix her ink up. Since then, she'd been back for five tats.

I mentioned that the derringers might sag a bit as she got older, but she shrugged it off.

Bitsy was telling her about our impending fifteen minutes of fame on *20/20* when I emerged.

"Brett, this is great news!" Charlotte threw her arms around me and air-kissed my cheek.

"Sure," I mumbled. "Let's get this show on the road."

Charlotte frowned at Bitsy, who shook her head and rolled her eyes. I saw it, but I pretended not to notice.

I led Charlotte to my room and showed her the stencils.

"They're perfect!" she said.

After pulling on my gloves, I applied the stencil, assessed the outline of the first derringer, arranged the ink caps, dipped the needle, and pressed the foot pedal. A tattoo machine is like a sewing machine; it's all in the foot action.

I ran the needle along the lines of the stencil, feeling Charlotte flinch only as the needle first touched her skin.

Getting a tattoo feels like a hundred bee stings all at once. It hurts for the first few minutes, and then the endorphins kick in and the excitement pushes away the pain.

It was a quick job, just an hour and a half for both tats.

"Fantastic," Charlotte said as she surveyed her arms in the mirror.

I wrapped her up in Saran Wrap; she knew the drill. Just before she left, though, she asked to see me privately.

Bitsy, who was in the midst of cleaning up for the night, raised her eyebrows at me, but I shrugged back. I had no idea what Charlotte wanted.

Once back in my room, Charlotte hesitated.

"What is it?" I asked.

She was a pretty girl, with sleek black hair and green eyes that sparkled. "I was wondering, well, if you ever, well, you know . . ."

"Spit it out," I said.

She smiled shyly. "I was wondering if you would be willing to take me on here, like an intern or something."

"What about being an accountant?"

She sighed. "I don't think it's in my cards. I bought my own machine, and I've been tattooing my friends."

I caught my breath. "Not a good idea, Charlotte."

"I know, but I just want to do this."

I had to stop her, and the only way was to agree to have her come in and talk it over with the rest of the staff. We hadn't had a trainee since I took over, but we'd all been starting out ourselves at one point. If Mickey hadn't taken a chance on me, I don't know where I'd be today.

Since I didn't want her to overlap with the TV crew, Bitsy scheduled her for the next week.

"What do you think?" I asked Bitsy as we watched Charlotte skip out of the shop.

Bitsy shrugged. "It's not like we don't have work we can give her. And she's a nice kid."

I was preoccupied, however, with the Murder Ink address on Elise's drawing. I didn't tell anyone about it. If I did, it could end up all over national TV, and I wanted to talk to Jeff Coleman about it first. It was conceivable that Elise had never shown up there, that she'd come to our shop first, but I figured some well-placed questions to Jeff would get me the answers I needed.

Since he was open until four, I'd head over there now.

Joel and Bitsy told me to go ahead home, they'd finish closing up. They'd decided I was a "gloomy Gus" and felt I was raining on their *20/20* parade.

It was more like a monsoon.

Sure, I should probably feel guilty about that, but they

were out of control, talking about outfits and Joel wishing he'd started Weight Watchers last week because he'd surely lose at least ten pounds right away, and you know how the camera puts weight on people.

Joel had completely forgotten about the creepy tattooed guy by now, but I didn't see anyone suspicious as I left the mall and went to the parking garage. I started the Bullitt up and headed out into the night.

The lights of the Strip sliced across my windshield, and I thought about putting the roof down, but decided against it. It was still pretty hot, and the air-conditioning felt good as it blasted against my face.

I was halfway up the Strip when my cell phone rang inside my bag. I dug it out and flipped it open, noting Tim's number on the screen.

"Yeah?" I asked.

"Brett? You on your way home?"

I didn't want to tell him about Murder Ink unless I knew Elise had been there or had some contact with them, so I sidestepped the question by asking one of my own: "Why?"

"You said that the picture of Elise Lyon on TV was definitely the woman who came into your shop?"

"Yeah. What about it?"

"You're absolutely sure?"

Something was up. "Why are you asking?"

"If I send you a picture on your phone, can you confirm or deny whether it was the woman who was in your shop the other night?"

"This is about that body in the car at the airport, isn't it?"

"I can't comment at the moment."

By his not commenting, I knew it was.

"What about Chip Manning? Why can't he identify her? What about her parents?" Yeah, what about them? Weren't the parents the ones who were always plastered all over the TV screens begging for information about their lost girl?

"Her father is on his way to Vegas now, but her mother's staying behind just in case she goes home."

For the wedding. If she still wanted to get married, she'd be there now. "So why me? I only talked to her for, like, ten minutes."

He sighed. "I'd rather not get her mother all upset—"

"Just in case it's not her, right?" I finished for him.

"Just do it, Brett, okay?"

"Okay, okay, keep your pants on."

"I'm sending it now."

I pulled over so I wouldn't get stopped by the cops for paying more attention to my phone than to the road.

I waited a couple of seconds, and a picture popped up on the screen. It wasn't a great picture, but I knew one thing: Elise Lyon's mother wouldn't be upset.

Because it wasn't the woman who'd come into The Painted Lady.

Chapter 11

"It's not Kelly Masters," I said.

"But it is," Tim said.

"What?"

"Her name is Kelly Masters. She's got ID on her; the rental car agreement is in her name. She's from L.A."

"What happened to her?"

"I really can't say."

I was ready to smack him. He couldn't tease me like this. "But you've already told me plenty. And I might find out on the news anyway."

"You might."

Something in his voice told me I might not. "You're not releasing anything about this, are you?"

"We need to find out the connection between Kelly Masters and Elise Lyon—"

"Because there is a connection, isn't there?" I interrupted. "Why else would Elise use Kelly's name?"

He was quiet a second, then, "You can't tell anyone about this. Promise?"

"A *20/20* camera crew is coming to the shop tomorrow to interview us about Elise Lyon," I said.

"You're kidding, right?"

"No. Wish I were."

"So there's even more of a reason to keep the lid on this, okay?"

"No problem." Not like I was ready to spill the beans to the media. And it was a good thing Bitsy didn't know about this. Or Joel. Ace wouldn't care, because Ace rarely paid attention to anything that didn't directly involve him.

I toyed with the idea of telling Tim where I was heading. Just as I decided to, he said, "Listen, I've got to run. I probably won't be home tonight." And he ended the call.

I stared at my phone, the picture of Kelly Masters staring back at me. Kelly was a pretty girl, too, but now that I paid attention to more than her face, I saw there was another big difference between Kelly and Elise.

Kelly had a tattoo on the side of her neck. I couldn't make out what it was, but it was definitely ink.

I punched Tim's number into my phone.

"What?" he asked, annoyed.

"Quick question about this picture."

"Shoot."

"Kelly Masters has a tat on her neck, right?"

He was quiet a second. Then, "You can see that?"

"It's my business, Tim." My turn to be annoyed. "What's it of?"

"What?"

"I can't make out what it is."

"What does it matter?"

"You never know. It might actually tell you a lot."

"Come on, Brett."

"Just humor me, okay?"

Tim sighed. "Will it get you off the phone?"

"Yes," I promised.

"It's an eagle. It's actually on the back of her neck, and what you see are the wings that come out on either side."

A shiver ran through me.

"Why does this matter?" Tim asked.

"It doesn't," I said, although it seemed like it most definitely did. But I wasn't one hundred percent sure about it, and until I was, I didn't want to say it out loud. "Thanks." And this time, I ended the call.

I sat for a second, staring out at nothing.

The tattooed guy, the one I'd seen in the mall. He had the same ink on his neck as Kelly Masters.

I had to park in the lot at the Bright Lights Motel, across the street from Murder Ink. The motel didn't live up to its name—the shabby building was mostly dark except for a faint glow behind a couple of windows covered by what could only be flimsy curtains—but the tattoo shop's lights were spilling out onto the sidewalk, its bloodred neon sign flashing. It wasn't the greatest neighborhood, and even though I knew Jeff Coleman, it was cold comfort, considering we couldn't stand each other.

A couple of people were walking around inside, but I couldn't see their features from where I was because the shop name was painted in large script on the window. With the neon, it was a bit redundant.

I got out of the car and locked it, shoring up some confidence as I jaywalked over to the shop and pushed open the door.

Jeff Coleman was working on a kid who looked like he couldn't possibly be eighteen. He barely had any facial or chest hair. From the looks of it, he was getting the entire cast of the original *Star Trek* on his abdomen.

To each his own.

"Hey, if it isn't the famous Brett Kavanaugh," Jeff said. "Slumming, are we?"

The *Star Trek* kid looked over at me. "Painted Lady, right?"

I recognized him now. We'd kicked him out last month when he showed up drunk and definitely underage with a bunch of his friends.

I ignored him, concentrating on Jeff. "I was wondering if I could ask you a couple of questions."

Jeff's machine stopped whirring.

"You want to ask me some questions?"

"Is there an echo in here?"

Jeff studied the *Star Trek* tat for a second. "Let's take a break," he told the kid as he peeled off his latex gloves and swung his leg over the swivel chair he was sitting on.

Jeff Coleman was a slight guy, shorter than me by a couple inches, and skinny. His arms were covered with ink, and I could see it just around the collar of his T-shirt, hinting at the tats on his torso. He was older than me, maybe around forty, and the lines in his face indicated he'd lived hard. The buzz cut on his head was salt-and-pepper, and his beard was scruffy, as if he hadn't shaved in a day or so.

He grabbed a pack of smokes and indicated I should follow him outside.

"What's up, Kavanaugh?" he asked as he lit a match, touching it to the cigarette that was now balancing precariously between his lips.

"Have you seen the news? The girl who's missing from Philadelphia?"

He blew a perfect smoke ring, his eyes never leaving my face as he leaned his shoulder against the side of the building.

"Saw it. Also saw you. She was in your shop?"

I nodded.

"Figures. Girl like that wants a custom design." He took a long drag off his cigarette. "What does she have to do with me?"

"The address of your shop was on the back of the drawing she gave me."

The smoke curled out of his nose and from between his lips. "Really?" His demeanor didn't tell me whether it was a surprise or not.

"She didn't come in here, did she?"

"And take one look at my flash and decide to go upscale instead?" Jeff chuckled.

"Come on, Jeff, I'm serious. Can you let the competition go for a few minutes?"

He studied my face for a second, nodded, and took another drag off his butt. "Okay. No, she didn't come in here. Although I wish she had. You're getting some great free advertising."

If I couldn't explain how I felt about that to my own staff, how could I possibly explain it to Jeff Coleman? I let it alone, let him think what he wanted. Elise Lyon may have written down the addresses of more than one shop—it had been only half a piece of paper, after all—and stopped checking out any others once she came into The Painted Lady.

Jeff tossed his butt on the sidewalk and ground it with the heel of his boot. "Is that all, Kavanaugh? Or do you want some ink as a souvenir of your walk on the dark side?" A smile tugged at the corner of his lips, but on him it looked more like he'd just bitten into a lemon.

I was about to say "thanks for nothing," but then I had another thought. I pulled my cell phone out of my bag, hitting a couple of buttons, and watched the picture of Kelly Masters pop up. I held it up so he could see.

"What about her? Did she ever come into your shop?"

Jeff's face turned white and he froze.

"What happened to her?" he asked, his voice tight, as if he were afraid to take a breath.

I didn't want to say. But maybe I'd get a straight answer if I did.

"She's dead."

He swallowed. "How?"

"Not sure. How do you know her?"

He didn't answer.

"Jeff, she's dead."

"Murdered?"

Tim hadn't said as much, but I was willing to bet something had gone down. "Yeah, possibly."

Jeff pulled another cigarette out of his breast pocket and lit it, his hands visibly shaking. I watched him take a long drag and then let it out slowly. As the smoke hung in the air between us, he said softly, "She's my ex-wife."

Chapter 12

Jeff swore he didn't even know she was in town. They'd been divorced for three years.

"She was living out in L.A. Went upscale after we split, got mixed up with celebrity life," he said. "Heard she might be getting married again."

"When did you hear that?"

Jeff was on his third cigarette. "Not long ago."

"Who'd you hear from?"

He shrugged. "I've got my ear to the ground."

I wasn't going to get anywhere with that. "She looks young," I said.

Jeff gave me a wan smile. "Younger than me, right, Kavanaugh? Sure, she was twenty-two when we hooked up. We were married five years. You do the math."

The look on my face elicited a smirk.

"You're wondering what she was doing with me."

I was, but I tried to be nonchalant. "None of my business."

"I pulled her out of a hole. She was a mess when we met—drugs, hooking. I helped her; she straightened out." He paused, took another drag on his butt. "And then she left."

Interesting.

"Did you do the tat on her neck?"

The question threw him. He was still trying to digest the fact that Kelly was dead. "The eagle, you mean?"

"Yeah," I said, like I'd seen more of it than just the corner in the picture on my cell phone.

He nodded.

"Did you do another one like it?"

"What?"

"Have you done others like it?"

Jeff frowned, not knowing where I was going with this. "I don't see how it matters, does it?"

I couldn't get the image of that big guy out of my head. "Might, might not," I said, hopefully with enough mystery in my voice so he'd think it really was relevant.

"Sure, I've done the eagle at least a dozen times. Probably more."

"How about a big guy, at least six-four, looks like a biker, shaved head? He's got a face full of tats."

It was the second time I'd rocked Jeff's world. He caught his breath, the smoke moving slowly out through his nose as he pulled the cigarette from his lips.

"What does Kelly's brother have to do with this?"

Her brother? Why would Kelly's brother be following me at the mall and watching my shop?

"Did he have something to do with Kelly's death?" Jeff asked.

I shook my head. "No, I don't know."

Jeff suddenly caught wind that I might be asking questions I shouldn't.

"Cops don't know about me, do they?" he asked.

"I just found your address on the paper a couple hours ago. I haven't told anyone." I paused. "You don't have any reason not to want the cops to come around, do you? Because they'll probably find out you're Kelly's ex-husband. That's their job."

"You really didn't know?" Jeff took another drag off the cigarette.

"No. I was just looking for a connection with Elise Lyon."

As I said it, I realized I'd found another connection between the two women. The first was that Elise was using Kelly's name; the second was Jeff Coleman's shop, if not Jeff himself.

"So you never saw Elise Lyon here?"

Jeff took a deep breath. "No."

"Did Kelly ever mention a friend named Elise?"

"You think Kelly knew her?"

I shrugged.

The *Star Trek* kid poked his head out the door.

"Jeff?" The booze was starting to wear off; I recognized the weariness in his voice.

"Be right there, Scottie." The door shut again.

Jeff tossed the butt into the street, and we watched the glow from its tip for a second before he said, "Listen, Kavanaugh, I'd appreciate it if you didn't say anything to your cop brother about me. They'll figure it out eventually, but I'd rather it was later rather than sooner."

"Why?" I blurted it out before I could stop myself.

Jeff chuckled. "Kelly and I didn't have the most friendly of divorces. But I really didn't know she was in town, and I didn't have anything to do with her murder. The cops will think I did. Ex-husband, always the first suspect."

He had a point, but how did I know he *didn't* kill her?

My hesitation must have told him I had doubts.

"Trust me, Kavanaugh. I loved her; I wouldn't hurt her. *She* left *me*." I could tell he was confused by that.

For a second, I flashed back to Paul, asking me, *Why*? He really had no clue. Asking me to quit my job at the Ink Spot, follow his career by giving up mine. I shook off the memory.

Jeff was still talking. "I want to do a little look-see into this myself, and if I don't have the cops breathing down my neck, I'll be able to do it a lot easier."

I couldn't resist. "If you find out anything, can you let me know?"

Jeff cocked his head to one side and studied me for a second. "Why?"

"Maybe I just want to find out what happened to Elise Lyon, and I've got a hunch there's a connection."

"A hunch? Who are you, Nancy Drew?"

Okay, maybe I deserved that. But it didn't deter me. "Elise showed up at my shop and told me her name was Kelly Masters."

I couldn't read his expression.

"So maybe there is something there after all," he said thoughtfully. "Sure, Kavanaugh, I'll play Starsky and Hutch with you, as long as you promise not to blab my name prematurely to that brother of yours. Agreed?"

"Agreed." I shifted my messenger bag to my other shoulder, crossing my fingers behind it so he wouldn't see, and asked, "So who would want her dead?"

He laughed, opened the door to his shop, put one foot inside. "The best question would be, who wouldn't want her dead?"

"What do you mean?"

"Let me worry about that right now."

"So Kelly had a lot of enemies?"

"Let's just say she would never be voted Miss Congeniality."

Again, the link between Kelly Masters and Elise Lyon seemed really remote.

He started to go inside, but I grabbed the door before it shut, causing him to stop in the doorway. "What is it, Kavanaugh?"

"Kelly's brother. What's his story?"

"I don't know where you met him, Kavanaugh, but my advice? Just stay away from him." He paused, and when he spoke again, his tone was soft, like he actually had a heart. "Matthew's bad news. You don't want to mess with him."

Matthew?

Chapter 13

So now I had two Matthews, or rather, a Matt and a Matthew.

Jeff Coleman's words floated around in my head, interrupted every second or so by the fact that Kelly Masters's brother, Matthew, was the guy watching me.

Matthew.

The object of Elise Lyon's devotion?

Maybe.

Or was it Chip Manning's driver Matt?

I had a hard time connecting Elise—from a well-to-do family in Philadelphia, about to marry one of the richest heirs in the world—with someone like Kelly's brother.

Where would she meet him? Did she hop a plane to Vegas, meet him in a casino or a bar here, decide she couldn't marry Chip but had to marry Matthew instead?

Something inside me wouldn't let me believe that. It just didn't fit.

Then there was Matt, the driver. That made the most sense. She would obviously have known him through Chip. Maybe Matt drove her around, too. Maybe he started her engine a few times. Maybe that was enough for her to realize Chip was never in the driver's seat.

My car analogies were getting out of hand.

Now I knew how Tim felt when he was working a case and didn't have all the answers.

It sucked.

Tim. He wouldn't be happy with me once he found out about my trip to Murder Ink to see Jeff Coleman. I thought about my promise to Jeff that I wouldn't tell Tim. It let me off the hook, but only temporarily. Even though no one knew I'd come here tonight—except for Scottie the *Star Trek* fan—Tim would find out Jeff was Kelly Masters's ex-husband and since Jeff was a tattooist and I was a tattooist, Tim was smart enough to figure that we might know each other and ask me about him.

It shouldn't be a difficult decision. Jeff Coleman was my sworn enemy; we hated each other. This was the first almost-civil conversation I'd ever had with him, and still he'd peppered it with constant reminders that he only ever called me by my last name. Like he was some sort of tough guy.

I could take him out.

But there had been something sincere about his voice when he talked about Kelly, and he'd definitely been surprised when he found out she was dead. If I went with my gut, I'd say Jeff Coleman didn't have anything to do with his ex-wife's death.

I didn't have to debate it too long, though, because when I got to the house, Tim wasn't there. I remembered he said he might not be home tonight.

I tugged off my tank top and skirt, changing into plaid pajama bottoms and a short-sleeved oversize T-shirt. It had been a long time since my burger, so I rummaged in the fridge and found some cheese and crackers. I poured a glass of Malbec and went to the sofa, clicking on the TV.

Hadn't I started my day here?

Elise Lyon was all over CNN. And MSNBC. And FOX. She was still missing. Chip Manning had joined his father in Las Vegas, and they were staying in the penthouse suite at Versailles. Elise Lyon's father had arrived in town; her mother was in Philadelphia not speaking to the press. A local tattoo shop owner had last seen Elise Lyon. See her in her shop in this incredibly unflattering footage.

They must have bought the film from Leigh Holmes's station. Great.

Nowhere was there any mention of Kelly Masters.

I finished my wine and felt my eyes droop. The day had finally caught up with me, and I had to get up early tomorrow for the TV crew's little visit. Fun.

I took the glass and empty plate to the kitchen, placing them in the dishwasher. Neither of us had eaten at home today except for breakfast, and it could be a few days before we had enough dishes in there to warrant using the water.

One of my biggest issues with Las Vegas is the water situation. By all rights, we shouldn't have any. We're in the desert, and the fact that water is in short supply is no mystery. Lake Mead, our water supply source, was down a hundred feet because of the drought, yet every resort and casino used so much water every day that we could probably fill another ocean in no time. Every time I looked at that fake canal that ran parallel to my shop, I tried not to feel guilty.

I shut the dishwasher, turned out the light, and went to my bedroom, where I fell on top of the covers and went to sleep immediately.

Regardless, I woke up sometime in the night when I heard Tim come in after all. He tended to have heavy feet, and I followed his footsteps in my head around the house as he got himself a glass of water in the kitchen and then went into his bedroom and shut the door.

I barely slept again, my nervousness about *20/20* bubbling up in my chest. How could I call it off? Could I do that to my staff?

When I got to the shop the next morning—Tim had managed to sneak out during one of my bits of sleep, thus alleviating my guilt about not telling him about Jeff

Coleman—Bitsy and Joel acted like it was Christmas, and even Ace wore a pair of jeans that didn't have a hole in the knee.

They all had dressed up like they were going to their First Communion. Bitsy had a new pair of trousers and a cute blue top that accentuated her blond curls. Joel's massive frame wasn't quite so overwhelming in a subdued charcoal rayon shirt and cream-colored slacks.

"What did you people do with my staff?" I asked as I surveyed them over my to-go coffee cup.

Joel circled me, his head shaking sadly. "Brett, you have to go get yourself something else to wear. I'll go with you."

I didn't think my print skirt and black tank top were awful. Why should I look different today?

When I voiced that out loud, Bitsy "tsk-tsked" me. Even Ace made a face.

I sighed. "Okay, Joel, take me out, dress me up."

The smile spread across his face as he clapped his hands. "Goody!"

"We're probably only going to be on air for about one minute, you know. No one will even notice what we're wearing."

No one got it. Joel shuffled me out of the shop and pointed me in the direction of Ann Taylor.

"You do realize that this sort of thing gives me hives?" I asked him as I showed off a wraparound dress with a print that clashed with my tats.

"Oh, shut up and deal," Joel said, handing me a pair of white cotton trousers and a flowing purple silk sleeveless top.

I got the top caught on one of my hoop earrings. Or maybe two of them. I wandered out of the dressing room with it stuck on my head, my bra and dragon exposed for all to see. Not to mention the tiger lily that stretched along the side of my torso from my breast to my hip. And the Celtic cross on my upper back.

Joel chuckled as he set the top free, and it settled on my frame like it was supposed to.

Joel stepped back and studied me, cocking his head from side to side. "Hold on a sec," he said, and he disappeared, reappearing a minute later with a pair of red patent-leather pumps with a heel that was at least four inches high. They rivaled the Kenneth Cole shoes; in fact, I liked them even better.

I slipped them on and stood slightly taller than Joel, who was nodding so hard I thought he'd turned into a bobble-head doll.

"That's it," he said, "that's the one."

I stepped in front of the three-way mirror and had to admit it looked good. I would never have chosen this for myself, but Joel had taste. The manager was nice enough to snip off the tags so I could wear the new clothes out of the store, and she bagged up the old ones.

We walked back to the shop, looping around the canal and passing Breathe, the oxygen bar. Ace sat on the end stool, the oxygen tube in his nose, a short Asian girl massaging his back with something that looked like a large fork.

Joel sighed as he shook his head at me. Ace was addicted to the aromatherapy oxygen, swore it gave him more energy. His eyes were closed, his face serene as he sucked in that air.

I just hoped they changed those tubes so Ace wasn't sticking someone else's snot up his nose every time.

My outfit got murmurs of approval from Bitsy. Since she'd canceled all our appointments until late afternoon, we didn't have anything to do, and Joel wouldn't let me finish my coffee because he thought I'd spill on my new white trousers.

He was probably right. I drank a Pellegrino.

The shop was gussied up, too, like the rest of us: A fresh spray of purple orchids had replaced the sad little white one on the front desk; the floor gleamed.

Ace came back about fifteen minutes later, his eyes alert.

"What time are they coming?" Ace asked Bitsy, who'd scheduled everything.

I didn't hang around to hear her answer; I went into the staff room and saw that all the piles of stencils I'd made had been filed neatly. I was getting too nervous to start the stencil I needed for later that day, so I turned on the TV, channel surfing until I saw a familiar face on CNN.

Elise Lyon was still missing.

But the media had caught wind of last night's twist.

"In a related story, a young woman named Kelly Masters was shot and killed and found in her car at McCarran International Airport yesterday afternoon," the anchor was saying.

Joel came in and started to say something, but I waved in his general direction, shushing him.

"Police believe Kelly Masters may have had some connection with Elise Lyon's disappearance."

I held my breath.

"Police found Elise Lyon's driver's license under the seat of the car."

Chapter 14

They *were* connected. Elise was posing as Kelly, and Kelly had Elise's license. Had Kelly planned to pose as Elise? What was the deal between them? Had they switched identities for some reason?

I didn't have time to ponder it any further, because the TV crew had arrived. The producer brought in a couple of camera and sound guys and proceeded to rearrange the area Bitsy and Ace had arranged the night before. Lights went up, blasting hot rays. I was glad my new blouse was sleeveless.

Bitsy coordinated it all. Ace, Joel, and I hovered in the background. Until the producer shouted, "Brett Kavanaugh? Who is Brett?"

I raised my hand like I was in fourth grade, and he came over to me. "This segment will be taped, and we'll air it tonight. Understand?"

I nodded.

"We need to mike you."

I indicated Bitsy, who I could see was chomping at the bit. "She was here, too. Her name is Bitsy Hendricks; she talked to Kelly—I mean Elise—too."

The producer glanced at Bitsy, and while I didn't see his expression change, I felt a distinct chill in the air. "We only have two minutes on air. We only have time for one of you."

He held the mike, which was attached to a small black box by a long wire. I put my hand on it and shoved it toward him. "Then interview Bitsy, okay?"

He didn't even look at Bitsy. "No. You. You're the owner." Like that made me the only grown-up in the room. I could see by the set of his mouth that he wasn't going to argue this with me, that he was right and I was wrong, so I nodded, shrugging at Bitsy, who looked like she was getting ready to call her lawyer to file a discrimination suit against ABC. I wouldn't put it past her.

The producer fastened the black box on the back of my trousers. "I'm going to feed the wire up through your shirt. Can you grab it and bring it up around to your collar?"

He got it halfway up without even touching my skin, and I managed to pull it up and out near my neck. He fastened the mike on my blouse and started to lead me toward the sofa when the door opened.

The Asian woman who glided into the room was half a foot shorter than I was, with sleek black hair pulled into a tight chignon at the back of her head. Her handshake was firm.

"Alison Cho, *20/20*," she said. "Where are we doing this?" She fingered the long strand of pearls that rested gently against a filmy cream-colored silk blouse. She may have been short, but she had a certain presence, a charisma about her that no doubt would be picked up by the camera.

"Where's Diane Sawyer?" Bitsy's voice echoed across the shop and bounced off the wall.

A flash of something—annoyance—was gone in a second before Alison Cho turned to Bitsy and smiled. "I'm doing the interview," she said firmly, ignoring Bitsy's expression, which clearly relayed that this was unacceptable, and turned to Joel and Ace, shaking their hands. Someone handed her a water, but she didn't open it.

They'd set up a chair for her across from the couch, and I settled in, jostling the black box at my waist a little. I shifted so I wouldn't lean against it, acutely aware that I couldn't slouch, trying to keep my back ramrod straight.

"Don't look directly into the camera," she advised.

I had no intention of looking at it at all.

Alison Cho had no issues with looking at the camera, though.

"Today we're speaking with Brett Kavanaugh, owner of The Painted Lady tattoo shop in Las Vegas, where Elise Lyon was last seen alive."

I hadn't thought of it that way, and it made me shiver.

Alison swung her head around and looked me straight in the eye. "What was her demeanor that night? Did she seem well? Or agitated?"

"She was fine. Relaxed."

The voice that came out of my mouth didn't sound like mine; rather, it was like I was somewhere else and hearing myself through a tunnel. My heart was pounding, and I hoped I wasn't sweating through the purple top.

"She came in for a devotion tattoo, correct?"

I nodded. "That's right."

"Please explain what that is."

"It's a tattoo that has the name of a loved one on it. Kelly—I mean Elise—wanted the name in a heart with two clasped hands." Maybe more information than anyone needed, but Alison seemed interested.

"She made an appointment for the tattoo?" she prompted.

I nodded again. "For the next day. But she didn't show up."

"And no one saw her again," she said ominously to the camera. "We have a copy of the devotion tattoo Elise Lyon requested," she said, holding up the sketch I'd drawn. Elise's original drawing was still in my bag, where I'd put it before heading to Murder Ink last night.

I instinctively glanced at Bitsy, who was frowning. She probably gave the sketch to the producer, thinking he'd put her on camera, and then he screwed her.

But Bitsy wasn't the only one getting screwed.

Chip Manning was, too.

Because the camera zoomed in on my sketch. Complete with the "Matthew" inside the heart.

Alison Cho didn't notice. She put the piece of paper in her lap and thanked me for my time.

It was over.

I stood up, trying to yank the mike and wire off my person, and was happy to see the producer come over to me. I assumed he'd help me out, but his mouth was set in a grim line.

"That drawing. It was the wrong one."

Alison's head snapped back. "What?"

"It was the wrong drawing." He looked at Bitsy, who'd come up next to me. "Why didn't you give me the right one? Was it because we didn't put you on camera?"

So Bitsy's attitude had not gone unnoticed.

From the look on her face, I could see she was going to say something she'd probably regret, so I jumped in. "It was the right one."

His gaze moved from Bitsy to me. "But it said Matthew. Not Chip, or even Bruce."

"That's right." I met his stare.

"You mean she wanted a tattoo with another man's name on it?" Alison was justifiably curious, her journalistic instincts kicking into full gear.

I took a page from Tim's playbook. "No comment," I said.

Alison Cho looked iike she'd just landed an interview with Osama bin Laden. "Do the police know about this?" she asked.

I shook my head. "I can't say anything else."

Alison turned to the producer. "Get the police spokesman on the phone. We need to get over there now and find out what this is about." She looked at me one last time. "This is your chance to have another few minutes on TV."

I tossed the black box to the producer. "I didn't want the ones I just had."

She smiled. "Suit yourself. Thank you for your time, and for letting us disrupt your business."

She was nice, I had to give her that, but I was glad when they were all gone and the shop was quiet.

"Do you think they'll get anything out of the police?" Ace asked.

"I don't know," I said. "Maybe. Maybe the cops will want the media's help in finding her, and this was a pretty interesting clue." I thought about the two Matthews again. If I'd found out about them so easily, then it wouldn't take the police long, either.

Ace and Bitsy moved the furniture back to where it belonged, and I grabbed the Ann Taylor bag. I needed to change before my first client came in. I didn't want to risk getting ink on my new trousers.

I had to admit that I was liking them. I wondered how they'd look on TV tonight.

Just as I was about to go into the bathroom to change, the phone rang on the front desk. Bitsy was in the staff room with Ace and Joel, so I picked it up.

"The Painted Lady," I said.

"Kavanaugh?" I recognized Jeff Coleman's voice.

"Yeah? What do you want?"

"I really thought I could trust you."

"What do you mean?"

"It's a good thing I've got better friends than you, friends who look out for me."

"What do you mean?" I didn't point out that we weren't exactly friends.

"Cops. They've got a warrant. They want to arrest me in Kelly's murder."

Chapter 15

"Where are you, Jeff?" I asked.

"No need for you to know that."

"I didn't say anything. I haven't even seen my brother since yesterday morning," I said. He didn't have to know I might have told Tim if I'd seen him.

Jeff was quiet a moment, then, "There's something going on."

"No kidding."

"Someone's setting me up. I heard the cops found my fingerprints in that car, the rental car. Couldn't have. I haven't seen Kelly. Didn't know she was in town."

"I believe you, Jeff." I didn't know what else to say. And strangely enough, I did believe him.

"There's something else, Kavanaugh."

I didn't like it that he called me by my last name, but he was a man on the run, so could I take that away from him?

"What is it?"

"That rich bitch? Guess the cops also want to talk to me about her."

"But I thought you hadn't met her."

"They found her driver's license with Kelly."

"I saw that on the news."

"What's going on, Kavanaugh? You show up at my shop last night and my whole world collapses. You're bad news."

"It's not my fault," I insisted. "Listen, Jeff, what can I do to help? Want me to talk to Tim? Where are you?"

He was so quiet I'd thought he hung up for a second, then, "There might be something you *can* do. But it's not talking to the cops."

I was afraid to press him, to find out what he wanted me to do. I shouldn't have been so generous, but it just slipped out. The sisters had taught us to be magnanimous to those who were in need.

Sister Mary Eucharista would've taken one look at Jeff Coleman and let me off the hook.

He wasn't about to let me off the hook, however.

"I need you to cover for me."

I wasn't liking the idea of this.

"Cover what?" I asked when he hesitated.

"I've got a high-profile client who won't come to the shop. He wants Mick Jagger's tongue on his ass. I'm supposed to be there at three. For obvious reasons, Kavanaugh, I can't be. But you can. I'll split the fee with you fifty-fifty."

"Why don't you just cancel?" Seemed reasonable to me.

"You don't cancel this guy. He won't call again if I do. He's paying a cool grand. It's easy money, Kavanaugh."

"Jeff, that's highway robbery. That Rolling Stones logo's got to be one of the easiest tats ever."

"He doesn't care. So I don't care. Will you do it?"

"Why me? Why not one of your staff?"

"Because the cops are watching the shop. I don't want them following anyone to this guy."

My curiosity was piqued. "Who is he? Howard Hughes?"

When Jeff told me who it was, a shiver ran up my spine. But not in a bad way. I couldn't say no.

"Where and when?"

He chuckled. "Knew you'd do it. Versailles. That new resort, the big one."

"I know it."

"The Marie Antoinette Suite. Three o'clock."

I hadn't taken my equipment anywhere in a long time and wondered whether I had a proper case for it. "Sure, okay," I said. "Can I just go up there?"

"He'll be expecting you. Just tell the guy at the desk that you're Minnie to see Mickey."

"You're kidding, right?"

"Serious as murder."

I cringed, but didn't argue. "Will you be okay?" I asked.

"Sure, don't worry. And thanks, Kavanaugh. I knew I could count on you."

He hung up without saying good-bye.

Bitsy was staring at me.

"Who was that?"

"Jeff Coleman."

"That scumbag?"

"His ex-wife was Kelly Masters."

Bitsy's mouth formed a perfect "O." I touched her chin and pushed up, closing her mouth.

"Why's he calling you?" Bitsy wanted to know.

I didn't want to tell her that I'd made a visit to Jeff's shop last night. "He knows Tim's a cop. He wanted to know if I had any inside scoop on her murder." As I said it, I wished I did. "Oh, by the way, do we have any sort of bag or case I can use for my equipment? Got a house call at three."

Bitsy's eyebrows shot so far up her forehead I thought they'd go into orbit. "What? I don't know anything about that."

"A friend of a friend," I lied easily. "Sorry, forgot to tell you."

Ace overheard our conversation. "I've got a case you can use," he said. "Used to do parties. It's under my table. I'll get it for you."

He sauntered off, and I asked Bitsy to stock the case while I was with my next client, who walked in just at that moment, letting me off the hook—but not for long.

I was in the middle of a Cinderella castle on the back of the client's thigh when the door to my room opened slightly,

Tim leaning around it. His shoulders were stiff in the sport jacket, his mouth set in a grim line. He caught my eye and cocked his head to indicate that I should come out.

"I need a couple minutes," I told the girl in front of me as I peeled off the latex gloves. "You want a soda or anything?"

She was texting someone on her phone and shook her head.

Joel mouthed, *What's up?* as I passed him, and I shrugged as I followed Tim into the staff room. He shut the door behind me.

"What do you know about Jeff Coleman?"

"Hi, hello, nice to see you for the first time in two days," I said, eager to put off this conversation, especially since I could feel my hands start to get clammy.

I wasn't a good liar.

He relaxed slightly, but kept his hands on his hips. "Sorry, but I've been pretty busy. I need to know what you know about Coleman. He's got a shop up near Fremont, and you always seem to know everyone."

As he said it, I realized it was true. I was never Miss Popular, but I always managed to keep up on who was who in the worlds I traveled in. It was always good to know who your enemies were, as well as your friends.

"Yeah, I know Coleman. He's a jerk." I said it too loud, and Tim came so close our noses were almost touching.

"Do you know where he is?"

I didn't have to lie this time. "No. Should I?"

"He was married to Kelly Masters."

I hoped I had what looked like surprise all over my face.

"You don't look like that's news to you," Tim accused.

So it was more like egg on my face. Figured.

"I might have heard something," I admitted.

"When was the last time you saw him?"

I shook my head, forcing myself to keep calm, even

though my heart was pounding. "Not sure," was all I could spit out.

He didn't believe me. So he tossed his cards on the table.

"Coleman's fingerprints were found on a gun in that rental car where we found Kelly Masters's body last night."

"Really?" It had been on the news that she'd been shot. Jeff hadn't said anything about his gun at the scene. My surprise was genuine this time. But Tim wasn't finished.

He threw the ace down.

"And we found traces of blood that match Elise Lyon's blood type in the backseat."

Chapter 16

Another little bit of information that Jeff neglected to mention when he called. Unless he didn't know. I'd checked the caller ID after I hung up with him, but the number registered as restricted. I had no way of getting in touch with him to find out if he was messing around with me.

"So, was Kelly Masters shot with that gun?" I asked.

"Yes."

I waited for more, but nothing else came. My thoughts ran around like a border collie in a field of sheep. "You're sure it's Coleman's gun?"

"It's registered to him."

"Why would he kill her with his own gun and then leave it there? I mean, the guy's not Ivy League or anything, but he's not stupid, either." Maybe whoever did kill her was framing Jeff, like he said. "And what does that mean? You found traces of blood?"

"What do you think it means?"

"So do you think Elise Lyon was shot, too?"

His expression told me his patience was wearing thin, but nothing more.

"Why are you here, then?" I asked. "Why aren't you out looking for Jeff Coleman?"

He ran his hand through his short hair, exasperated. "I thought maybe you might know where he hangs out."

"Oh, because he's in my crowd? Because we're both tattooists, we must hang out together? Tim, I hate to tell you this, but it's not a *club*. We're just business owners. Yeah, we run into each other from time to time, but I can't stand the guy." All of this was true, so I didn't have to feel guilty about any of it.

Tim sank down onto the chair next to the light table, wringing his hands in his lap. "I'm sorry," he said. "It's just that there's a lot of pressure on this one. You know, with the media, Bruce Manning, we're under the gun." Considering the situation, that might not be the best phrasing, but I opted not to mention that.

I pulled Bitsy's stool over and sat next to him. "I don't mean to get on your case. I'm sorry, too. But I don't really know how I can help you. I don't know where Jeff is."

"We've got a warrant."

"I know."

The words were out before I could take them back. Tim frowned.

"How do you know that?"

I tried to be nonchalant. "Word gets around, you know."

"No, Brett, it doesn't. Unless you have friends in high places, and as far as I know, I'm as high up as your friends go. Who did you hear it from?"

I couldn't keep this going. I just didn't like Jeff enough.

"He called me."

"When?"

"A little while ago. He said he was in trouble, asked me to take a client of his he couldn't cancel. I said okay." And the more I thought about it, the more I felt like I'd made a deal with the devil. But I couldn't turn down the cash. Or the client. I mean, any woman would want the job.

"Where was he?"

"I don't know, and before you ask, his number was listed as restricted on the caller ID."

Tim had gone all rigid, ready to pounce out of his chair

toward the phone at the front desk. He relaxed slightly, but he was still on alert. Like the way a cat is when the bird flies away, but maybe, just maybe, it'll be back.

"I can't believe I'm sitting here asking you about this and you talked to him but you won't tell me until I trip you up. You're not hiding anything, are you?" His face was dark, and I recognized his expression. The last time he'd looked like this was when Mary Ellen Judson had messed around with his best friend, Aidan, but pretended nothing had happened even when he asked her about it, even after Aidan had told him about it.

Sister Mary Eucharista knew the power of guilt. It was kicking my butt.

"I'm sorry," I said softly, not making eye contact.

"If he calls again, I need to know. You need to get some information out of him."

So now I was a narc. Sort of. "Sure." I got up. "I've got to finish that tat out there."

Tim and my guilt followed me out of the staff room.

"Oh, and don't talk to any media again. That Leigh Holmes snippet made it onto the cable networks."

Bitsy was on the phone, jotting down an appointment, but as Tim spoke, she glanced up at me. I knew what she was thinking, and I had to tell Tim.

"Uh, Tim, you're a little late with that," I said.

He took a deep breath. "Why don't you just tell me everything, Brett? Why do you make me pull it out of you?"

"That thing for *20/20*, remember? I told you they were coming. They were already here. Not a couple of hours ago. They're doing a piece tonight on Elise Lyon's disappearance."

He looked like he'd just gotten off a ship after a two-week cruise and couldn't get his balance. "What?"

"*20/20—*"

"I heard you. What sorts of questions did they ask?"

"It really wasn't a big deal," I said quickly. "It was some

reporter named Alison Cho. She just asked about Elise's visit here."

"But she showed the drawing," Bitsy piped up. Lucky for me, she'd just gotten off the phone. Right.

"What drawing?" Tim looked at Bitsy, knowing she'd give him the straight answers he'd been looking for from me.

"The devotion tat Brett was going to do." Bitsy's eyes skipped from Tim to me and back again.

"What is it?" he asked, and I shook my head behind him, trying to tell her to stop right there.

Bitsy has a problem with keeping secrets. She can't. So no one usually tells her anything they don't want spread around. That's why when she said, "You know, how it said Matthew and not Chip," I wasn't totally surprised.

Tim whipped around to face me again. "That's going to be on TV? Why didn't you just tell her it was the wrong one?"

"I said no comment." I cocked my head at Bitsy. "But Ms. Truth Teller here couldn't keep her mouth shut."

Tim looked like he was about to explode. "If anyone here," he said loudly, "talks to the media or anyone else besides me about Elise Lyon again, I swear I will find a way to arrest you."

And then he walked out.

"What's up his butt?" Joel called out from his room.

"Nothing," I said, and headed back to Castle Girl.

Because of Tim's visit, I barely finished the ink in time before I had to go to Versailles to cover for Jeff. I grabbed the case that Bitsy had put together for me.

"Where are you going?" she asked.

"Yeah, just what is this mysterious job you've got?" Joel had sneaked up behind me, as much as a three-hundred-pound man can sneak up on anyone.

I'd been busting at the seams to tell someone, and I couldn't keep it to myself any longer. This was too good not to share.

"Jeff Coleman asked if I could fill in for him with a client who doesn't want to go to his shop."

"Why can't he do it?" Joel asked.

"Because he's on the lam," Bitsy said, then immediately put her hand over her mouth.

"You were eavesdropping," I accused her.

"Wouldn't you?" Bitsy asked through her hand.

She had me there.

"Okay." I sighed, and I told them who the client was.

Joel's body rocked slightly, as if he were about to swoon. Exactly how I'd felt when Jeff told me, and I had no idea how I'd react once I actually had the man's bare butt under my fingertips. I hoped the sweat from my hands wouldn't seep through my gloves and cause the machine to slip. That was all I needed, to make a mistake on the guy's ass. Granted, it wasn't exactly in a spot where he'd notice.

"I have to go now," I said, pushing my way past Ace and out into the mall.

In the parking garage elevator, I was sandwiched between an elderly woman in a bright pink velour sweat suit—didn't anyone tell her it was a hundred degrees outside?—and a guy who looked like he was on his way to a Young Republicans meeting, complete with a three-piece navy pin-striped suit, red tie, and buzz cut. And they looked at me like I was the freak.

When I stepped out of the elevator, though, I started to freak. Quietly. To myself. Because the big, bald, tattooed guy in the sleeveless jean jacket was leaning against a concrete pillar about halfway to my car.

Chapter 17

The pink sweat suit and the Young Republican slipped past me, going in the opposite direction. I didn't want to face this guy in a parking garage by myself. I didn't want to seem afraid, either, even though he could probably smell my fear, mixed with exhaust, from here.

I could just pretend I forgot something and get back in the elevator. I could use the case as a weapon. I wondered whether Bitsy had packed it in such a way so that if I had to swing it at him, my stuff would be okay.

I could just ask him what he wanted, why he was watching me. But while I could confront Willis, the cop, outside my shop, that was clear-cut. He was a cop. I knew cops. I felt comfortable around them.

Sure, this was a big tattooed guy. Not like I hadn't encountered one of them before, either. Not like I hadn't inked one of them myself.

But this particular guy? There was a vibe about him, a sinister, creepy vibe that hit me in the gut when I'd seen him the first time, then outside my shop, and now. He wasn't just a guy I was running into. There was more to it. What there was, I wasn't sure, but I didn't want to be alone in a dark, cavernous parking garage with him. I preferred to question him when surrounded by people, in a public place.

He had to be Kelly Masters's brother, Matthew. Jeff's

warning about him only solidified how I felt about this. I wondered if he thought I knew something about his sister. Although the first time I saw him, no one had found her dead.

I was grabbing onto any straw I could to make sense of this.

And while I'd hesitated, he started walking toward me.

I stopped breathing for a second as I debated what to do. Turn back or just barrel past him and take my chances?

Suddenly, the elevator door opened behind me, and a young couple stumbled out, their smiles indicating that either they'd hit a jackpot at the tables or they were anticipating a little afternoon delight. I didn't care which, because they were going my way, and I managed to put them between me and Matthew as we walked, so I felt safe. They didn't pay any attention to me.

We shuffled by, and I felt Matthew's eyes on me as I clicked my key fob and slid into my car, dropping the case on the seat next to me. I didn't even wait to put on my seat belt, just fired up the engine and felt the Mustang skid slightly as I peeled out of the spot.

I thought I'd hit him as I spun around, but he was gone.

Like a ghost.

I kept looking in the rearview mirror as I pulled out of the garage and headed toward Versailles, which had been built on part of the lot where the old Frontier had sat before it was imploded. Another hotel and casino was scheduled to go up on the property, too. Vegas was just squeezing them in on the Strip. Cranes and bulldozers and construction crews were just a matter of course. Sin City had become Crane City. Soon there would be no empty lots left.

Despite the space restriction, Versailles still managed to look sprawling. Gardens that imitated the ones at the real French palace were in front, rather than behind, and hedge animals danced along the elegant drive up to the circular entranceway. A fountain sporting sculptures shaped like mermaids made me start thinking about that water short-age again.

I debated self-parking, but my experience with that was dubious. The parking garages were mazes of arrows that made you think you were going in the right direction but somehow you always managed to end up at the exit or the valet parking lane. It was easier to valet park, cheaper—free—to self-park. It depended solely on the level of frustration I was willing to endure.

Today, my endurance was at an all-time low. So I pulled up into the valet parking lane.

A valet in a white-and-gold footman's uniform, complete with white wig, tights, and big-buckled shoes, pranced up to my door as I eased the Mustang to a stop. I climbed out, grabbing my case, and handed over the keys.

"Nice tat."

The valet's words were whispered, as if he'd get in trouble for admiring the garden on my arm. But it *was* Monet, and it *was* France. I should get some sort of points for that.

I nodded my acknowledgment and skipped up the steps, not prepared for what I would encounter inside.

The opulence of the magnificent lobby was staggering. Mirrors lined all walls; ornate chandeliers dripped real diamonds—I'd read that somewhere—from the ceiling. Huge sprays of loose orchids—not the sad little orchids in our shop; these orchids were on steroids—sprang out of spectacular, gilded china vases on white marble tables with thick mahogany legs.

The marble floor was rippled with golds and browns and creams, ending in a busy carpet to the left, where the casino began. The slot machines were all lined up like little soldiers, ready for anything. Since they'd done away with actual coins, the familiar *clink-clank* of the old days was gone; the only white noise now was the rhythmic *ding-ding* as the wheels turned, along with the piped-in music.

Tasteful signs with cursive gold lettering pointed guests

to the front desk, concierge, elevators, gaming area, shops, restaurants, and pools.

I sidestepped one of the flower displays, drinking in the scent as I lugged my case over to the front desk.

The guy was in costume, like the valet out front, this one with a permanent-marker mole sitting on the top of his cheekbone. I wondered if I should tell him I could make that really permanent. I did, after all, have my needles and ink with me.

"May I help you?" he asked, with a distinct French accent.

I wondered if he'd been imported for this very purpose.

I felt like a moron, but I leaned forward and whispered, "Minnie to see Mickey."

His face lit up like one of the chandeliers. "Yes, yes, miss."

I felt someone touch my arm and stared straight into the face of another costumed Frenchman offering to take my case. I clutched it a little tighter. "No, thanks," I declined. "I can carry it."

For some reason I felt that if I handed it over, I might not get it back, and I didn't want anyone here knowing what was inside, since I was on this Top-Secret Mission.

The Frenchman waved me into a special elevator, separate from the bank of elevators that would bring regular people—well, incredibly rich regular people—up to their rooms. The elevator was also mirrored, and I began to feel like I was being watched again, although this time it was definitely just me watching myself. And maybe hotel security. Cameras were everywhere, even if you didn't see them. A little disconcerting.

The doors slid open at a floor that was undesignated. The French footman—because that was what he looked like—stretched his arm out and turned up his hand, indicating I was to disembark. So I did.

The doors shut behind me, with the Frenchman behind them, and I stood alone in what I assumed was the Marie Antoinette Suite.

The pale yellow wallpaper was speckled with tiny pink roses and interrupted with elaborate white molding, the chandelier balanced delicately over yet another orchid spray on yet another marble table. I was uncomfortable and began to understand why the French had a revolution.

I took a couple of steps and peered around, seeing no one.

"Excuse me?" I said into the silence, venturing a little farther into a living room area. A grand piano sat next to a long floor-to-ceiling window overlooking the gardens, and beyond them, the Strip. It would be a great view at night, especially with all the lights.

I moved into the suite step by step, saying, "Excuse me?" as I went.

Still no answer.

The adulation that rushed over me when Jeff had said this guy's name and the thought that I would get up close and personal with his ass were quickly dissipating. He could only be crazy. How else to explain "Minnie" and "Mickey"? And this cat-and-mouse in the suite? Would he have done this to Jeff? Was this some sort of sick misogynistic thing?

I moved through the bedroom and saw the open bathroom door. All the lights were on. I still didn't hear anything, though.

I was going to see his naked butt anyway, so I decided against shyness and poked my head into the bathroom. I was tired of this and just wanted to get to work.

I realized, though, that my easy five hundred wasn't going to be so easy.

He lay slumped over the edge of the Jacuzzi bathtub, his head lolled on its side, an eye staring up at the ceiling. There was no water in the tub, and I was pretty sure he was dead.

But it wasn't the celebrity I'd been expecting to see.

I had no idea who it was.

Chapter 18

I didn't want to put my fingerprints anywhere, so I hit the elevator button with my elbow. I had a minute or two before the doors opened, and I took a couple of deep breaths to try to calm down. I immediately thought of Jeff Coleman and how he'd sent me over here. Did he know about this? Had he set me up?

I wanted to give him the benefit of the doubt, but I was having a hard time with that.

The elevator finally arrived, and I again hit the lobby button with my elbow and felt the drop in my gut. When I stepped out, a footman—a different one this time—was waiting. He was frowning.

"Is there a problem, miss?"

"You might say that. There's a body up there, in the bathroom, in the bathtub." As I said it, I started to feel a little woozy.

I sank down on the floor, dropping my case at my side, and put my head between my knees.

"What's the problem?"

It was a baritone, with an English accent.

"She says there's a body in the Marie Antoinette Suite," I heard the footman whisper.

"Who are you?" I felt his breath on my cheek, and I looked up into deep brown eyes that twinkled at me.

"Brett Kavanaugh. The Painted Lady."

His mouth quivered slightly, as if he wanted to smile but stopped himself in time. I felt myself get warm all over as his eyes now moved to my arm and then across my chest to the dragon's head, but it wasn't an unpleasant feeling. In fact, just the opposite.

"Yes, Miss Kavanaugh, I see that. What were you doing in the Marie Antoinette Suite, and what did you see up there?"

I glanced behind him to see a crowd starting to form. I cocked my head and said, "Maybe we should just go up there and I can show you."

His hand was under my elbow—sending a small electric shock through me that I told myself was just from the carpeting, but from the way he was looking at me, I wasn't totally able to convince myself of that—and he gently helped me up, leaning down slightly to pick up my case with his other hand. "Let's," he said simply and nodded at the footman, who fetched the elevator for us.

Once inside and going up, my stomach doing more flip-flops, I noticed the stranger was slightly taller than I was and had a sort of rakish, Hugh Jackman look about him. His hair was blonder, streaked with natural highlights, brushed back to emphasize the angles of his face. I figured he was mid-thirties or so. He wore a navy suit with a red tie but carried it off better than the Young Republican I'd seen earlier.

"Who are you?" I asked.

He did smile then.

"Simon Chase. I'm the manager."

"I thought everyone here had to be French."

His eyebrows arched slightly. "It *is* a bit of a sacrilege to have an Englishman here, but Bruce Manning likes my résumé."

"And I guess what Bruce Manning likes, Bruce Manning gets," I said, happy to have a small distraction from what we were about to walk in on.

"Perhaps now that you know who I am, you can tell me why you're here, Miss Kavanaugh."

"I was here to give a guy a tattoo, but when I showed up, I didn't see the guy I was supposed to see. Instead, I saw some other guy dead in the bathtub."

"Are you sure he's dead?"

"He didn't look alive." As I remembered, I took a deep breath and hoped I wouldn't get woozy again.

The amusement disappeared off his face, and his mouth set in a grim line. "Well, we'll see about that."

I got the sense he didn't believe me —like I would make something like that up—but before I could say anything further, the doors slid open and we were stepping back into the suite.

I smelled it then, the faint pungent scent that I hadn't noticed the first time because I'd been too hopped up about my celebrity encounter. Simon Chase smelled it, too, and his nose wrinkled, leading him toward the bathroom. I followed, not only to make sure the body was there, like I'd said, but to keep an eye on my case, which he was still carrying.

Simon Chase turned at the door, his hand again taking my elbow and steering me back out into the living area. "I see what you mean." He looked over at the footman, who was standing sentry at the elevator. "Please call nine-one-one. But we need to be discreet. Have them meet you at the loading dock entrance, and bring them up that way, please."

The footman nodded and stepped backward into the elevator, the doors closing.

Simon Chase let go of me then, put my case on the floor, and sank down on the back of a plush sofa, facing me.

"So, Miss Kavanaugh, you were here for a job. To tattoo a gentleman. But not that gentleman in the loo?"

"No. Not him." And I told him who was supposed to be the recipient of the Stones logo, without going into the intimate details of my assignment.

Simon Chase didn't stop the smile this time, which spread from his lips up to his eyes. I was feeling slightly unnerved. It had been a long time since I'd felt an attraction like this, and if my radar was working properly—I wasn't one hundred percent sure it was—it seemed he was reciprocating.

"That particular guest left yesterday, Miss Kavanaugh. I find it difficult to believe he would arrange this, since he knew he would be leaving."

My mind was racing. Again I wondered if Jeff had set me up. Then again, maybe he'd been set up. He was the one who was supposed to be here, not me. He *had* told me that he thought someone was framing him in Kelly's death.

"I'm actually covering for someone else, another tattooist," I admitted.

"So he's the one who arranged this?" I could tell that he, too, wondered if I'd been set up.

"I really think he thought it was his client who called and made the appointment," I said, surprising myself by defending Jeff. But my gut told me Jeff wouldn't set me up like this, despite our tenuous relationship. Would he? Seemed my gut was a little ambivalent.

"Who's in there?" I asked.

"So you really don't know?"

"No. Is it a big secret?"

"I suppose not." Simon Chase got up and walked around to the window, his back to me for a second before he turned to face me.

"His name is Matt Powell. He's Chip Manning's driver."

Chapter 19

Before I could react, a loud cacophony of cheering swept through the window from somewhere below. I must have looked puzzled, because Simon Chase beckoned me over.

A crowd of what looked like French peasants was racing toward the front of the building. If I wasn't mistaken, they were waving sticks of French bread.

"What is it?" I asked.

"They're storming the Bastille. Every afternoon at three. You've just missed Marie Antoinette telling them to eat cake."

"You're joking, right?"

"This is Versailles. Have you been in the casino?"

I shook my head, unable to rip my eyes away from the production going on outside.

"Guillotines."

I looked at him then. "What?"

"The slot machines. When you hit a jackpot, the blade crashes down on top of the machine. It's not real, of course, so no one will get hurt."

Sometimes the illusions went too far. But he seemed rather proud of his guillotines, so I kept the thought to myself. Instead, I changed the subject.

"So why would Chip Manning's driver be here?"

Simon Chase took a deep breath. "When your client

left yesterday, Chip moved in here. He usually stays in this suite when he's in town, but his visit this time was, well, unexpected."

Because he was supposed to be on his honeymoon with Elise.

"You're the woman on the telly, aren't you?" Simon had finally made the connection.

"That's right."

"You saw Elise."

"Yes." I didn't quite know what else to say. If he'd seen the bit on TV, then he already knew what I knew.

Fortunately, the conversation had to stop at that point, because the elevator doors opened and the footman led two detectives, a couple of crime scene forensics guys like the ones you see on TV, and two paramedics and a gurney into the room.

Simon Chase became all business. He showed them where the body was. One of the detectives tossed a glance back at me, and I recognized him as one of Tim's buddies. Great.

"She found the body," I heard Simon saying from the other room.

I felt my stomach drop with those words, and when I saw the detective—what was his name?—come out to talk to me, it got worse.

"What happened here, Brett?"

He was on a first-name basis with me, but I was in the dark about his.

"I was supposed to see someone else, a client, and when I got here, I saw this guy instead." That was it in a nutshell.

He wanted more than that.

"So someone commissioned you to, well . . ." His voice trailed off as he tried to figure out just what it was I was supposed to do.

"It was a house call," I filled in for him. "Someone who wanted a tat. But that client wasn't here. The guy in the bathroom was."

"Who was the client?"

I told him, and his eyebrows shot up, a grin dancing across his face. "Really?"

"But he wasn't here," I repeated. "So I went downstairs, and Mr. Chase came back up with me."

The elevator doors opened again, and a big, white-haired man bounded into the room.

"What's going on here?" he demanded, looking straight at Simon Chase.

I didn't need anyone to tell me *his* name. He was Simon Chase's boss, Bruce Manning. I'd seen him enough on TV myself to know that.

"I'm afraid there's been an incident," I heard Simon murmur, taking Manning's elbow much like he did mine earlier and steering him toward the window, next to the piano, away from the activity.

Why is it that an English accent will make anything sound civilized—even death?

"We're going to need to take your fingerprints," the detective was saying to me.

Brian. That was it. That was his name.

"Sure, I guess so, but I didn't touch anything. I used my elbow to push the elevator button." I paused. "Does this mean he was murdered? He didn't just keel over in the tub?"

Brian didn't look too happy with me. "We're going to need to take them, just in case."

I knew what that meant: just in case I was lying about why I was here, who I was supposed to see. Just in case I happened to have killed that guy in there.

And as I was thinking that, Brian pointed to my case, which Simon had put on the floor next to the plush sofa.

"I need to check that out."

I pulled it out and unlatched it, opening it to reveal my inks and needles wrapped nicely in their one-time-use packages and the tattoo machine. Brian poked around, lifting up the latex gloves, also in packages. The state of Nevada wouldn't find any health violations with me or my shop.

Without saying anything, Brian took the latex gloves and needle packages and went into the other room. I wasn't sure I liked the idea of that, especially since I wasn't sure what he was up to.

Bruce Manning's voice filtered into my head.

"I want to know what that driver was doing in here."

"Does it matter now?" Simon's voice was barely above a whisper.

"He shouldn't be in here without Chip."

"Where is Chip?"

Good question. I tried not to be obvious, watching them out of the corner of my eye as they huddled in the far corner of the room.

"Why is that woman with the tattoos here?" Bruce Manning obviously didn't feel compelled to answer Simon's question; either that, or he didn't know where Chip was. Maybe both.

"She says she was supposed to see the previous guest." The whisper was a little louder now, and while Manning's back was to me, Simon was looking in my direction—straight at me, actually. And he winked.

It was a tiny wink, but a wink all the same, and I got warm all over again, suppressing a smile.

"That's ridiculous," Manning said, swinging around now and spotting me hovering near the sofa. In three strides he was next to me, and I had no choice but to stand tall.

I was at least two inches taller than he was.

But what he lacked in height, he made up for in stature.

"Young lady, you had no business in this room."

"On the contrary, sir, I did."

His head swiveled to look at Simon Chase. "Is she telling the truth?"

Simon cocked his head at me, studying my face, and then said, "I believe so."

"Well, then, you've got a security issue here, Chase, and I demand you take care of it. She should never have been allowed up here, regardless, without you knowing about it."

"I'll look into it, Mr. Manning," Simon said, his voice measured.

"Is there a reason you're still here?" Manning bellowed at me.

"There is." Brian the detective was standing behind me, still holding the gloves, but now they were out of the package. I had a bad feeling about this.

"Did you put a pair of these gloves on earlier?" he asked.

All eyes were on me, and I shifted slightly.

"No. Why would I? I hadn't even seen my client."

Brian's face was stonelike. I couldn't read it. His words, though, came through loud and clear.

"A pair of gloves like this was in the tub. And a package exactly like the one you have in your case is in the trash can."

Chapter 20

"You've got to be kidding," was the first thing out of my mouth, which probably wasn't the smartest thing to say.

"What are you implying?" Simon Chase's voice surprised me, as he approached Brian.

Brian looked from me to Chase and back again. "Perhaps we need to take this downtown," he said.

"You should take her into custody now," Manning demanded.

I glared at him. "Can I at least get a phone call?" I heard something in my voice that was not conducive to speaking to police officers.

"We'll call your brother for you," Brian offered, but it wasn't more than an official gesture.

"I think I'd rather call him," I said, reaching for my messenger bag, which was still slung around my shoulder.

I don't know if it was my sudden movement—maybe he thought I was going for some sort of weapon—but Brian body-slammed me and I fell back over the top of the sofa and did a sort of backward somersault. Before I landed between the sofa and the massive coffee table, however, I felt a strong arm around my shoulders, helping me up.

Simon Chase asked, "Are you all right?"

I nodded, adjusting my skirt and shirt and messenger

bag, combing my fingers through my hair. "Thanks," I murmured, glancing at his profile, which was really quite striking. So he was chivalrous, to boot. Not like Brian the detective, who just stood there, staring.

"I think you owe Miss Kavanaugh an apology," Simon Chase demanded of Brian.

I was liking him more and more.

Instead of saying he was sorry, Brian shoved a cell phone at me. "Call your brother."

I took it before he changed his mind and went across the room, in front of the magnificent marble fireplace that dominated the far wall. I hadn't paid much attention to it before, but as I heard Tim's cell ringing, I studied the painting above the mantel. It was a splash of colors in the Impressionist style. But it was merely an imitation, and not a very good one at that.

"Kavanaugh."

That's right: He wouldn't know it was me because it wasn't my phone.

"Um, Tim? It's Brett."

"Brett?"

"I'm in a bit of trouble, I think. At least your friend Brian of the LVPD thinks so."

Silence, then, "Why is that, Brett?"

"He thinks I have something to do with the body found in the bathroom in the Marie Antoinette Suite at Versailles."

More silence.

"Why would he think that?"

Yeah, why would he? Except for a pair of latex gloves you could buy at any Wal-Mart. I didn't say what I was thinking this time, though. I had to tread lightly with Tim. He didn't like it that I kept ending up on his turf.

So I ran through the afternoon's events as quickly as I could, without even taking a breath. When I was finished, he said, "Okay, I'll be right there."

As I closed the phone, I felt someone behind me. I expected to see Brian, but it was Simon Chase. His brow was furrowed, like he was worried about me or something.

"Everything all right?"

I nodded. "My brother," I said, indicating the phone. "He's a detective. He's going to be here shortly." I tossed my head toward the painting. "You know, the Impressionists didn't paint until the nineteenth century. Your interior designer was off a century with the decorating. Or did she perhaps just choose it because of the colors?"

His eyebrows slid up slightly. "And you know about paintings, Miss Kavanaugh?"

I liked the way my name sounded when he wrapped his accent around it. Not like when Jeff Coleman barked it at me.

"I have a degree in fine arts from the University of the Arts in Philadelphia, concentrating in painting."

The eyebrows slid even higher. "That explains the tattoo on your arm." He smiled, a sly little smile that made me tingle unexpectedly. And what he said next was even more unexpected: "But what about the dragon over your breast?"

The way his tongue lingered on the word "breast" took my breath away for a second. It was completely inappropriate, considering there was a dead guy in the next room and Brian thought I was some sort of person of interest. But I couldn't help myself. He was the sexiest guy I'd met in a long time.

Maybe it was just the accent.

No, it was the whole package. I was ready to storm his Bastille.

"I like Chinese dragons," was all I could spit out. I was sure he saw right through me, but to his credit, he didn't call me on it.

"So you're a fan of Asian art? Or French Impressionists?"

"Neoclassicists." I said it before thinking.

Again with the eyebrows. "Really? Who?"

"Jacques-Louis David. *Death of Marat. Death of Socrates*."

"You're into death, then. You must feel right at home here."

He was flirting with me. A little "yay" echoed through my head, but I merely smiled. "At least he's French."

"Yes, he has that going for him." Simon Chase's eyes twinkled. "So why don't you have Marat on your arm?"

I thought about the painting: Marat slumped over the side of the bathtub, the blood on the sheet underneath him, the bloodstained letter in his hand. So real it was as if you could touch him.

It was just like the guy in the bathtub just yards away. Sans the letter and the blood. Coincidence?

I shivered with the thought. "A little too gruesome to wear," I admitted.

"Water lilies are more cheerful?"

"You could say that." I was distracted by the police officers who had started to dust for prints.

Simon noticed. "Perhaps we could continue this conversation over dinner sometime."

"If I'm not in the big house," I said grimly, only half joking.

"I'll bring you a cake with a saw inside so you can break out," he teased.

"Will you have a car waiting?"

"A big black Cadillac. That's the car of choice, isn't it, for you convicts?"

"Or a Town Car."

"Oh, those are nice, too."

It was as if we were the only two people in the room, until the elevator doors slid open and my brother walked into the suite.

Before I could say anything to him, Brian pulled him aside and whispered something in his ear. His expression didn't change, but his eyes flickered slightly as he looked at me. Something was wrong, and I didn't think it was just the latex gloves.

Brian let go of Tim's sleeve and went back into the other room. Tim approached me, but he now seemed to notice Simon, who held out his hand. "Simon Chase, manager."

Tim nodded, shaking his hand. "Detective Kavanaugh." He was through with pleasantries and turned back to me. "Brett, I need to talk to you."

Simon cleared his throat. "I need to speak to Mr. Manning anyway." And he went in search of his boss, who had disappeared into the other room as well.

"What is it now?" I asked Tim. "You know, I really just came here for a job."

"I believe you, but we've got to go through the motions."

"What motions?"

"Fingerprints. We have to confiscate your case."

I had a momentary panic attack. "My tattoo machine is in there."

"Don't you have another one?"

"That's my favorite." As I said it, I realized it sounded stupid, but it was true. That particular machine fit perfectly in my hand; it was just the right weight. "What's the problem?"

Tim nervously shifted from foot to foot, not very good at hiding his emotions from me.

He sighed. "We need to check the machine. The needles. The victim? His neck was punctured. That's how he died."

I had a bad feeling about this.

"Brett, there's a tattoo needle stuck in his neck."

Chapter 21

All my needles were still in their sterilized packages, but so were my latex gloves, so that wasn't a good argument for my case. I watched as the forensics officers swept the room with the black dust. Bruce Manning could barely hold in his anger, but I noticed Simon Chase was very good at calming him down.

"Why isn't she in custody?" Manning demanded at one point, indicating me.

My brother, to his credit, said, "We have no real evidence to arrest her."

That should've made me feel better, but Tim still wouldn't let me leave, despite that lack of evidence. Except for my case that had needles and gloves in it. Perhaps he meant physical evidence that I'd actually stuck that needle in Matt Powell's neck.

Even though the suite had almost as many square feet as our house, there were only three rooms: the big living area, the bedroom, and the bathroom, which by itself was about the size of our garage. I wanted to find a corner so I could call Bitsy and tell her I wouldn't be back for the rest of the day. However, privacy was out of the question.

"I could take her down to my office," Simon Chase offered, hearing me arguing with Tim about it.

Tim looked grateful, although slightly suspicious. "Okay,

sure, but you have to bring her right back up here after she makes her call." He looked around the room. "I don't have an extra body to send with you, so you'd better behave," he told me.

I stuck my tongue out at him. Habit. Simon smothered a grin.

"You two have an interesting relationship," he noted when we were safely in the elevator.

I'd been savoring the quiet. I hadn't realized how noisy it was in the suite.

"Don't you have siblings?" I asked.

He shook his head. "Only child."

"Lucky you."

He must have sensed I wasn't in the mood for any more banter, because he didn't say anything else. When the elevator finally eased to a stop and the doors opened, he led me down a long hall, opening a door to a small office. A woman sat at a desk in front of a computer. She looked up when we came in, and a long, sexy smile spread across her face. She was gorgeous, with those long black tresses and a bodice that was aching to be ripped, just like in romance novels. Not that I read romance novels. I'm just saying.

"Penny, we'll be in my office."

I followed Simon to a door in the back that I hadn't noticed. When he opened it, an office the size of the Marie Antoinette Suite overwhelmed me. It wasn't decorated in the same way; it was more retro, with a long Scandinavian desk and funky lights and a red leather couch that looked like it belonged on the set of Dan Tanna's *Vega$*. The long windows along the back wall gave me a view of the mountains, reminding me about Red Rock and how I could totally use a hike right about now to work off this stress.

What I didn't notice at first was the person at the bar—a full bar with glasses and bottles and a sink—over to the left. When he spoke, it startled me.

"What the hell's going on upstairs?"

I recognized him now. Chip Manning. Son of Bruce and

cuckolded fiancé of Elise. He'd had a few, from the way the amber liquid sloshed around in his glass as he swayed toward us.

Simon took his arm, steadying him and settling him onto the couch. Chip put his glass on the coffee table, leaned forward, and shouted, "Why doesn't anyone tell me what's going on? My father left me here, told me to stay, and he's been gone, I don't know, at least three drinks."

Maybe four or five, but who was counting? And obviously Manning had known where his son was but had chosen not to say.

"There's been a situation." Again, that British accent made a murder sound like Sunday in the park.

Before he could elaborate, though, Chip noticed me for the first time.

"You!" He stood up and pointed his finger at me. "What are you doing here?"

Simon positioned himself in between us, like Chip was going to come after me or something. "She needs to use the phone. Why don't we step outside for a moment?" And in one easy swoop, Simon pulled Chip around the table and steered him out of the office, nodding at me as he closed the door after them.

Now that they were gone and I was alone, my head started swirling. What was up with the guy upstairs? It certainly sounded like a tattooist had been there. Granted, anyone could get tattoo needles; you could order them off the Internet. But odds were that it had been a tattooist.

I really wanted to find Jeff Coleman and ask him some questions.

First, however, I had to call the shop.

Bitsy answered.

"Hi, it's me. I'm not going to be back today."

"You've got a seven-o'clock."

"Cancel it."

"What? You never cancel. And she was rescheduled from this morning. What's wrong? Did something happen on that house call?" She paused. "Hey, I get it. He fell madly in love with you while you tattooed his butt and you've found one of those Elvises and you're going to get married in one of those awful chapels and you'll be all over the tabloids this time tomorrow."

"Wish it were true, Bits. But no, I've gotten held up, and Tim needs me for something. I'll be in in the morning."

"Tim needs you? Hey, wait—"

I hung up, then shut the phone off, knowing she'd try to call me back. I didn't have Jeff Coleman's cell number, and he wouldn't be at his shop if he was skulking around the city hiding from the cops. But maybe someone there would know where he was. I turned the phone back on—I would need to recharge the battery later—and dialed his shop.

"Murder Ink."

Somehow the name of his shop had become prophetic.

"I'm looking for Jeff."

"He's not here." The voice was curt.

"It's Brett Kavanaugh. He sent me to cover for him on a job, and there was some trouble."

Silence, then, "What sort of trouble?"

"I need to talk to Jeff. How can I reach him?"

"How do I know you're really Brett Kavanaugh?"

Everyone was a bit paranoid these days.

I wasn't quite sure, either, how to answer that. I couldn't exactly prove it over the phone, and my personal cell number would show up on their caller ID, not my shop's number. "You'll just have to trust me," I tried.

"Sorry, lady," and he hung up.

A knock at the door, and Simon Chase poked his head in. "Are you all set?"

"Yeah," I said, shutting my phone off again.

Chip Manning came back in with Simon and collapsed on the couch. He'd left his drink outside. He pointed at me again, wagging his finger like Sister Mary Eucharista used to.

"Why didn't you tell me?" he asked, tears in his eyes.

"Why didn't I tell you what?"

"She wanted a tattoo."

"We already had this conversation, Chip," I said flatly.

"But she loved Matt. You knew that. It was what she wanted. Why didn't you tell me that?" He started to sob. "Where is she? Where is Elise?" He lay down, his face against the cushion.

I looked at Simon Chase, who shrugged. I didn't quite know what to do. Chip was drunk and brokenhearted.

He swung his head around and looked at me with one eye open. "Do me," he said.

"Excuse me?"

"Give me a tattoo. I want it to say 'Elise.' I want it"— he rolled over and pulled his shirt up, tapping a hairless chest—"here. I want to feel the pain. I deserve it." Rolling over again, he closed his eye, and in seconds he was snoring loudly.

I stifled a chuckle.

"Maybe you should do it."

I looked at Simon Chase, who was staring at Chip.

"Do what?"

"I can go upstairs, get that case of yours, and you can tattoo him right here, right on this sofa. I heard him tell you to."

It was tempting. "I demand up-front payment," I said. "I don't think he's in any condition—"

"How much?"

"What?"

"How much?" He was serious.

I thought about the fee I'd lost earlier. "A thousand," I said.

"Do you take cash?"

This had gone on long enough. "As much as I'd like to—and I like a practical joke as much as the next guy—I really can't."

"How about a temporary one?"

Our eyes met and we both started laughing.

"Now that's a good idea," I said. "I could make a stencil; he'd think it was real."

The phone on the desk startled me, and I jumped. I noticed Simon didn't. He probably got calls interrupting him all the time. He went over to his desk, and I watched him for a few seconds, until Chip made a sort of snorting sound. He rolled over, and as he did, I noticed something on the tails of his shirt. I peered more closely and saw small, reddish stains that seemed at first to blend in with the pink stripes.

They sure looked like blood to me.

Chapter 22

I wasn't a stranger to blood. The sight of it didn't make me all queasy. Especially little splashes. I wiped more blood than this off a tat while I was working.

I thought about Matt Powell upstairs. I hadn't seen any blood, but that didn't mean there wasn't any. He was stabbed in the neck. Had to be some. These stains couldn't be from that—could they? Chip said he knew about Matthew, that he knew about the tattoo I was supposed to give Elise. How? As far as I knew, it wasn't on TV yet. Had he found out anyway, like he'd found out about me—from his father, who was alerted by the police? Had he confronted his driver and the situation got out of control?

While it was a believable scenario, it didn't explain the tattoo needle or the gloves. How would he get those? Chip didn't seem that enterprising. In fact, I was having a hard time seeing in him what Elise had. Money could only go so far. Which was probably why she turned her sights elsewhere.

But then my train of thought veered onto another track. Where had Chip been this afternoon? He was drunk now, but was that just a reaction? Was it a cover-up, an alibi?

I was watching way too much TV.

"Mr. Manning is bringing your brother down to fingerprint you."

Simon's voice startled me. He noticed.

"Where were you just now?"

I tried to laugh, but it came out sort of funny, and his deep brown eyes unnerved me with their intensity. "Nowhere," I said. I didn't want to voice any suspicions about Chip unless I was sure. At least not to him.

He stepped closer, close enough so I could feel his body heat, which made me catch my breath. He was smiling, his hand reaching up—

The knock at the door made us both jump backward, away from each other. First time I'd seen him a little flustered. Part of me was sorry—I'd wanted to see where this was going—but the other part was glad. Because I wasn't nearly emotionally ready for something that seemed prematurely potent.

Manning came in first, bellowing at Tim, "You have to wrap all this up; there's media in the lobby, they've got their spies, they know something's happening."

Tim smiled serenely. I recognized that smile. It was the one he gave my parents whenever they asked why he wasn't married, why he and Shawna didn't patch things up, she was a nice girl, she would make a wonderful mother.

"We'll do all we can to avoid the press," he assured Manning.

It was at that point that they both noticed Chip passed out on the couch. Tim raised his eyebrows at me and I made a motion like I was drinking.

Manning seemed to lose a little of his bluster, looking disconcerted now instead. "How long has he been like this?" He focused on Simon.

"We came in and he was drunk," I offered, causing Manning to turn and study me like I was an exhibit at the city zoo.

"Haven't you caused enough trouble already, young lady?" he asked.

I opened my mouth to say something smart—I really didn't like that he kept calling me "young lady"—but Tim caught my hand, which stopped me. He had his fingerprint case in his other hand, and he asked Simon if he could use the desk, he would be neat about it.

With Simon's permission, we crossed the room and left Simon to Manning.

Tim rolled my fingers in the ink and pressed them one by one onto the print sheet.

"You might want to take a close look at Chip's shirt-tails," I whispered.

"What?" He stopped midhand.

"Stains. Red stains. I don't know if it means anything."

Tim glanced back at the trio on the other side of the room, Chip's snores now resonating through the air. "You know what you're implying, right?" His annoyance came through, but there was also a tinge of curiosity.

"He knew that a Matthew had captured Elise's heart. Maybe he thought it was his driver," I suggested.

Tim finished up with my hands and gave me a cloth to wipe my fingers. I needed more than that. I needed some soap and hot water. I also realized I needed a bathroom.

"Take a look," I whispered.

Tim's expression changed slightly as he approached Manning, and I asked Simon if there was a bathroom I could use. He directed me to a door in the corner.

I was almost afraid to actually use the facilities. The sink was a crystal bowl that sat demurely on the blond marble vanity, a gold faucet perched over its top. I hoped it wasn't real gold, but I wouldn't count it out. This place had cost a fortune, and it was obvious no expense was spared.

I scrubbed my hands until they were red but with no more sign of ink. As I turned the water off, I lingered a moment to savor the decor. The door wasn't all that sound-proof, I discovered to my chagrin, but it allowed me to eavesdrop.

Tim was trying to get Chip's fingerprints while he was passed out.

Manning was arguing that he couldn't do that legally; he'd call his lawyers and slap a suit against him.

Simon Chase's soft English murmur was indecipherable, but both Tim and Manning quieted down.

I stepped out of the bathroom to see all eyes on me.

"We'll get out of your way now," Tim said to Simon Chase, shaking his hand. He turned to Manning. "I'm sending a uniformed officer down here to wait for your son to wake up. We'll want to ask him some questions." Tim indicated that I should follow him, so I did, tossing back a quick, "Thanks," to Simon Chase, who gave me another wink that made me blush.

"Can I go home?" I asked Tim once we were back out in the hallway, heading toward the elevator.

Tim bit his lip, like it was a tough decision to make. Then, finally, "It doesn't look good, you know, the needle, the gloves."

"You can't possibly think I killed that guy, do you?"

Tim's mouth set in a grim line. "No, I don't think you killed him. And we've questioned the guy at the front desk and the elevator guy who brought you up here. They verify the time you came in. We'll check the video, too."

The video of the front entranceway, which would show what time I came in. The illusion was also one big *Candid Camera*, the black domes in the ceiling catching it all. I couldn't fault Tim for having to double-check. It was his job.

Tim was still talking. "But I want you to promise to go straight home. Otherwise, I'll put out an APB on you. I'll be there in a few hours, and we can talk then."

"It did look like blood, didn't it, on Chip's shirt?"

Tim stared me down before saying again, "Go straight home now."

He thought it was blood, too. He also didn't think I had anything to do with what happened to Chip Manning's driver, Matt. Otherwise he wouldn't let me go anywhere.

"I might stop for something to eat," I said, realizing I was starving.

"Make it takeout."

Tim took the elevator back up, and I took it down into the massive, mirrored lobby. The flashing lights of the slot machines reminded me of the guillotines Simon Chase had told me about. I couldn't leave without seeing those.

I followed the tasteful, yet at the same time gaudy, path through the casino a little ways. Despite the elegant and over-the-top decor in the hotel, this was a casino: loud, patterned carpeting meant to lift your gaze up to the machines and tables, where you'd lose all your money in a matter of seconds. Or in the unlikely chance that you'd hit the jackpot, like the guy over to my left, a guillotine blade would come crashing down on top of the slot machine, the whine of the bells and whistles announcing that today there was a winner.

It was pretty cool, the guillotine.

The cocktail waitresses all had high white wigs decorated with buttons and bows, their breasts bulging out of the white satin corsets, the skirts hacked off to reveal shapely legs in white fishnet stockings and four-inch white patent-leather heels.

I wondered how they could move in those costumes, but they seemed to have it all under control.

I started back out, pondering where I'd get a bite to eat. I was thinking of something more than a burger—I had just been fingerprinted by the police, even though it was my brother, and I needed a civilized meal to remind me that I wasn't some sort of criminal.

I was so lost in thought that I didn't see him at first.

But then I did.

Out of the corner of my eye. He was standing behind one of the guillotines, his shaved head with the eagle tattoo giving him away. I lifted my hand without thinking about it, then caught myself midwave.

He took a step toward me.

And I ran.

Chapter 23

He was gone by the time I went back with a security guard, who proceeded to give me the riot act about how I shouldn't cry wolf, because he didn't have time to run around looking for big, bald, tattooed guys who weren't there.

I thanked him for his time and gave the valet my ticket for my car.

What was this guy watching me for? If he was Kelly's brother, as I imagined he was, it also brought up another question that kept circulating in my head: What was the connection between Kelly and Elise Lyon? I found it hard to believe that Elise had come here to abandon Chip, met up with Kelly, and they decided on a lark to switch identities.

Well, then again, it *was* Vegas. Weirder things had happened.

But I wasn't sold on the idea.

I needed to find Jeff Coleman. In addition to wanting to find out if he'd set me up, or, as he'd told me, someone was framing him, I also wanted to quiz him a little more about Kelly Masters. He might know something he wasn't aware of.

Unlike the tattooed guy, I wasn't afraid of Jeff Coleman. Even if logic told me maybe I should be a little warier than I was. But it was Jeff. His bark was worse than his bite.

I'd told Tim I would go home. And I would.

After I went over to Murder Ink to interrogate Jeff's staff about his whereabouts.

Just call me Miss Marple.

I climbed into my Mustang after tipping the valet a dollar. He stared at it with pursed lips, and I had the sense that I might not get great service the next time around. Maybe I should've played one of those slots and tried for a couple extra bucks.

I'm just not that into gambling.

I kept looking in my rearview mirror to see if I was being followed. I wasn't quite sure what to look for, since I *was* being followed—by a lot of other cars that weren't familiar to me. Matthew could be in any one of them, and I wouldn't be the wiser.

I hooked my cell phone into my hands-free and called the shop.

"Everything okay?" I asked when Joel answered. "Where's Bitsy?"

"She ran out for some takeout for dinner."

On cue, my stomach growled.

"Where are you?" Joel's voice was full of worry.

I told him about what had happened, now that I was out of earshot of anyone but my own self. He had appropriate "ohs" and "ahs" and caught his breath when I described Matt Powell's body and then Simon Chase.

"He sounds dashing," Joel said of the latter.

"Dashing" was a good word. I had to remember that one.

"So where are you heading now?" Joel asked when I was finished with my story.

I was halfway to Murder Ink. I didn't really want to tell him I was going to try to track down Jeff Coleman. If Tim happened to call and ask where I was, then Joel would be completely in the dark and he couldn't be called a liar.

"I'm going to get something to eat and head home," I said, spotting one of my favorite Mexican spots in a strip mall. So much for my civilized dinner. No time for that when I didn't have much time. I made a sharp turn, irritating the guy behind me, who laid on his horn like there was no tomorrow.

I just waved at him, a little finger waggle.

"Listen, Joel, I'll see you in the morning, okay? Tell Bitsy she's doing a great job."

"And Ace and I are not?" He was teasing me.

"Sure, you know you are," I said, hitting END on the phone and getting out of the car.

I still glanced around furtively, like Matthew was going to jump out of the shadows from behind a car, but besides a family of four and a young couple who were also heading into the restaurant, there was no one else.

The flaky white fish accented with cilantro and wrapped in soft tortillas were to die for. I scooped up a generous bit of the salsa in crunchy chips that were obviously not store-bought. Throwing caution to the wind, I drank a Corona. I justified it by telling myself I'd been through a lot. Even with the beer, my meal didn't cost ten dollars. Gotta love it.

Jeff Coleman's shop was closed when I walked over from the motel parking lot. The sign in the window advertised that it was open, but the door was locked. I hooked my hands around my eyes and peered inside, seeing nothing but shadows.

"He's out of town."

The voice made me jump, and an elderly woman, tiny, maybe five feet tall but no taller, with her white hair piled on top of her head in a loose bun, stood behind me. Her sleeveless dress showed off swirls of ink on her arms, tattoo sleeves extending to her wrists, an elaborate design across her chest, and even more tats on her legs. She wasn't blind to my scrutiny.

"Taught him everything he knows," she said, indicating the shop.

"Jeff Coleman, you mean?"

She nodded, holding out her hand. "Sylvia Coleman."

Coleman?

A slow smile spread across her face. "Yes, dear," she said, answering my unasked question. "He inherited the business from me when I retired." She pulled a key out of her pocket and stuck it in the door. "Might as well come in. It's hotter than hell."

We stepped inside, the air-conditioning making the hairs on my skin stand tall, but not in a bad way. Sylvia indicated I should follow her to the back of the shop, where she pushed back a curtain so I could go through. It was Jeff Coleman's office, cluttered with stencils, flash, piles of boxes of baby wipes, latex gloves, and disposable needles. My eyes lingered on the latter. Maybe I should swipe some of them, see if they matched the one sticking in Matt Powell's neck. A closer look, however, told me that they were the same brand I used, the same ones the cops had in my case. Figured.

"Sit," Sylvia said as she plopped into a swivel chair behind the desk.

I obeyed her, balancing on the edge of a metal folding chair.

"I'm Brett—" I started.

"Oh, I know who you are. I keep tabs on everyone in this business in this town." She may have been petite, but her voice was big. Like Bitsy's. Maybe all little women felt they had to compensate. "Jeff said you probably would be coming around, which is why I've been keeping an eye out."

Jeff knew I'd try to find him? Did that implicate him in any way? I still had more questions than answers.

Sylvia was still talking. "I'd tell you where he is, but we don't know if we can trust you."

When a second passed and she hadn't said anything more, I felt it was safe to respond. "I'm not sure I can trust *him*."

She snorted. "Of course you can, dear. Why wouldn't you?"

A mother's love can go so far and be so blind.

"I just need to talk to him," I tried.

"We've heard about what happened over there at that big new place," Sylvia said. "Jeff's trying to figure out who's setting him up."

Word traveled fast. Must be that "source" who told Jeff there was a warrant out for his arrest.

"It's got to have something to do with Kelly," I suggested.

Sylvia gave me a look that indicated she thought I might be a few clowns short of a circus. "Well, of course it has something to do with her."

"I've been seeing her brother around."

She waved her hand in the air dismissively. "Oh, him."

"He's been following me. Jeff said I should watch out for him. That he's bad news."

Sylvia leveled her gaze at me, studying my face for a few seconds before her eyes slid to the dragon's head. "You need more ink," she said flatly. "How can you run a shop if you don't even have tats yourself?"

I glanced down at my arm, then at the dragon, knowing how it curved around my torso to my back, its tail touching the lilies on my side. I'd been thinking the same thing, but hadn't figured out just what I wanted. It had to be perfect.

Sylvia was reaching under the desk. "I can do it now. Only two hundred." Her words were muffled, but her tone came through loud and clear.

I stood up. "I'm not here for that. I just wanted to talk to Jeff."

Sylvia put a tattoo machine on the desk and smiled serenely. "You're a nice girl. But I can't tell you where he is."

"Can you tell me about Kelly, then?"

The change of subject startled her.

"What about her?"

"What was she like?"

Sylvia stared at a spot somewhere on the ceiling before answering. "She had some troubles."

"Jeff told me she had a drug problem."

"That wasn't the only thing. She was a hooker. I told Jeff he should be careful. Sometimes you can't change a leopard's spots."

"Is that what happened? Did she go back to hooking?"

Sylvia leveled her eyes at me, trying to figure out what to tell me. "You could say that."

Could say what? On one hand, Sylvia seemed like she had all her balls in the air. On the other, her cryptic answers made me wonder if she had a touch of dementia. When I didn't say anything, she continued.

"Jeff pulled her out of the gutter. She did clean up nice, have to give her that. Pretty girl. Maybe a little too pretty." Sylvia snorted. "He trained her here, teaching her how to tattoo; she was pretty good. That's how women got started, you know."

I knew. I knew about the circus women who ended up marrying the men who'd tattooed them. How their husbands trained them as tattooists so they'd have help in their shops and they didn't have to pay them. I wondered if Sylvia Coleman had learned the trade from her husband.

"So she worked here?" I asked instead, my curiosity stronger about Kelly right now.

"This"—Sylvia waved her arm around in the air, indicating the shop—"wasn't in her plans. Even if it was in his. He wanted to spend his life with her. He wanted kids with her. They tried for two years. But she couldn't. She had a condition." I hoped she wasn't going to start going into medical explanations. That was all the information I needed.

"Did they get divorced because of that?"

Sylvia smiled sadly. "She just left him one day."

"So you didn't hear from her again, either, after the divorce?"

She shook her head. "I wasn't exactly close to her. But I wasn't surprised when she left. Once she got straightened out, once Jeff gave her back her life, she was antsy. He thought a baby would change things, but she got tired of waiting for that. I couldn't talk sense to my boy—had to just let it play out."

Go figure, but I actually felt sorry for the guy.

A creaking sound made me catch my breath. The curtain began to move, and I saw a pair of black cowboy boots. Sylvia stood expectantly, and my heart hammered in my chest.

Chapter 24

"The sign says closed, but your door was unlocked." He was about twenty, baby-faced, with tattoo sleeves running down both arms.

Sylvia stood, shaking her head. "I keep forgetting things," she mumbled, indicating that I should follow her out into the shop.

I watched as she began preparing the young man's calf for ink, shaving it carefully as she talked to him about what he wanted: a basic cross with a crown of thorns wrapped around its top. She found the flash hanging on the wall and noted its number, shuffling through a pile until she pulled it out, a ready-made stencil.

"I don't know how much more I can help you," she said to me as she transferred the stencil onto his calf, leaving its outline that she would trace with her machine's needle.

I wanted to stay, to talk to her more. Not necessarily about Jeff—she wasn't going to tell me where he was—but just to watch her, a previous generation of tattooist, a woman tattooist who'd had to suffer far more discrimination than I ever did. Those women who came before me were pioneers, breaking into a male-dominated profession and breaking all the rules. Women like Sylvia gave me an option after I held that somewhat useless art degree.

She was concentrating, her reading glasses perched on her nose so she could more clearly see the lines she had to follow. I needed to head home before Tim got there, so he wouldn't have another reason to be upset with me.

I was also tired; it'd been a long day.

I thanked Sylvia for her time, and as I turned to leave, I heard her call my name, so I looked back.

"Come back and I'll find something nice for your other arm," she said. "A garden should be balanced."

I promised her I'd call.

The tinkle of a small bell rang in the distance as I pulled the door open and stepped outside into the heat. The sun was starting to go down, but the air still wrapped itself around me, suffocating me. The car took just a few minutes to cool off, and I eased the Mustang out of the lot and into the street, heading for home.

The white Dodge Dakota stuck out like the proverbial sore thumb behind me. Every time I looked in the rearview or side mirrors, there it was, looming large behind me. If I stopped short, he'd run right into me.

After about five miles, I knew for sure I was being followed. And he wanted me to know that, staying close, not hanging back behind any other cars. I tried to make out the driver, but couldn't. Only a shadow.

My cell phone was still hooked into the hands-free device, and I stuck it on my head, dialing Joel.

"Talk to me," I said.

"Where are you?"

"Have you ever met Jeff Coleman's mother, Sylvia?"

"Did you meet her? Isn't she fabulous?"

"So you do know her."

"Everyone in the business in Vegas knows Sylvia." He paused. "Hey, how did you meet her? I heard she retired."

"She was at Jeff's shop."

"You went there?"

I quickly told him about the visit, keeping an eye on the Dakota behind me.

"Interesting about Jeff and Kelly," he said. "I knew he'd been married, but didn't know more than that."

I told him that I was suspicious Jeff had set me up at Versailles.

He pointed out the other side of that coin: that whoever had killed Matt might have been setting Jeff up.

Neither of us could decide which was right.

"I'm being followed," I finally conceded.

"What?"

I'd turned off the highway and the Dakota was close enough so I could smell its exhaust. "A Dodge Dakota. Followed me all the way from Jeff's shop. But not exactly trying to keep it from me."

"Do you think it's that guy who was following you before?"

"It crossed my mind."

"Why don't you just stop and find out what he wants?"

It was a simple question, and one I'd been considering. It wasn't like I was alone on the road; there were plenty of other cars.

"Okay," I said, tired of the game. "But stay on the line, okay?"

"I've got my hand on the landline. I'll call the cops if I hear something."

I pulled over, easing the Mustang off to the side of the road, but as I opened the door and started to step out, the Dakota sped past me, so close I thought he'd take my door off, so fast I couldn't read the license plate.

I watched the taillights as the truck slowed for a light and made an executive decision. I closed the door and put my foot on the accelerator—the mouse now following the cat.

"What's going on?" Joel asked in my ear, and I told him. "Don't lose him!" he said.

I was trying not to, but I'd gotten stuck behind a couple of elderly drivers who decided the speed limit was way overrated. The Dakota turned a corner, but by the time I got there, it was gone.

I sighed. "Lost him," I said to Joel.

"Want to come back to the shop and we'll get a drink?" he asked.

The idea was tempting, but my heart was racing. "I just want to go home and lock the doors and put on my sweats," I said. "I'll see you tomorrow."

"If you need to talk again, just call," Joel said before hanging up.

The Dakota didn't reappear, and I managed to make it home without any more drama. Tim's car was absent from the garage, so I let myself into the empty house, savoring its familiarity.

Cheese and crackers beckoned from the fridge, and the bottle of Malbec was still half-full. I poured a glass before settling down in front of the TV. The clock reminded me that it was just about time for *20/20* and the exposé about Elise Lyon.

Alison Cho was giving the introduction just as I hit the remote.

"Elise Lyon had it all: youth, beauty, money, and she was going to marry the son of one of the richest men in the country. But she threw it all away, running from her fiancé to Las Vegas a week before her wedding, where she was last seen in a tattoo shop asking for a tattoo with the name of a man no one had ever heard of."

The screen filled with a close-up of the devotion ink I'd drawn, "Matthew" prominent, larger than life.

"Who is Matthew?" Alison's voice-over emphasized. "Is she with him now? No one knows, because after visiting The Painted Lady, Elise Lyon was never seen again."

The commercial was for Viagra. I muted the TV, mulling the dramatics, the mystery perpetuated by the media. Granted, I had a personal interest in Elise Lyon and Kelly Masters, but most of the country wouldn't even know about her if the media hadn't pounced on the story, like they had so many stories like this one. She was, as Jeff Coleman had insensitively put it, "a rich bitch," but she was also, in a sense, the princess who threw it all away to go slumming in Vegas. The public would eat it up.

I went into my bedroom and found my laptop, bringing it into the living room, turning it on, and logging into the wireless Internet—another post-Shawna splurge for Tim. Too bad he couldn't break up with her twice; maybe I could get him to buy us both iPhones and GPSs.

I Googled Elise Lyon.

A wedding announcement from the *New York Times'* Sunday Styles section popped up in the search, and I clicked on it.

> *Elise Lyon, 26, daughter of the world-renowned architect Richard Lyon and his wife, Madeline, of Philadelphia, will marry Bruce "Chip" Manning Jr., 31, of New York City, son of developer and entrepreneur Bruce Manning Sr. and his wife, Helene, on June 29. Richard Lyon most recently designed Versailles, Bruce Manning's new resort in Las Vegas. The couple met through their parents at a cocktail party in Manhattan.*
>
> *Elise Lyon attended Mary Baldwin College in Staunton, Virginia, studying psychology, and Chip Manning is vice president of marketing for his father's holdings in Atlantic City and Las Vegas, based in his father's offices in New York City.*

Doing the math, I quickly deduced that if Elise Lyon had gone to college when most high school graduates did and then graduated on time, it seemed unlikely she had pursued any sort of career path, otherwise the story would've said so. These stories were big on pointing out the high-powered jobs that the brides and grooms held. Maybe marrying Chip Manning, who was most definitely on a career path with his father's empire, was her calling.

I didn't get it. But I'd been working since I was sixteen.

I knew enough about Bruce Manning Sr. to skip the rest.

The voice on the TV tugged at me. I looked up from the laptop to see Alison Cho asking me questions. Joel had been right about the outfit. It totally worked, but I didn't look like me. At least not the me I knew. I heard my voice and wondered if I really sounded like that.

The phone rang.

"Brett? Brett? Why didn't you tell me you were on TV?" My sister's soft, hurried voice echoed in my ear.

I'd conveniently forgotten she was obsessed with the news shows. "It happened so fast, Cathleen," I tried.

Cathleen was the first to leave the nest—and the East Coast. Her husband was a software engineer, and they moved to Southern California ten years ago, right after they got married. Even though they were just a few hours away, we never saw each other. Cathleen thought I was a bad influence on her six-year-old daughter, who'd decided after my last visit that she wanted a tattoo of Tinker Bell on her arm.

"You should've called. Where's Tim? Why didn't he call? You were the last to see her? What was she like?"

I wanted to tell her to just hang up and let me finish watching the show, but she wouldn't stop asking questions. To shut her up, I told her everything that was being said, at about the same time.

Except for one thing.

"A man named Matthew Powell was found murdered in Chip Manning's suite at Versailles earlier today. Police will not say whether Matthew Powell, who was Chip Manning's driver, was Elise Lyon's Matthew."

But by saying that, Alison Cho certainly implied it.

My sister was still babbling. I ignored her, my eyes trained on the TV.

I wasn't prepared for the next statement.

"Police have confirmed that they have brought Versailles manager Simon Chase in for questioning."

Chapter 25

I told my sister I would have to call her back. I hung up even as she was arguing with me about it.

I sat on the couch and took a drink of wine. I wished I liked something stronger, but the wine was going to have to do.

Simon Chase? What did that mean, they were questioning him? Did the police think he had something to do with Matt Powell's murder? I thought about how he'd brought me up to the suite to see what I'd seen. If he'd already been there, he certainly hadn't shown it.

He'd egged me on about inking Chip's chest. Maybe he did know more about this than he was letting on.

I shivered, thinking about how he'd flirted with me.

My brain started going backward, like a video in rewind, through the events of the last couple of days, trying to get Simon Chase out of my head.

I thought again about Jeff Coleman. And Kelly Masters. I wanted to find the connection between Kelly and Elise. They seemed separate, but they weren't. They couldn't be.

I pulled my laptop out again and Googled Kelly Masters this time. I found a MySpace page, but it wasn't her. It was a Kelly Masters at NYU who was advertising her Wiccan religion. An accomplished harpist named Kelly Masters had gone to Juilliard and now played with the Boston Symphony. And then there was the Scientologist named Kelly Masters who had a YouTube video, preaching L. Ron Hubbard's words much in the same way Tom Cruise did, but to her credit she didn't jump on anyone's sofa. I shuddered and hit the button to go back to the previous screen.

A small item in *Entertainment Weekly* from a year and a half ago caught my eye. A picture of a woman whose features were similar to the picture on my cell phone— without being dead, obviously—accompanied two paragraphs about a Kelly Masters from Los Angeles who'd won a modeling contract with a top agency after some reality program on an obscure channel no one watched. Alive, she was very pretty in that skinny-model sort of way.

I couldn't see a tat on her neck.

I couldn't be sure if it was the same Kelly Masters. Jeff had said she'd been living in L.A. the last he knew, so it was possible. But he also said he hadn't seen her for a long time, so she could've been anywhere.

Except when I went to the next page, another small item popped out at me. Kelly Masters had been stripped of her modeling contract because she'd lied about her age during the competition. She was too old.

It was just a segue into the next hit. A tattoo shop site. Planet Tattoo. I clicked on it.

The shop was in Malibu; it advertised that all the hot celebrities had gotten tats there, prominently featuring the one I was supposed to ink earlier today.

And in the center of the screen was a photo of their star tattooist: K-C, who wore a wide, sexy smile, a black bustier, black leather pants, and eagle wings spread across her neck. A short bio said that K-C had trained in Las Vegas—but there was no credit for her ex-husband—and that she had won a modeling contest previously.

She should've been stripped of her title solely for choosing the moniker "K-C." Those TV tattoo shows were creating monsters.

Did Jeff Coleman know his wife was the Tattooist to

the Stars? He certainly hadn't indicated that, and neither had Sylvia. Kelly Masters had truly moved on, but it didn't answer my original question: What was she doing in Las Vegas with Elise Lyon?

I stared at the Google search bar for a few seconds.

I couldn't put it off any longer.

Googling Simon Chase brought up a slew of hits. Lots of news stories about Versailles, how Chase had been working for Manning in his Atlantic City casino before coming to Vegas.

I read through as much as I could, piecing together Chase's history.

He'd grown up outside London, but not too much information was available about his life until he came to the United States, where he got his master's in business administration from Harvard, hooking up with Bruce Manning early in his professional career. Not a bad star to hitch a ride on if you were ambitious.

And he was as ambitious in his off hours as he was on the job. He was a playboy, always with a different beautiful woman on his arm. I clicked on "Images" and saw him with celebrities, actresses and musicians and pop artists.

I picked one at random, clicking on the picture to make it larger.

The picture was taken on a beach, with palm trees and white sand. Chase was wearing a pair of khaki Bermuda shorts and a flowing cotton button-down shirt that was unbuttoned, revealing the physique I'd suspected when I met him. He had his arm slung over the shoulder of a woman wearing the scantiest of bikinis, her long dark hair pulled up and off her face, her features stunning and pink with sunburn.

Her body was turned to his, her neck swiveled in such a way that I could see it.

Eagle wings spread across her neck.

It was Kelly Masters.

My breath caught in my throat and my fingers froze above the keyboard.

Did he know Kelly Masters was dead? She was in Vegas; so was he. Had they hooked up here? Jeff said he'd heard she was getting married. Could it have been to Simon Chase?

Now I was even more embarrassed that I'd been taken in by his English charm. That his good looks had clouded any objectivity I would normally have had. But he had been suave and sophisticated and smart and funny, and, well, I'd been totally attracted to him.

The police were questioning him in Matt Powell's murder. What about Kelly's? Did the police even know Chase had a history with Kelly?

I wanted to know more. I hadn't found enough. I hit the arrow to go back and found myself again among links for Simon Chase. I hit the "next page" button three or four more times before a link caught my eye.

The *New York Times*. An engagement announcement. But it wasn't Simon Chase and Kelly Masters.

It was Simon Chase and Elise Lyon.

Chapter 26

The date told me the announcement had been published two years ago. Chase was working in Atlantic City at the time; Philadelphia wasn't too far away. Maybe he and Elise had met there. At the time of the engagement, Elise was twenty-four and Chase was thirty-six. He was older than I'd thought, but some men aged better than women. It wasn't fair.

I wondered what had happened to break them up.

Elise seemed to have a habit of falling in love and getting engaged. First Simon, then Chip, then Matthew. She was a busy girl. And Chip's statement about her affair a few months ago indicated she obviously had some commitment issues. Maybe she was one of those girls who just liked the idea of falling in love and getting married but couldn't follow through.

I'd been accused of that, but my story was more complicated. Paul and I met in a Manhattan club during the run of his first off-Broadway show. He played the Claus von Bulow part in a stage production of *Reversal of Fortune*. Let's just say he was typecast. At first, I found him charming and clever and attentive. However, over the next three years, Paul managed to snag some prime parts, feeding his ego and eccentricities. His needs had to come first; his art was more important than mine. I ignored that for a long time, thinking I could live in the shadow of his success, until I realized I couldn't. Tim was the only one I'd confided in; when he split with Shawna, he gave me the out I needed.

I pushed my memories aside. This wasn't about me. I focused again on my computer.

I hadn't seen the engagement announcement for Chase and Elise when I Googled her before, but I'd stopped searching for anything after I saw the one for her and Chip.

And then it struck me.

The connection I'd been looking for between Kelly and Elise was Simon Chase. I wondered if the police knew about that. Maybe they didn't before, but since they were now "questioning" Chase, maybe they had found out.

If they had, however, why were they still looking for Jeff Coleman? Oh, right. The gun with Jeff's fingerprints on it had killed Kelly. And I'd told Tim that Jeff was supposed to be in that suite at Versailles.

If Chase were guilty, then it would've been easy to set Jeff up there. Chase knew who would be staying in that suite and when, and if Jeff hadn't talked to that high-profile client too many times it would be easy to disguise his English accent and pretend to set up a job.

The more I thought about it, the more sense it made.

I couldn't believe I had flirted with a murderer.

I shut my laptop and realized I'd missed the rest of the *20/20* program.

I finished my wine and ate a couple more crackers before lying back on the couch and closing my eyes. I didn't mean to fall asleep, but when I awoke to the sound of the front door opening, I jumped up.

Tim looked like he hadn't slept for a week.

"What time is it?" I asked, the TV still flickering behind me.

"Two a.m. What are you still doing up?"

"I was watching *20/20* and fell asleep."

He spotted the laptop on the coffee table. "Checking e-mail?"

I nodded, uncertain whether I should tell him what I'd learned. I'd start out with baby steps. "The TV said you were questioning Simon Chase."

He pulled off his tie, which had been hanging rather slackly around his neck. "Yeah."

"Why?" I tried to keep from sounding too anxious.

"The press are a bunch of idiots," Tim said. "We asked Chase to come downtown to answer some questions formally for us about that suite, who was staying there, what the situation was with the victim. He wasn't a person of interest, but the reporters jumped to conclusions." He ran his hand through his hair, making it stand on end. "By the way, you're off the hook. We didn't find your fingerprints in that room, and the videos showed you definitely arriving when you said you did."

"You didn't really think I had anything to do with it?"

"Of course not. But I was surprised that since you were there, we didn't find a print anywhere."

"I hit the elevator button with my elbow. I know better than to touch anything at a crime scene." I said it like I was at crime scenes all the time, like I wasn't just picking that up from *CSI*. "What about Chip Manning? Did you get his fingerprints? Did you find out anything about the blood on his shirt?"

"His fingerprints are all over that suite, but it's not a surprise, since he was staying there." Tim paused. "We got the shirt. We're testing the stains. Thanks for the tip."

I was about to tell him what I'd learned on the Internet about Chase and Kelly and Elise, but his expression changed slightly, and I knew something was on his mind.

"What's wrong?" I asked.

"Time of death. Matt Powell wasn't killed today."

"You're kidding. When was he killed?"

"Medical examiner thinks maybe sometime yesterday."

"Chip Manning stayed in that room with a dead guy?"

"He was moved. We found carpet fibers from the room all over his body."

"So he was dragged through the suite and stuck in the tub?" I made a face. "That's really sick." I had another thought. "But how could someone get a body into the hotel without the cameras picking up on it?"

Tim smiled at me as if I were a simpleton. "Matt Powell had a smaller, much smaller, room on another floor."

I got it now. "So he was killed there and put in Chip's room? Was it to implicate Chip?" My thoughts were moving faster than a hamster on a wheel. "But even if he was moved, the cameras would've filmed it, right?"

Tim's expression told me that he was one step ahead of me, but he had no intention of sharing.

I had another thought. Once I started, there was no stopping me. "Hey, Chip was at my shop yesterday morning. He said Matt was waiting for him in the food court."

Tim's interest was piqued. "Really? Did you see him?"

I remembered how Joel and I had tried to catch up with Chip but lost him. "No. Do you think he was setting up an alibi?" I sounded like I really knew what I was talking about. Hey, maybe that Starsky and Hutch crack Jeff Coleman had made wasn't so far off the mark.

Tim didn't answer. But I was on a roll.

"Do you think Chip killed his driver because his driver was Elise's lover?"

Tim pursed his lips and shook his head. "Can't speculate."

I had another thought. "You know Kelly Masters's brother's name is Matthew, right? Maybe he's got something to do with this."

Tim frowned. "How do you know him?"

"I've seen him a couple of times. He showed up outside my shop the other day, and he was in the casino at Versailles when I left."

"Is he bothering you?"

"He's sort of a creepy guy. I don't like the idea of running into him. I get a bad vibe from him."

"But has he done anything? Approached you?" Tim's tone was laced with worry, but as I thought about his questions, I realized Matthew hadn't attempted to talk to me or follow me. Not that I knew. He'd just been *there*. And I hadn't been able to see the driver of that truck. Maybe it wasn't him at all. Maybe it was just a guy in a truck who just happened to be going my way. Maybe in my paranoia I'd jumped to conclusions.

I shook my head.

"If he does bother you, you should let me know."

I nodded. "Okay. But you know, I'm not sure Simon Chase is entirely innocent in all this," I said.

Tim made a face at me. "And why is that?"

"I don't know if you know this, but Simon Chase dated both Kelly Masters and Elise Lyon a couple of years back."

Silence, then, "Yeah, we know that."

"Really?"

"Why do you sound surprised? If you know it, why shouldn't we? Anyway, Chase told us."

"And you let him go?"

Tim sighed. "We don't have any evidence to hold him, Brett. I'm going to bed. I'm beat." He disappeared into his room, leaving me to clean up my dishes and shut the TV off before heading to bed myself, my head swirling with everything that had happened the last couple days.

Tim was already gone when I got up in the morning. I opted to get a muffin and a coffee in the mall rather than eat breakfast at home.

Bitsy had opened. Sometimes I wondered if she ever got any sleep.

"So, tell me about yesterday," she said. "The news said—"

"The news is a little skewed," I said.

I was still telling her about it fifteen minutes later, when Joel and Ace came in. Joel carried a box of doughnuts and stuck it on the light table, grabbing a glazed one.

"Figured we'd need some sugar today," he said, although

Bitsy and I shared a look that told me she was thinking the same thing I was: Joel never needed an excuse to eat doughnuts.

Ace nibbled on a cinnamon doughnut as I started my story over for them. Joel didn't say anything about the Dakota and me calling him. I was glad about that, since I'd pretty much decided it had meant nothing after all.

Bitsy wandered off into the front of the shop, because she didn't need to hear the story again, and she picked up the phone when it rang. She stuck her head in the doorway, her grin wide, and said, "It's an Englishman for you, Brett."

I caught my breath. I only knew one Englishman.

"Hello?" I asked when I picked up the receiver.

"Miss Kavanaugh?"

My back was so stiff with tension I thought that if I moved it would snap in two. "Yes?"

"This is Simon Chase. I hope you don't mind my calling you at work, but I didn't have any other numbers for you."

"Oh, that's fine." My voice didn't sound like me. I could hear a distinct affected English accent. I was turning into Madonna.

"I was wondering if you'd be able to have lunch today, here at Versailles, with me."

My brain zipped through a million reasons why not, but I heard myself saying, "I'd love to."

What was wrong with me?

"Would one o'clock be good? I'll make a reservation at Giverny."

I was confused. Giverny?

He sensed my hesitation and chuckled. "Of course, Giverny means more to you than just a restaurant."

Monet's home. The site of the garden that decorated my arm.

"You know, by calling your restaurant Giverny, you're again violating the century that Versailles was famous for." I just couldn't help myself.

"I was waiting to see if you'd pick up on that, and I would've been surprised if you didn't." His tone was flirty, playful. I wished I knew whether it was sincere. The worst thing was, I didn't really care.

I told myself I could ask him some questions at lunch; that could justify my desire to see him again regardless of my newfound suspicions about him.

"I'll meet you at the restaurant," I said.

"Cheers." And he hung up.

I stared at the phone. Bitsy took it out of my hand.

"I take it you have a date."

I nodded.

"I saw him on the news. He's a good-looking guy."

I nodded.

"Where is he taking you? And you can't just nod this time."

"Giverny, the restaurant at Versailles."

"Get the filet," Joel said from behind me. "They do something with a horseradish sauce that's to die for."

"I'll consider it," I said, not sure that horseradish went with a first date.

I mentally slapped myself. First date? With a playboy who dated a dead woman who was connected with a missing woman and a dead body?

Ace had another doughnut in one hand and a cell phone banging out Springsteen's "Born to Run" in the other. He handed the phone to me, and I recognized it as mine.

Tim's number was displayed.

"Hey, Tim," I said, turning to go back into the now deserted staff room. "What's up?"

"I need you to put out some feelers about where Jeff Coleman might be," he said. "We really need to find him."

"Why the urgency?"

"We just got the autopsy reports back on Kelly Masters." He paused. "She was four months pregnant."

Chapter 27

"What do you think that has to do with Jeff? I mean, they've been divorced a while."

"That doesn't mean anything. He could be the father, or someone else could be. Maybe he killed her in a jealous rage."

Even though Jeff Coleman was smarmy, I doubted he'd kill his ex-wife, knowing she was pregnant with another man's child. "What about Simon Chase? Maybe it's his baby."

"Listen, Brett, can you just let me do my job? If you hear anything about Coleman, I need to know right away." And he hung up.

It was those fingerprints on the gun again. Tim had a good reason to think it was Jeff. Physical evidence usually doesn't lie. But I couldn't shake my gut feeling that Chase might really be involved with all this. Maybe it *was* his baby. Maybe Kelly was in Vegas to see him. I remembered how Sylvia said Kelly couldn't get pregnant. But sometimes miracles happened, didn't they? There were stories like that all the time.

Joel was still eating doughnuts.

"If you hear anything from anyone about where Jeff Coleman might be, can you let me know?" I asked him.

Joel shrugged, and I thought that was the end of it.

I turned as my next client came in, a woman who'd just turned forty who wanted a butterfly on her shoulder. I love midlife crises. They're good for business.

But Joel stopped me, touching my shoulder and baptizing me with a little doughnut dust.

"I heard that Jeff Coleman's holed up outside town at a Super 8." He rattled off the address.

"Who'd you hear that from?"

He smiled, creating dimples in his cheeks. "Everyone's talking about how the cops are looking for him."

I could go out there after I had lunch with Chase. Which meant that I'd have to take my car again. That valet wouldn't be happy to see me, but maybe he wasn't working today.

"You can't go alone." Joel's dimples had disappeared. "I'm going with you."

"You don't have to do that."

"I know, but I'm going with you."

"I'm seeing Chase first."

"And I'll pick you up at Versailles at two. That should give you enough time for lunch."

I wanted to take my car, but Joel put a finger over my lips before I could say anything.

"You can walk over to Versailles, save some gas, and I'll pick you up at two. End of conversation. You were followed yesterday; someone's watching you, and I don't want you to go alone. What if Coleman's behind all this?"

I'd dismissed my fears when I talked to Tim, but Joel had a point, so I nodded. Chase could be behind this, too. I wasn't ready to let my friends know about my suspicions. "Okay, fine. I'll meet you at two in the lobby."

The butterfly didn't take me too long, only about an hour. It left me time to contemplate my outfit. I couldn't go in the tank top and jersey skirt I was wearing. It was way too casual. I'd left my white trousers and purple silk top here yesterday, along with the fabulous red shoes. But walking in those shoes wasn't a good idea. I tried on the slacks with my Tevas, and the pants dragged a little on the ground, but I'd have to live with it. I dumped the red heels into my messenger bag.

Joel "tsk-tsked" when I emerged, frowning at the bag.

"It's all I've got," I said, "and I don't have time to shop."

He conceded, but it was difficult for him.

I indicated my skirt and tank on the table. "Bring those with you, okay? I want to be comfortable when we go see Jeff."

It was hot outside, and the silk top was sticking to my chest. The dragon looked like it was crying, but it was just tears of sweat. I was afraid my trousers would have sweat marks all over them, and in unfortunate places. By the time I reached Versailles, my makeup had slid off for sure, making me feel as if I looked like one of those melting faces at the end of *Raiders of the Lost Ark*.

It's a dry heat.

Right.

I didn't go straight to the restaurant when I got to Versailles. Jarred by the mirrors and my reflection, I found the ladies' room tucked in a little corner just past the front desk around the corner from the casino.

A very busty young woman with a tall wig of white hair piled on top of her head was applying a thick layer of red lipstick. Her face had been powdered almost as white as the wig. She grinned at me when I walked in.

"Nice tat," she said, lifting her short skirt—she must be one of those cocktail waitresses—and showing off Sylvester the cat and Tweety Bird on the side of her thigh.

I'd admonished Tim for thinking that there was some sort of tattoo "club," but anyone with ink invariably noticed everyone who shared their penchant for the needle.

I ducked into one of the stalls—not your typical restroom stall, either, but one with a white-paneled door and gilt knob. The toilet was European, with a little golden bulb you had to pull up on in order to flush. I was surprised there wasn't a bidet.

The cocktail waitress was still primping when I emerged and surveyed my face in the mirror. It *had* melted a bit, and I rummaged in my bag, pulling out a small Baggie with some lip gel, blush, foundation, and mascara. My hand caught on the red patent-leather pumps, and I dropped them on the floor.

"Great shoes," the waitress said, "but your face is a mess."

Nothing like being blunt.

"Let me help." She frowned at my Baggie, then washed my face with a wet, cold towel—a real one, not paper—pulling the remains of my makeup off. "Have to start over, sweetheart."

Within seconds, she'd put foundation on, then a little blush. She took my mascara wand and expertly created lashes where there had been none. She squirted some hair gel from her own bag and ran it through her fingers and then through my hair, making it spiky. It matched the tats and the rows of silver earrings in my ears, but not the purple silk blouse.

"I feel like two people," I said, mostly to myself.

She laughed. "You look great."

"Thanks," I said, holding out my hand. "Brett Kavanaugh."

"Robbin Seipold."

I took one of my business cards out of my bag and handed it to her. "Robbin, come into the shop and your next tat's on me. For making me look great for my date."

Her eyes grew wide. "Really?"

I held my finger and thumb an inch apart as I smiled. "A small one."

"Better than nothing," she said with a grin. "Lunch date, huh? I've got one after work. Rich guy."

"Better rich than poor."

"This one's really rich. Runs this place. I brought him a cocktail and we got to talking. And then he asked me out."

It had to be Chase. Who else ran this place?

I kicked off my sandals and stuck my feet into the red shoes, my lunch date even less appetizing now.

"Hey, Robbin, really, stop in when you want," I said, eager to get out of there.

My mood didn't improve, either, as I approached Giverny.

Standing just beyond the restaurant entrance was Simon Chase.

He was arguing with the bald tattooed guy. Matthew.

Chapter 28

I hid behind a huge plant in the hall, watching them. I couldn't hear what they were saying, even though I was trying. People were passing me, talking, laughing, interrupting.

"What are you doing here?"

I stiffened, turning slowly, not recognizing the voice.

Chip Manning's head was cocked to one side, a twitch playing at the corners of his mouth.

"You're that tattoo woman. You found Matt yesterday. You saw Elise."

"Yeah."

"Why are you hiding?" He peered past me, not waiting for an answer, then chuckled. "Checking up on Simon?" He stepped closer to me, and I could smell the booze on him, but he wasn't acting drunk. It might just be left over from yesterday.

"I'm meeting him for lunch," I tried to say casually, but it felt like I had a piece of wool wrapped around my tongue.

"Then why are you spying on him?"

"I'm not spying on him. I thought I saw something on the ground over here." I made a stupid show of looking around, then putting my hands up and shrugging. "Guess not."

"Elise spied on him, too."

A little tidbit of information I hadn't asked for, but it was interesting all the same. "Really?" I prodded.

"She was crying when I met her. He broke her heart."

I made a little "mmm" sound.

"And then she fell in love with me. Elise had a habit of falling in love with the wrong men."

"Until you."

He looked a little startled by that, as if it hadn't even occurred to him before. "Well, yeah, I guess so, sure."

He didn't sound so sure to me, but I was willing to give him the benefit of the doubt.

"Still haven't found her?"

His eyes skirted around me, past the plant and over to where Chase was still arguing with Matthew. "No. Police say she could be anywhere."

"Not in Vegas anymore?"

"Might not be." He was still focused on Chase.

"Do you have any idea why she left in the first place?"

His gaze swung back to me, his face dark with rage. "Why would I know that?" And he stormed off, leaving me more than a little confused. What had just happened here?

I should've asked him about Matt, his driver, but I'd lost that chance. I mulled over his comments about Simon Chase and Elise. So he'd broken her heart. He probably broke Kelly's heart, too. Maybe worse.

I shivered, and it wasn't just from the air-conditioning.

Sister Mary Eucharista was sitting on my shoulder again. She didn't think it was a good idea to have lunch with Simon Chase, or to have anything to do with him ever again.

I debated taking her up on her advice. I had no business prying into Simon Chase's life, running around trying to find out what I could about a missing woman. I had my own business to run.

But my curiosity was getting the better of me, not to mention my hormones. I watched Simon Chase from my hiding spot and remembered the way his eyes twinkled. Oh, why not. I'd get a nice meal out of it, anyway.

Just as I decided I'd come out of hiding, Matthew whirled around, his face looking much like Chip's had just seconds ago. He saw me, his expression changing with the recognition, but just shook his head and walked away. Chase had already gone into the restaurant; he didn't see me—or Matthew's reaction to me.

The entrance to the restaurant had frosted-glass walls with illuminated Monet water lilies reflected on them, sort of like a very upscale and tasteful PowerPoint presentation. I walked in, and the water lily theme was repeated along the far wall, with realistic weeping willow trees adorning the far corners of the room. The ceiling was painted like the sky, with clouds and a hint of sunset. Illusion. It was all about illusion.

Chase was talking with the maître d'. His face brightened as he saw me, and he lightly touched my shoulder and gave me a kiss on each cheek—very European. I smiled and hoped I didn't look as flustered as I was. His touch had sent an electric shock through me, despite my resolve to resist his charm.

This wouldn't do. I was here to find out if he was a murderer. I couldn't get all warm and fuzzy just because he turned me on by just looking at me. Granted, it could be argued that the *way* he looked at me would've unnerved any woman.

"You look gorgeous," he said softly in my ear, and the warmth of his breath caressed my neck, causing me to again blush.

I reminded myself about Robbin, how she was going to see him later. That cooled those hot flashes.

We were seated at a corner table, away from everyone else. The waiter handed me a menu, but before I could take it, Chase took it and gave it back. He didn't look at me as he said, "I'd like a bottle of Domaine St. Nicolas, 2004. We'll each have a Caesar salad and the filet."

The waiter scurried off, nodding. Looked like dinner for lunch today.

"I hope you don't mind, but the wine is a Pinot Noir/Cabernet Franc blend from Feifs Vendéens in Brem on the coast south of the mouth of the Loire. It's superb."

I had no choice but to believe him. "That's fine," I said, sipping my water.

"And I took a chance that you're not a vegetarian."

"Who could be?" I asked flippantly. His gaze was unnerving me again.

He leaned back in his chair. "You must think I'm terribly pretentious."

"I don't stereotype," I said. "Don't like double standards."

"That's why I like you."

If I were in eighth grade, I'd be writing *Mrs. Simon Chase* over and over on my paper-bag book cover.

"You like a lot of women," I said, meeting his eyes.

He grinned. "You've been checking up on me."

"Why not?"

"Why not, indeed. So, ask your questions. I'm an open book."

I wasn't so sure. "You like celebrities, actresses. Models. Tattooists." I let my tongue linger on the last word.

"You want to ask me about Kelly Masters."

"You knew her real name?"

"That 'K-C' business was just that: business. In her personal life, she was Kelly." He took a deep breath. "So why do you want to talk about her and not Elise?"

"Elise isn't dead." My words surprised even me, but they didn't faze him.

"Do we know that?"

I wasn't completely sure I'd heard him right. "Know what?"

"That she's not dead."

What was he implying? Did he know something I didn't?

"You were the last to see her alive, I understand," he said.

"The last one who'll admit it." The banter was putting me off guard. I was comfortable with Chase; he made me feel I could say anything.

Before I could add more, however, the waiter arrived with the wine. He made a great show of opening it, his hands trembling slightly as he offered a taste to the man who ran the place. Chase lifted the glass to his nose, sniffed, then sipped, swishing the wine around in his mouth before nodding.

The waiter poured me a glass, then poured more into Chase's. He left without meeting my eye.

Chase lifted his glass, and we clinked.

"To delightful company," he said, his eyes smoky as his tongue gently licked the rim of the glass. I wanted to be that glass, and he knew it. I was a lousy detective.

"So when was the last time you saw Kelly?" I asked.

Chase cupped his glass in his hand, staring at me over the top of it. "Four days ago. She was very much alive."

"Did she tell you she was pregnant?"

The glass wavered slightly. "What?"

"Did you know Jeff Coleman?"

"Slimy little bastard," he said. "But good at his job." He tipped his glass toward me.

"He's the one who sent me over here," I said. "He was supposed to be here, not me, yesterday."

"I suppose he has some explaining to do," Chase said.

The salads arrived, perfect crispy Romaine with parmesan shavings and a tangy anchovy dressing.

"Did you know Matt Powell?" I asked.

"Of course."

"Did Elise know him?"

"Of course." He took a sip of wine. "You think Matt was Elise's lover?"

"The name fits the tattoo."

"So his murder was a little tit for tat?"

Clever. I nodded. "It would make sense."

"So who killed him?"

I thought about it a second, taking the time to savor my salad. "Chip, maybe."

Simon laughed. "He couldn't kill anyone. He can barely get through a day. I tried to tell Elise . . ." His voice trailed off.

"What did you tell Elise?" I asked, fork in the air. "You warned her not to marry Chip? Do you think she got cold feet and ended up here with Matt Powell and decided to marry him instead?" As I spoke, the scenario felt right. Except for one thing. Kelly Masters. "When did Elise meet Kelly?" It wasn't completely a non sequitur.

He didn't indicate that the change of subject bothered him. "As far as I know, they never knew each other."

"So they didn't meet through you?" I tried to read his face, but it showed me nothing.

"Kelly and I were over a long time ago," he said. "As were Elise and I."

"Did you see Elise when she came to town?" I asked as the waiter took our salad plates away.

Chase poured more wine for each of us—had I really finished the glass?

"I haven't seen Elise in over a year," he said. "She wouldn't exactly seek me out."

"What happened between you?" I wanted to see if he'd corroborate Chip's story.

He didn't say anything, just stared at me for a few seconds, then, "What happens to any relationship when two people have nothing in common except great sex?"

I wasn't quite sure how to respond, and he asked another question before I could.

"Is that what happened with you and Paul Fogarty?"

I caught my breath. How had he known about Paul?

He was smiling, his eyes flashing. "You're not the only one with a computer and resources, you know, Miss Kavanaugh."

The filet arrived then, medium-rare, bursting with juices, on a bed of mashed garlic potatoes, the horseradish sauce not overpowering but complementing the meat. I didn't want to tell him anything about Paul—or our sex life, which was none of his business, thank you very much—but that sabotaged my own questioning. We ate in silence, each sneaking little peeks at each other over our forks.

We were at an impasse.

He knew it, too.

"Dessert?" he asked, pouring more wine.

"I'm stuffed," I said. "I need to get back to the shop." As I said it, I looked at my watch. Two thirty. I was supposed to meet Joel out in the lobby at two. My face gave me away.

"Do you have a train to catch?"

I put my napkin on the table next to my plate. "Actually, I really do need to get back. I'm late as it is." I tried a smile on for size. "I'm the boss. I can't have my staff doing all the work while I'm out playing."

I stood up, and Chase stood up, too, walking around the table and taking my arm, again sending a spark through my skin. His lips brushed my cheek, and I could feel desire rush through my body.

"I hope we can do this again," he whispered.

"I don't see why not," I said, my voice tinged with that faux accent. "Thank you for everything." I didn't trust myself to look at him before I grabbed my bag off the back of my chair and stumbled on those high heels out of the restaurant. I could feel his eyes on my back the whole time.

I hadn't learned much. And I'd forgotten to ask about Matthew.

I had just reached the lobby when a hand clamped itself hard around my shoulder.

"Just what do you think you're doing?"

Chapter 29

Bruce Manning didn't bother to disguise his irritation.

"I was just having lunch," I said. "Can you take your hand off me?"

He didn't move it. "The last time you were here, someone turned up dead. You spoke to my daughter-in-law and she disappeared. I see a pattern."

I wasn't so sure. It was tenuous at best. But his grip was strong, and I was trying not to flinch.

"Future," I said.

"Future what?"

"She is your future daughter-in-law. She hasn't married Chip yet."

The semantics escaped him as he scowled. "I see you've bewitched my manager."

Bewitched? What century did he live in?

"I'm no witch," I said, twisting my shoulder to try to release his grip.

"You're as bad as she was," he muttered, the pressure tightening and pain shooting through my arm.

"Who?" I asked when I caught my breath. "Did you hurt Elise, too?"

"I don't like your insinuation. I'd like you to stay out of my hotel and casino. I'd like you to tell my manager that you can't see him anymore. If I see you, I'm going to call the police." His voice was low, but he kept his face neutral. Anyone watching us probably wouldn't suspect he was threatening me.

"You don't scare me," I whispered.

"I should. Now get out." And as quickly as he'd grabbed me, he released me, my arm dangling by my side.

I reached up and rubbed my shoulder. It had gone slightly numb. "I'm waiting for someone to pick me up."

But Bruce Manning had already dismissed me and walked away—toward Simon Chase, who was watching the whole thing. Manning flicked his hand at Chase, who turned to follow him, but not before I saw his raised eyebrows, a question as to whether I was all right. I nodded.

I didn't care that Bruce Manning was one of the richest and most powerful men in the country. All I cared about was that he'd hurt me, in public. I could try to press charges, but I'd be laughed out of court. I'd be a fool to go up against him; it would be his word against mine.

Still, I could tell Tim and maybe he'd be able to give me some advice.

I moved farther into the lobby, glancing around for Joel. I didn't see him. But I did recognize the woman hovering behind the gigantic spray of flowers.

Sylvia Coleman.

"Your young man came to the shop," Sylvia said when I approached her. "Dear, do you know he's gay?"

It took me a second to realize she was talking about Joel. "He's not my young man."

She grinned. "That's a relief."

"Where is he?"

"Who?"

I wondered again about dementia. "Joel. My young man. He was supposed to meet me here."

"Oh, yes, dear, I know. He's in the men's room."

Why was she here? Did Joel bring her? Why had he gone to Murder Ink? We were supposed to go to that Super 8.

As I was asking myself those questions, he somehow

managed to appear without my noticing his approach. "How was lunch? Did you have the filet?"

I tugged on his arm, asked Sylvia to excuse us a moment, and led him a few feet away. Keeping my voice low, I asked, "What's going on? Why are you here with Sylvia?"

"I just thought I'd run past there before I picked you up to see if I could get any more information. She was hanging around, bugging everyone."

"So you decided to do them a favor and have her tag along with you so she could bug us?"

"She said she'd bring us to Jeff."

That stopped me. Okay, I could live with this. "He's not at the Super 8?"

"No. Why would he be there?" Sylvia's voice startled me. She'd sneaked up behind us. "It's not nice to keep secrets," she admonished me.

No kidding. But there were a lot of them floating around these days; what was another one?

"You can take us to him? I really need to talk to him," I said.

Sylvia grinned. "He wants to talk to you, too." She looked up at Joel. "Him, well, not so much."

"She's not going without me," Joel piped up.

Sylvia crossed her arms over her chest. "Well, then maybe no one will go."

At that moment, I saw Bruce Manning out of the corner of my eye. He was heading back our way with Simon Chase. I grabbed elbows and steered Joel and Sylvia through the lobby and out the front revolving door.

"What's going on?" Joel asked.

"Let go of me," Sylvia demanded, trying to wrench her arm free.

Who was bullying whom now? I dropped their elbows and apologized. "It seems I've been banned from Versailles," I said with a slight twitter. "Bruce Manning has made me an enemy for life."

"Oh, dear, he's full of hot air," Sylvia said, pooh-poohing

me. "He's a nice man, just a little too full of himself sometimes."

"And how do you know Bruce Manning?" I asked sarcastically.

"I happen to know him at least as well as you probably do," Sylvia said, puffing up her chest. "He was just in the shop this morning. He wanted to know where Jeff was, too."

Chapter 30

So the cops and Manning were both after Jeff Coleman. Interesting.

"Let me guess," Joel said, his expression showing his surprise at this revelation as well. "He didn't want any ink, did he?" The valet had come over, and Joel handed him his ticket.

Sylvia looked slightly uncomfortable and didn't answer.

"What did he say he wanted Jeff for?" I pressed.

She shrugged. "He didn't exactly say."

"What *did* he say?"

"He came up in one of those big black cars and asked if Jeff was there. I said no, he was out of town. He didn't like that, but then asked if someone named Ellis, Ellen, something like that, had been around."

I raised my eyebrows at Joel.

"I told him I didn't know any Ellis, that Jeff didn't either, and if he wanted a tat, I could do a nice skull on his chest for five hundred. He left then."

I could picture Sylvia wielding her tattoo machine, the ink on her arms and chest and legs most likely intimidating Manning and making her look taller than her five-foot frame.

So Manning had wanted to know about Elise. Why would he assume Elise would've been to Murder Ink? Unless he knew about Kelly Masters's connection to Jeff.

The valet pulled up with Joel's Toyota Prius. I didn't know how he managed to squeeze his body into the driver's seat, but somehow he did. He said he wouldn't drive anything else; he had to conserve energy and use less gas. Water was my issue; climate change his. But I guess you could argue they were one and the same.

I let Sylvia sit up front next to Joel and settled in the backseat, my knees up under my chin. "Where are we heading?" I asked as Joel eased the Prius down the drive and past the hedge animals.

Sylvia shifted in her seat so she could face me. "Circus Circus."

Joel made the appropriate turn out of the drive. I pondered this. Circus Circus looked on the outside like a red and white–striped circus tent. The big neon sign sporting a clown creeped me out—mainly because all clowns creep me out, one reason why I never go to Circus Circus even though the roller coaster in the Adventuredome is supposed to be pretty cool.

None of us said anything for a few minutes as we made our way up the Strip.

"Uh, Brett?" Joel broke the silence.

"Yeah?"

"Look out the back, will you?"

Sylvia and I turned at the same time, peering out the back window.

A white Dodge Dakota was behind us.

"Is that the same truck that was following you?" Joel asked.

All big trucks looked alike to me, although the possibility of coincidence was unlikely. Again I tried to see if I could recognize the driver, but the window was tinted slightly and the sun was glaring off it, so it was impossible.

"I have no idea," I said.

"Who is following you, dear?" Sylvia asked.

"A bald guy with an eagle tattooed on his neck." ——

"Oh, that's just Matthew."

I remembered that she hadn't been concerned about him when I'd spoken to her before, either. "What's his story?"

"He just has a bit of a temper. You have to know how to handle him."

"How is that?"

"Be nice to his sister."

Kelly? "You know Kelly is dead, right?" I asked tentatively. That possible dementia kept rearing its ugly head.

Sylvia sighed and shook her head, her expression indicating that I was a sad excuse for a human being. "I wish you wouldn't doubt me. And I wish you'd come in for that other sleeve. Really, dear, a naked arm is like a naked breast. It just shouldn't be out in public."

Joel glanced back and rolled his eyes at me.

We reached Circus Circus, and Joel pulled into the front, even though the self-parking was in the back. The Dakota drove past.

"Maybe it wasn't Matthew after all," I said.

"Why would it be Matthew?" Sylvia asked.

"Because he's following me." I spoke slowly, as if to a small child.

"But Matthew drives a Harley. He doesn't own a truck."

Okay, I guess I should've asked Sylvia about that earlier, but it didn't occur to me that she would know what type of vehicle Matthew drove.

We drove in circles trying to find self-parking. Joel finally gave up and pulled up in front of the hotel entrance. Joel handed the valet his keys, took a ticket, and we headed toward the entrance with Sylvia leading the way, scurrying so quickly I was afraid we'd lose her. Joel was panting by the time we got inside, where the air-conditioning enveloped us and immediately gave me goose bumps.

I took off my sunglasses and sped off after Sylvia, who was navigating the slot machines like a rat in a maze.

"Come on," I urged Joel, who was huffing and puffing hard enough to blow down a house.

I was dubious about Sylvia's state of mind, but we had no choice but to follow her lead, to trust that she really was taking us to Jeff and not on a wild-goose chase.

We took the escalator up, turning right at the top. It was set up like Main Street, USA, with fake trees and kiosks selling everything from cheesy jewelry to candy to temporary tattoos.

We reached the entrance to the Adventuredome, a bright, enclosed space that sort of looked like the big ball at Disney's Epcot, but turned inside out. Carnival rides were laid out in front of us, and we skirted around to the right—it was circular, with rides and booths, the scent of cotton candy in the air. I got caught behind a group of four teenagers jostling one another and laughing. Sylvia's head bobbed up and down ahead of me as she went around the curve, then disappeared. I turned to Joel, who was barely keeping up beside me.

"Stay here, and I'll find her," Joel said.

"No, I want to go with you. This place is a nightmare." I wasn't kidding. SpongeBob was bigger than life, right in front of me, advertising his 4-D ride.

"Stay here," Joel said again. "I'll be right back."

I watched his large body lope away until I couldn't see it anymore.

A stroller slammed into the back of my legs, and I stiffened, sorry I'd let Joel go on ahead. There was no apology from the woman steering the small Hummer. I smelled popcorn and sugar and heard screams from the roller coaster that wound its way across the ceiling overhead. I stared up at it, trying to follow the tracks to see where the twists were, but it disappeared into a fake mountain.

His voice made me jump.

"So, Kavanaugh, who do the cops think killed that guy? You or me?"

Chapter 31

Jeff Coleman looked like he hadn't slept since I'd seen him the other night. Black smudges accented his eyes; his five-o'clock shadow was more like ten o'clock.

I didn't care. "What are you doing? Did you send me over to Versailles knowing I'd find a dead guy in the bathroom?"

Jeff glanced around at all the tourists who'd brought their kids to Vegas like it was some sort of Disneyland. Yeah, there was a roller coaster, but it was just the backdrop for the blackjack and roulette tables, the slot machines. A few years back, Vegas wanted to become a family destination, but somewhere along the way it realized that was a sham. Adventuredome was one of the few leftovers. Even the MGM had shed its amusement park and *Wizard of Oz* identity in favor of topless showgirls.

He took my elbow and led me out of the path of the crowd, next to the airplane ride for toddlers. "You've got to believe me, Kavanaugh. I had no idea."

I studied his face, looking for a lie, but I couldn't see it.

"So what's going on?"

"I don't know. All I know is, someone took the gun I keep at my shop and apparently planted it with Kelly's body to incriminate me."

"Why do you have a gun in your shop?"

He chuckled. "Kavanaugh, you don't have the same walk-in clientele I have. And you don't stay open past midnight."

Point taken.

"Did someone break into the shop?" I asked.

Jeff sighed. "My mother forgets to lock the door. No one needs to break in."

I remembered how Sylvia had left the door unlocked when I was there.

"There were latex gloves and needles in the bathroom in that suite," I said. "Was anything else missing from your shop?"

He frowned. "I don't know. Gloves and needles? Really?"

"They confiscated my case."

Jeff rubbed his chin thoughtfully. "Whoever killed that guy didn't know you were going to be there, but thought I was. I don't get it. Why set me up? I didn't even know the guy who was killed."

"But you knew Kelly, who had a tie to Elise, who knew the guy who was killed."

Jeff made a face at me. "And Professor Plum was killed by a candlestick in the parlor."

"Funny, ha, ha."

"Yeah, but we're missing some parts of the story, Kavanaugh."

I debated whether I should be the bearer of the bad news, but I had no choice. "Kelly was pregnant," I said. "Four months."

His face turned white, his eyes wide. "That's impossible."

"My brother told me," I said. "So I don't think it's just a rumor. The cops want to ask you about it."

He couldn't seem to get his bearings. His eyes skirted around. "I couldn't get her pregnant before. Why would they think I could now?"

"Beats me," I said softly. "So are you sure it was her and not you—the problems, I mean?"

Jeff nodded. "That's what the doctors said."

"Did you do an in vitro or anything like that?" I knew my question was deeply personal, but I was curious.

For a second I thought he was going to tell me to mind my own business, but then he said, "We started the process, but it just seemed too complicated after a while. She was young, not even thirty. She told me maybe it would straighten itself out." He paused. "I guess it did."

"But she left you."

He nodded. "Yeah."

"You trained her," I said. "I found her on the Internet. She was inking some pretty big celebrities."

"She was a fast learner. Could've used her in the shop." His expression was wistful as he thought about what might've been. Go figure, but I was feeling sorry for him.

"So why leave you and reinvent herself in L.A.?" I asked.

Jeff snorted. "No clue. But she got to rub elbows with celebrities."

She did more than rub elbows with Simon Chase.

"What about her brother? You know, I think he's been following me around."

"Following you? Like some sort of surveillance?"

I hadn't thought of it that way. "I don't know." I told him about the few times I'd seen Matthew.

When I was done, Jeff said, "I don't know what he's up to, but he's been around. Heard he was in a bar fight, almost killed a guy. I'd be careful around him."

No kidding.

"Why don't you just turn yourself in?" I asked him. "Just tell the police what you've told me. Someone stole your gun, probably stole the gloves and needles, too. You're getting set up, and by hiding, they think you're even guiltier."

"I want to know *why* I'm being set up before I go to the cops."

"Maybe you're just an easy target," I suggested. "Spurned ex-husband, you know the drill."

"They could get that casino manager for the same reason," he muttered.

"Simon Chase?" I couldn't keep the surprise out of my voice. "You know about him?"

"A mutual acquaintance told me about it. Like I wanted to know." Bitterness seeped out of his words. He shook his head. "Listen, Kavanaugh, can you keep your ear to the ground? I'll check in with you. See if you can find out anything on your end, and I'll try to see if I can figure out what's going on."

I opened my mouth to protest, and he put two fingers across my lips.

"Give me a day or two, and then I'll talk to your brother, okay? Just give me that much time."

I pulled my head back, away from his fingers. I didn't see that I had much choice, and what was another couple of days? Kelly and Matt were dead already. Strangely, I trusted his story, the whole thing, from the stolen gun to his belief he was being set up.

I nodded. "Okay, a couple of days. And do me a favor, too, all right? If you hear anything about Kelly's brother and why he's following me, let me know?"

Jeff grinned. "Deal."

"Brett!" I heard my name yelled across the sea of people, and I saw Joel lumbering toward me.

When I turned back to where Jeff had just been standing, he was gone.

Chapter 32

Joel dropped me at the Venetian before taking Sylvia back to Murder Ink. Jeff's story was swirling in my head, and I had a funny feeling that I had all the pieces, but I still couldn't figure out how they fit together.

"Nice to see you," Ace said sarcastically when I walked into the shop.

Uh-oh.

Bitsy slapped his hand. "She had a date with a rich Englishman. How could she say no to that?" She looked up at me and winked. "Didn't think lunch would take that long."

"Had a little encounter with Bruce Manning," I said. "Apparently I've been banned for life from Versailles."

Ace chuckled. "What does that mean? Banned? Like, forever?"

"Yeah. Guess so."

"What happened?" Bitsy jumped in.

"He didn't like it that I found a body in his hotel. Guess he's holding it against me personally. He also didn't like it that I had lunch with his manager, or that Elise came into my shop."

"So he's blaming you for everything that's going on?" Bitsy asked.

"Pretty much." I didn't really want to talk about it anymore. I just wanted quiet. I went into the staff room and pulled a Coke out of the fridge.

Ace draped himself against the doorjamb as I settled in to work on a sketch at the light table.

"Yeah?" I asked.

"Sorry. About before. But you haven't been around too much the last couple days."

"I know." I didn't need to conjure Sister Mary Eucharista for the guilt I was feeling. "It's just been a little crazy. It'll get back to normal now."

"You sure about that?"

I smiled. "No."

As I sketched, I thought about Simon Chase and Bruce Manning and Jeff Coleman and Kelly Masters.

And about where Elise Lyon might be. I hoped she was still alive.

Which reminded me . . .

I pulled my cell phone out of my bag and dialed Tim's number. He picked up on the second ring.

"What do you want, Brett?" He was working and didn't want me to bother him.

"I heard Kelly Masters's brother, Matthew, almost killed someone in a bar fight."

"Are you doing some sort of genealogical tree?"

"Don't be snippy. I'm just trying to help."

"Have you seen him again?"

I told him about seeing Matthew at Versailles with Simon Chase. "Maybe they're in on it together," I suggested.

"In on what?"

Good question.

"Did he approach you? Threaten you or anything?" Tim was asking.

"No."

"Then just try to stay out of trouble. And stay away from Versailles." It was the way he said it that made me take pause.

"You didn't hear from Bruce Manning, did you?" Mr. Big Shot who had friends in high places.

He was so quiet I thought I'd lost the connection, then, "Just stay away from Versailles, okay? Just go about your life as normal."

It was futile to try to explain that my life had been far from normal the last few days. All I could do was agree. "Sure, fine." I felt compelled to add, "I can't believe Manning called you."

"You ruffled the wrong feathers there, Brett."

"I didn't do anything," I tried.

"That's not what he thinks."

I sighed. "You know, I really don't think Jeff Coleman had anything to do with any of this."

"And why do you think that?"

"I just do."

"Nice that you have a lot of faith in him, Brett, but I don't. He sent you over there. I'm not convinced he wasn't trying to set you up."

"I don't know about that—"

He cut me off. "The victim yesterday? The one you found? He had a tattoo, you know."

"I didn't see one."

"You wouldn't, with the way his body was positioned. But it was there. A heart, with clasped hands underneath it. And the name Elise."

Chapter 33

I tried explaining that anyone could use a tattoo machine. It didn't have to be a trained tattooist. But Tim seemed to think this was a more professional job.

"I'd like to see it," I said.

"What?"

"I'd like to see the tat. I think I can make that call better than you."

"I am not letting you into the morgue. He's been autopsied. You can't see that."

"I'm not seven years old, Tim." Although we were both acting like kids. I forced myself to relax, breathing out of my nose for a second. "All right, I don't have to see the body, but can I see a picture? You sent me one of Kelly— why not of this?"

"I don't want to send it over the phone."

"Why not?"

"It's evidence, Brett. Last time I needed an ID, so it was different. The phone's just not that secure."

"That's lame. Nothing's secure these days. Someone could lose the picture in the evidence room." I'd seen that sort of thing on TV. I continued to make my case: "I could help you. But you're right about not sending it over the phone. I won't be able to really see it that way. E-mail it to me."

He hesitated so long that I thought I'd lost him, then,

"All right. I know you won't let up until you see it. I'll e-mail it to you. I can't do it right now, but within an hour or so, okay?"

I agreed. But I wasn't finished with him yet. "So you think this guy was Elise's lover?"

"Seems that way."

"But why would Jeff kill him? Jeff didn't know her, so why would he care if Elise was messing around with the guy? There doesn't seem to be much motive here." I didn't watch *Law & Order* for nothing.

"Just let us do our job. I'll send you the picture." And he ended the call.

I wasn't convinced Tim had this figured out. But he had to put on a good show, since it was his job to sort it all out and solve it. Me, well, I just fell in the middle of it, so it didn't matter what I knew.

I finished up the stencil in time for my client, and I spent the next hour tattooing the Chinese characters for love, prosperity, and hope on a guy's upper back, trying to be careful not to get any ink on the white trousers, since my other clothes were in Joel's car and he was still out. But I managed to be neat, and I could've done the tats with my eyes closed.

Which was almost the case. I was exhausted when I finished. All the stuff that happened the last few days had finally hit me, and the endorphins had disappeared, leaving me dragging. I considered a Red Bull, but I wasn't sure I needed that much of a boost. A coffee would do.

I thought about food, too, but lunch still sat in my stomach. I never eat so heavy in the middle of the day.

Ace ran out to get coffee for all of us, which was when I realized Joel wasn't in the shop yet.

"Hey, Bits." I poked my head into the office, where she was straightening up the file cabinets. "Where's Joel?"

She shrugged. "Not my day to watch him." She glanced at the clock on the wall. "But he's got a client in half an hour, so he'd better be back."

I dialed his cell, but it just rang and rang, kicking into voice mail. I left a message.

I mulled over where he could be. He said he'd drop Sylvia back at Murder Ink. On a whim, I decided to call over there.

No one answered; there wasn't even a machine pickup. That was odder than Joel not answering his phone. A business should always have a machine answer if no one was there. And why wasn't anyone there? They were open till four a.m. Unless having Jeff on the lam was incentive for his staff to take a little vacation.

I mentally kicked myself for not finding out where Sylvia lived or hung out when she wasn't in her son's shop, even though there'd been no reason to until now. A walk through the phone book told me nothing. I pulled up a people search on the Internet, but nothing there, either.

I decided I should check e-mail while I was online, since Tim had said he'd send that picture.

He sent three.

The first was a close-up of the tat. So close so I couldn't tell exactly where on the body it was; it could be the chest or the back, a place with little body fat and taut muscles. There was no hair, but if it had just been done, the hair would've been shaved beforehand. It did look professionally done, not by a scratcher—a disreputable tattooist or amateur. The heart was neatly outlined, the letters in careful calligraphy, the clasped hands incredibly well-drawn.

It was practically identical to the one I'd drawn for Elise, except her name was substituted for "Matthew" in this one.

If I didn't know better, I'd think that whoever did this ink had seen my drawing. But my drawing hadn't been made public until that night, on *20/20*.

I clicked on the second picture, the tat slanted and elongated by the angle. The skin looked otherworldly; it must be from the autopsy. I shivered and clicked quickly on the third picture.

It was of the crime scene, the bathroom at Versailles, but the body had been rolled back against the back of the tub, the shirt unbuttoned to reveal the tat in the center of Matt Powell's chest.

Right in the same place Chip Manning had shown me on his own chest where he wanted the exact same ink.

It struck me then.

Chip must have seen my drawing.

Chapter 34

Because of the quality of the ink, Chip couldn't possibly have done the job himself. And I couldn't be sure whether the tat was done before Matt was killed or posthumously. If the skin was alive, it would be pink around the edges. I didn't know what it would look like if a corpse was inked.

I heard heavy breathing.

Bitsy was looking over my shoulder at the screen. She tapped it with her finger a few times.

"That's your drawing. Why does it say 'Elise'?"

"Someone stole the idea."

"Copycat."

No kidding.

I twisted a little in the chair so I was at eye level with her. "You didn't show this to anyone else, did you? I mean, besides *20/20* the other day."

Bitsy's chin went up in the air slightly, put out that I would even suggest that. "*I* didn't." It was the emphasis on the "I" that made me take notice.

"Who did, then?" My attempt to keep my tone light wasn't very successful, and she frowned.

"Ace had a difficult client."

"Difficult in what way?"

"Difficult in that the guy didn't know what he wanted

except he wanted his girlfriend's name in a heart. You should be happy. Imitation is the purest form of flattery."

"Yeah, yeah, yeah. Who was the client?"

She sighed and went back to the file cabinet, dragging that stool after her. She climbed on top of it, pulled out the top drawer, and shuffled around in the papers until she held up a manila folder. "Here it is." She hopped down off the stool and flipped through the file. A small smile tugged at the corners of her mouth. "That's right. After all the crap he put Ace through, he never did get the ink."

"What's his name?"

"Matthew Powell."

I hung my head back and stared at the ceiling. "You're kidding."

"No, should I be?" She shoved the folder in front of me, on top of the computer keyboard.

I glanced at the page of notes Ace and Bitsy had both made, as well as the information Matt Powell had provided. "He had a pretty good memory," I said, pointing at the screen. "He must have taken the design and had it done somewhere else."

Bitsy's eyes grew wide. "That's him? That's the guy?"

I nodded. "He's the guy I found at Versailles. When did he come in for the tat?"

"It was a couple days ago."

It could explain how Chip had seen it, but when I thought about it further, why would Matt have shown his devotion ink to his boss when he was messing around with his boss's fiancée?

Maybe Chip had seen the ink and killed him. That would explain the blood on his shirt. But I was still stymied as to how he could've gotten the tattoo needles. They're just not something that's in everyone's medicine chest or utility closet. Sure, you could order them off the Internet, but that took some thought, and it would take at least a day or two to get them.

I needed Elise. She held the key to all of this, since she

was where it all started. But where was she? Had that actually been her blood in the trunk of Kelly Masters's rental car? And if so, was she dead somewhere or had she escaped?

I was going at this all wrong. I kept focusing on the results of Elise's actions, not on what made her run in the first place. That could tell me everything. And it just might stop these bodies from popping up.

I had half a mind to call Tim, but he'd just tell me again to mind my own business and stay out of his. Problem was, when I'm the last person to admit seeing a missing woman and I encounter a dead person who is somehow linked to that same missing woman, it becomes more of a personal quest to find out exactly what's going on.

"Joel's still not here," Bitsy announced, her words interrupting my inner monologue. "What do I do with his client?"

I pushed back my chair and got up. "I'll take him. But keep trying Joel's cell. I don't know what happened to him."

Every time the phone rang, I jumped. Which wasn't exactly comforting to the guy who was under my needle. He'd conceded to my replacing Joel, but there was that tinge of uncertainty, confirmed whenever I turned off the machine to see if I could hear whether it was Joel on the phone.

Bitsy wasn't as concerned, but two hours later it was clear that Joel was most definitely missing.

"What is it about this place?" Ace muttered. "Are we all going to end up going missing? Is it going to be some weird thing, like in *Invasion of the Body Snatchers* or something?"

"If it was *Invasion of the Body Snatchers*, there would be two of each of us," Bitsy said matter-of-factly, as if this were a definite possibility. "There would be pods all over the place."

"Listen, guys, I know I haven't been around much the last couple of days, but I think I know where I can at least find out where Joel might be," I said, planning to take a trip over to Murder Ink. I'd run into Sylvia over there before; why not tonight?

"He's a big boy, Brett," Ace said. "Don't you think he can take care of himself?"

No, I didn't. And the look on my face must have said it all, because they both nodded.

"Call us when you find him," Bitsy made me promise as I went out the door.

A long line of tourists waited for a gondola ride just across the canal from the shop. St. Mark's Square was bustling more than usual tonight. I heard some opera singers in the distance; a musician playing a mandolin stepped into my path. I moved around him, eager to get on my way.

I smelled food, a mix of Chinese, beef, and chocolate that was not entirely unpleasant, and for the first time since my huge lunch I felt hungry. The thought of lunch made me think again about Simon Chase. He said he hadn't seen Elise, but I had seen him talking to Kelly's brother, Matthew.

Bruce Manning had said I was banned from Versailles, but he didn't say I couldn't call over there.

I punched the numbers for information and got Versailles's main line. I asked for Simon Chase, expecting to hear his secretary Penny's voice on the other end when it picked up.

"Yes?"

It was him. Chase. Answering his own phone.

"Oh, hello," I said as casually as I could.

"Yes? May I help you?"

He hadn't recognized my voice. A slight disappointment rushed through me, but then I admonished myself. Why would he recognize my voice? After only one dead body and a lunch?

"It's Brett."

Silence, then, "Oh, yes."

"Manning kicked me out. Said I couldn't see you, either."

"Oh, yes," he repeated. "I'm sorry about that." There was something funny about his voice, something not normal. Sort of like my Madonna accent.

"I forgot to ask you something at lunch."

"I'll have to get back to you."

Because I didn't just fall off the turnip truck, I got it. "Is Manning there with you?"

"That's right. I'll call you back." And the phone went dead.

Rejection in any form is never easy, and I told myself I shouldn't take this personally. I stuck my phone back in my bag and walked into the parking garage. I stiffened when I saw movement to my right, but it was only a family of four heading back to their car. My Mustang was just to the left.

I unlocked the door and slid onto the seat, sticking the key in the ignition. But before I turned her over, a flap of paper stuck under my windshield distracted me. I hated those flyers for local businesses, especially in a mall parking garage. I leaned around out the window and snagged it, ready to crumple it up and throw it on the floor.

But the image on it made me stop.

It was my drawing of the devotion tat. But instead of "Elise" or "Matthew," it now said "Brett."

Chapter 35

Someone was playing games with me. At first, I thought it was Bitsy or even Joel, but in light of the discovery of Matt Powell's ink, this was more than a sick joke. Elise was missing and Matt was dead. What did that mean for me? Who was sending me a message? And, more important, why?

Springsteen's "Jungleland" blared from my bag, startling me. After a second, I realized what it was and pulled out my cell phone.

It wasn't a call, but a text message.

Meet me in my office. 15 min. Simon.

He must have seen my cell number on his caller ID.

I eased the Mustang out of the parking spot and wondered how I could go up to Chase's office without Manning seeing me. I pulled into another spot and texted back: *Banned how will I get there brett.*

Within minutes, Springsteen belted out "Jungleland" again and I read, *Minnie mickey.*

That old song and dance? Really? I tossed the phone into the seat next to me and peeled out of the garage. A small part of me—a very small part, but a part just the same—was tingly with the thought of seeing Simon Chase again. So I wasn't sure if he was a murderer, and I knew he was a playboy, but he looked mighty fine.

No Dodge Dakotas followed me as I made my way to Versailles, and once I got there, I saw a small sign for self-parking, so I veered to the right before the valets caught sight of me. The parking garage was surrounded by those hedge animals, and I kept close to the edge, just in case Bruce Manning happened to look out a window and see me coming.

The lobby was more difficult. Those mirrors showed hundreds of me, and if circumstances were different, I might be making sure my hair and makeup looked good. As it was, I ducked behind one of those big flower arrangements when I saw Chip Manning emerge from the hallway where the elevators were tucked away.

A woman with platinum blond hair styled in a flip like Marilyn Monroe was right behind him, and he stopped to let her catch up. She wore a tight-fitting dress that hugged all her curves. Chip put his arm around her waist.

I blinked a couple of times. She looked familiar, but I couldn't place her. They were laughing, her face tinged with a blush as he whispered something in her ear.

He hadn't wasted any time.

They came closer, and I ducked so I was now eye level with the marble table, the orchids hanging over my head. A quick glance in the mirror told me that hiding wasn't my number one accomplishment, but insanity might be. However, I stayed put. Especially since Bruce Manning had come around the corner.

From the look on Chip's face, I could tell he wanted to Be the Table, too, but he wasn't close enough to blend in. As it was, he pushed the poor girl he was with aside, and she stumbled, slipping on the newly waxed floor and landing with a thud on the other side of my table. She frowned at me as Bruce Manning helped her up. I had stopped breathing.

"Are you all right, young lady?" Manning asked.

"I'm fine—"

"Chipper, I need you upstairs now." Manning didn't give

two hoots about that girl. His feet started walking away. Chip went after him, scurrying to keep up.

I peered up over the edge of the table. The girl looked perplexed at being abandoned, and I wanted to say something, but I couldn't afford to have Manning turn around and find me here. I didn't want to risk getting banned from Versailles a second time. What would happen then? Would he hoist me on top of one of those slot machines and lop off my head? Or would he let the Bastille crowd run me down?

I might have been overreacting, but the man had scared the crap out of me. And even though I was here at Simon Chase's request, I didn't think it would bode well for Chase, either, if Manning found me here.

I approached the front desk when I was sure Manning was far out of sight. The concierge recognized me from yesterday.

"You—" he started.

I put my finger to my lips and shushed him. "Minnie to see Mickey," I whispered, feeling like an idiot.

A knowing look crossed his face, and I began to wonder just why that little code had been devised. Perhaps they thought my tattoo story was a cover for a real painted lady. Great. I totally had to think about renaming my shop.

Unlike yesterday, I was put in the elevator alone. I punched the floor for Simon Chase's office—I hoped it was the right one, if memory served—and the box lurched upward. When the doors opened, I stepped into silence.

The office was at the end of the hall to my left.

I tapped on the outer door. It wasn't shut all the way. I peered around it, but saw no one. Penny was probably gone for the day, since it was after five. I stepped inside, closing the door behind me.

The door to Simon's office was slightly ajar, but I didn't hear anything inside.

A cold chill crept up my spine.

Maybe I shouldn't have put my fingerprints on that door. Because I was having some serious déjà vu.

I strained my ears to pick up any sound at all.

Nothing, except my heart pounding in my chest.

I didn't want any more surprises. If I tiptoed out of here, no one would be the wiser. I went back the way I came. Because the door was shut, I had to put my hand back on the doorknob.

I twisted it.

Twice.

My hand slid off the knob both times.

Throwing caution to the wind, risking the noise, I jiggled it. But nothing happened.

I was locked in.

Chapter 36

A phone rang somewhere in the distance, and I realized it was in Chase's office. I counted four rings before it stopped.

I tiptoed—as well as one can tiptoe in heels—back over to the door to the inner sanctum. I nudged the door with my toe and it moved inward slightly, enough so I could see most of the office, except for the area just behind the couch. I nudged the door a little more, getting a little braver, since it really did seem as though I was alone.

Still, the blood hammering in my ears meant I was expecting the worst.

A few steps and I was in Chase's office. I tentatively moved around the couch, sighing with relief when I didn't see anyone behind it. A quick look around the rest of the room didn't turn up any bodies, either, and even the bathroom was empty.

It wasn't until I'd completely cased the joint that I began to realize that I shouldn't be alone here. I should've just stayed outside in the hall.

I went over hypotheticals: a) Chase would show up and apologize for locking me in, even inadvertently; b) Manning would find me and have me arrested for breaking and entering, even though I hadn't actually broken anything; c) Chip would come in for an afternoon cocktail and demand again that I tattoo his chest.

Of course, Door Number One was the best-case scenario, but with my luck, it would be one of the other two.

I went over to Chase's long mahogany desk and plopped
my butt in his leather chair that felt like butter. I spun
around a couple of times like a kid, then took my phone
out of my bag.

I hit a few buttons and checked the text messages again,
to make sure Chase had asked me to be here in fifteen minutes, which was what I remembered.

That was what the message said, but then I had another,
paranoid thought. When Simon Chase had called me at the
shop for lunch, I'd jotted down his number from the caller
ID and stuck it in my cell phone. Just in case something
happened and I had to let him know plans had to change.
Right.

I scrolled through my contacts list and found it.

But there was a problem. The number those text messages had come from wasn't Simon Chase's. Which was
why it hadn't shown up on my caller ID. I hadn't even questioned it.

I hate it when paranoia is justified. My chest felt like it
had three-ton weights on it. Who had sent me those text
messages? But more important, from my new vantage
point, I was in a man's office uninvited.

I surveyed Simon Chase's desk as I thought about how
I'd definitely been set up this time. And for what reason?
Why did someone want me to come here? There was no
dead body.

The message light on Chase's fancy phone was blinking
at me. Right. The call that had come in while I was hovering
outside the door.

I had nothing else to do, so I grabbed a Kleenex out of
the box on the corner of the desk, wrapped it around my
finger—my prints could still be here from yesterday, but I
wasn't going to take any chances—and hit the button that
said MESSAGES. Seemed clear-cut.

"Chase, we need to take care of that little problem."

I recognized Manning's voice. "Meet me in the lobby at six."

I glanced at my watch. It was almost six now. Too bad Chase wasn't here to get his message and take care of whatever it was Manning was concerned about. But how did I know he wasn't on his way back from wherever he was?

I debated whom I should call. Definitely not Tim. He *would* arrest me, probably, and keep me under house arrest for the next five years. Joel was always the first person I thought of, and so out of habit I tried his number, even though he hadn't been answering his cell for a while now.

"Hello?"

Hearing his voice startled me so much I almost slid off that slippery chair.

"Hey."

"Hey, yourself. Didn't get your messages. I left my phone in the car by accident."

"Where did you go?" I was acutely aware that my voice was bouncing off the walls echo-style in this room, so I lowered my voice. "I've been looking for you."

"Took Sylvia home, and she ended up making an early dinner for me. She told me some crazy stories about the old days."

"Crazy" was the right word for Sylvia.

"You know, I had to take your client," I said, barely above a whisper.

"I'm sorry; I forgot about him."

"I took care of it," I said, whispering now. I didn't much care at this moment whether Joel missed a client or not, although we'd revisit this later, when I was out of this jam.

"Thanks. Hey, why is your voice so quiet? Where are you?"

I told him, and I told him how I had ended up here. "I need someone to get me out before Chase or Manning shows up and finds me here."

"Why would someone pretend to be Chase and ask you to go there?"

I had no clue.

"Why don't you text back and ask?"

"Now there's something I hadn't thought of. Text the murderer, or whoever he is, and ask directly what's up."

Joel was quiet a second, then, "Why not?"

Had to admit, the idea was growing on me. But first things first.

"Just come and get me, okay?" I paused. "Tell the guy at the front desk that you're Minnie to see Mickey." Considering Joel's suspected persuasion, that wasn't far from the truth.

"That's stupid."

"Yeah, it is. But it'll get you up here."

"Where exactly do I go?"

I told him which floor and gave him directions to Chase's office. "How soon can you be here? I really can't have Chase find me."

"Why don't you just tell him what happened?"

"Because that's like Lucy trying to explain to Ricky why she's sitting out on the ledge."

"All right, all right. I'm only about ten minutes out. Hang tight." And he ended the call.

Hanging tight was about all I could do. Except . . . well, I was in Chase's office, and there really should be a twelve-step program for snooping. With nothing on top of the desk, I tried the drawers—forgetting the Kleenex until it was too late—but they were locked. Looked like I wasn't going to be falling off the wagon.

There wasn't even a computer or a laptop or anything that looked remotely interesting. Except maybe the bar.

The little fridge wasn't locked, and it was well stocked with Heineken and Corona. I took a bottle of the latter, twisted off the top, and shoved a slice of lime I found in a little bowl down the neck. It fizzled as it sank, and I took a long drink. It was cold and satisfying. I took another swallow. I'd have to slow down, though, because if I didn't watch out, I'd end up passed out on the couch like Chip.

Bored, I paced the room, eyeing a door that was probably a closet. I had nothing better to do, so I pulled on the knob.

It was more than a closet. It was the size of my bedroom, with about fifty monitors flickering gray and white images of the casino floor, the lobby, the restaurants, even the restrooms.

Nothing was hidden in Vegas; little black domes in the ceilings of every resort and casino displayed the good, the bad, and the ugly. Everyone was watched constantly. Cheating was not to be tolerated, at least in the gambling sense.

I suspected that this wasn't the only room with monitors; Versailles probably had a whole floor of security personnel checking them out. This was probably a backup for Chase's own personal pleasure.

I scanned the casino monitors, watched some people playing blackjack, roulette. I didn't understand craps, even though Tim had tried to explain it hundreds of times. He said it was the only game you could actually really win.

The lobby flickered with reflections off the mirrors, and something familiar caught my eye. Joel was lumbering through the front revolving door; he made better time than he'd expected. My heart jumped with the thought that I'd be out of here soon and no one would be the wiser.

I was getting used to the silence when the phone on Chase's desk rang again, the unexpected sound causing me to spit beer on myself. Great. Now I'd smell like a brewery when Joel got here. He'd think I was enjoying myself. Hey, get locked in a casino office and have a kegger.

Chase's voice blared through the office, and I ducked behind the door before I realized that it was his message machine. I must have hit the speakerphone button earlier. I relaxed a little.

But the next voice made me tense up.

"Simon? It's Elise. Meet me where the Elvises hang out. Seven o'clock."

Elise? Elvises?

But before I could wrap my head around it, another noise—a familiar noise—crashed into the silence.

I tightened my grip on the bottle for lack of any other plan.

Because it was the door. The outside door. I heard it open.

Chapter 37

Joel couldn't have made it up here that fast. Panic rose in my chest, and without thinking, I ran back into the monitor room and shut the door behind me. Maybe not the smartest thing to do, but getting caught wasn't high on my list of priorities at the moment.

Heavy footsteps.

"Chase?" The big voice bounced off the walls. Manning.

I heard him open the bathroom door. Guess he didn't much respect people's personal privacy.

It didn't bode well for me, since this room was the only other option, and when the footsteps came close, I held my breath, hoping I could just flatten myself against the wall behind the door and not be noticed.

The knob turned, and a sliver of light sliced into the room, cutting across the monitors. Seconds felt like hours, then—

"Bruce?"

I hadn't heard Simon Chase come in because I'd been too distracted by Manning, who pulled the door shut with a slam.

Their voices were muffled, like they were talking inside a tunnel.

"You were supposed to meet me in the lobby." Manning wasn't happy. But was he ever? "I left you a message."

"I didn't get it. I've been downstairs." I imagined Chase going over to his desk to check his phone. The red light was blinking.

"We really need to take care of this." The urgency was clear in Manning's voice.

"I understand, but can you trust me on this? It's better if he just goes back for a while. He can come back later. In a month or so. When it's all died down."

I wondered if they were talking about Chip. Maybe Chip really did kill Matt Powell.

My foot had fallen asleep. I shifted a little, the pins and needles shooting up through my calf and causing me to slip. The bottle slid out of my palm—I'd almost forgotten that I was holding it—and I squatted, trying to catch it, but it landed with a thud on the floor.

"Did you hear that?"

I held my breath again at Manning's words.

"Hear what?"

Nothing for a couple of seconds; I let my breath out softly through my nose.

"Guess it was nothing. Anyway, Chase, I expect you to take some action on this. Show me what you can do for me."

"You know I will, Bruce."

A loud knock interrupted, and I froze.

"Yes?"

"Oh, well, oh . . ." It was Joel. He was here for me, but he didn't expect a party.

"Yes, yes, we have an appointment, don't we?" Chase's English accent wrapped itself around his words. Smooth, very smooth.

Chase told Manning that he had to attend to this right now, but he'd be with him in about half an hour, would that be all right?

"Aren't you—"

Chase cut Manning off as he continued his good-byes. Finally, a door shut.

Not even a second later, the door next to me swung wide, and Chase stepped in, circling around a second before spotting me.

"What are you doing here?"

I didn't say anything.

"I heard a noise, and when your friend came in, I figured it might be you. What are you doing?"

"Why didn't you come in, then? When you heard me?" It was easier to ask the questions than answer them.

He gave me a look that made me think he wasn't going to play along. But then, "I thought at first it might be Penny. She wasn't at her desk. Manning wouldn't like it if he knew she was in here."

"What, is she spying on people for you?" I glanced over at the monitors. Seemed like Penny's résumé had more than just secretarial skills on it.

"What are you doing here?" he asked again, this time ignoring my question.

I slipped on a little spilled beer and leaned down to pick up the bottle as I followed him out into his office. "I got locked in. I got a text message from you saying to meet you here, but then I realized it wasn't from you, but by then it was too late, I was in here, the door was locked, I couldn't get out." The stream of consciousness flowed freely out of my mouth. I put the bottle on the bar, Chase not even seeming to notice I'd helped myself.

"I didn't text you," Chase said, looking from me to Joel, whose expression told me he was having a hard time figuring out what was going on.

I shrugged. "I know that now. But I didn't know it before. The person who texted me said I should do the same thing as yesterday, tell them downstairs about Mickey and Minnie, and here I am. If Manning sees me, I'm dead." Immediately I regretted my choice of words, but in their confusion, no one seemed to notice.

"You're right about that," Chase said. "What was the number?"

"What?"

"The number the text message came from?"

I dug my phone out of my bag and hit some buttons, showing him.

"It's not my number."

"I know."

Chase hit a button on the phone and listened a couple minutes before handing it back to me. "No answer, no voice mail."

I couldn't help myself. "What's up with this Mickey and Minnie business?"

"I have no idea," he said, but something crossed his face, something that told me he knew exactly what it was all about.

"Does everyone use the same code?" I couldn't help but push; it was too intriguing. Did they do that at every resort in Vegas? I'd never heard anything about it if they did.

"I have no idea what you're talking about," he repeated, and his face didn't give him away this time.

We stared at each other a couple of seconds. I opened my mouth, then shut it again.

"What?" he asked.

"Well, you might have gotten a phone call while I was here." I paused. "And it might have been on speakerphone."

Chase cocked his head to one side, studying me. "And who might it have been?" Without waiting for me to answer, he stepped around his desk and picked up the phone, hitting the MESSAGE button. He listened to Elise's message, then set the receiver down carefully, not looking at me or Joel, but staring out the window.

"So she's alive," I said softly.

His head swung around, his eyes meeting mine. "I'll get you out of here without Manning seeing you."

"Where are the Elvises?"

Chase shook his head. "I'm getting you and your friend out of here. I'll call you."

Right. That's what they all say. And then they never do. I wasn't born yesterday.

He must have seen my thoughts written all over my face, because he smiled as he came over to me and ran his finger along my cheek, causing goose bumps to rise, among other things. "I really will call you," he promised, then looked up at Joel, all business now.

Joel was trying not to snicker, and I shot him a look.

"Did you valet park?" he asked us.

We both shook our heads.

"That makes it easier."

Chase took my elbow and led us out through his office and Penny's office and into the hall. Instead of taking us to the elevator we'd both come up in, he brought us around the corner and down a flight of stairs to another elevator.

"This will take you out to the loading dock out back," he said. "When you get there, go outside and walk around to your left to the parking lot. Don't stop to talk to anyone. Just look like you're supposed to be there, and they'll leave you alone."

The elevator doors opened, and Joel stepped inside. Just as I was about to follow him, Chase put his arm across the door, his body so close to mine I could feel his heat, his deep brown eyes mesmerizing.

"Don't think about hanging around to follow me."

I opened my mouth to say I wasn't—even though the thought had crossed my mind—but he stopped me by leaning in, his lips brushing mine, his tongue most definitely in play. He tasted like cognac, and I caught my breath, but this time it was in a good way.

He pulled away too soon. It was a tease, and his fingers lightly ran down my arm and cupped my hand, caressing my palm.

"I'll call," he whispered, then stepped back.

I sidestepped him and joined Joel in the elevator, the doors closing on Simon's face, and we fell with a jolt.

To his credit, Joel didn't start chuckling until the doors opened again.

"He likes you," he said. "And it looks like you like him back."

"What are we, in seventh grade? Can we just get out of here?" I felt the flush crawling up my neck, and I needed a distraction.

"What's up with Elise?"

I filled Joel in as we followed Simon's instructions, passing a few Mexicans loading and unloading whatever it was they had delivered back here, but no one bothered us.

"I think we have to follow him," I said.

"I think you're right."

At least we were on the same page with this one.

Problem was, we weren't exactly sure just where Simon's car was, what he drove, or how we'd follow through on this plan. And we had two cars, since we'd both driven here.

"Do you know anything about Elvises and where they hang out?"

"Brett, there's an Elvis on every corner here."

No kidding.

"Bitsy might know," Joel offered. "Remember last year she dated that Elvis? The little-person Elvis? I'll call her." He pulled out his cell and dialed. I heard him tell Bitsy he was okay, Brett had overreacted, but he needed to ask her if the Elvises in town had a place they hung out. He listened a couple seconds, thanked her, then closed his phone.

"Got it," he said. "Let's take your car. It's right here. I'm parked all the way over on the other side of the garage and up a couple levels."

"Where are we going?"

"Viva Las Vegas."

"Where?"

"It's a club off the Strip on Charleston. It's all karaoke, all the time, and it's all Elvis songs. Bitsy says she's never seen more Elvises in one place than there."

"But it's a shot in the dark." The thought of karaoke

alone made me shudder; the idea of Elvis karaoke was enough to make me run screaming from the room.

"It's the only shot we've got."

We climbed into my Mustang, and as I maneuvered our way out of the Versailles driveway, I discovered we had another problem.

The white Dodge Dakota had parked itself on my butt again as we pulled out onto the Strip.

Chapter 38

"**L**ose him," Joel instructed.

"Lose him? What are we, on *Miami Vice*?"

"This is the Bullitt car, isn't it?" Joel asked with a tinge of sarcasm. "Wasn't that the best car chase ever in movies? Steve McQueen on the streets of San Francisco?"

"Now you want a car chase?" I gripped the steering wheel tightly, glancing in the rearview mirror at the Dakota and then through the front windshield at the line of traffic in front of me. "No way. No freakin' way."

"You're no fun," Joel muttered, and I could've sworn he was serious.

Joel told me when to turn right and left, and the Dakota was following the directions beautifully. Like he knew where we were heading.

Either that or I was going so slowly it was much too easy for him.

For a few seconds I did consider trying to "lose him," but since I'm a law-abiding citizen who drives the speed limit, I couldn't bring myself to actually do it.

It was now around seven o'clock, and the sky had started to change slightly from its daytime look. I hoped it was too early for karaoke, but when we pulled into the parking lot at Viva Las Vegas alongside about a hundred shiny silver motorcycles, I knew there was a party going on inside. We could hear it, too, as we stepped out of the car, no longer in our air-conditioned cocoon. I could even feel it against the bottoms of my feet, the bass thumping like an earthquake. Not that I knew what an earthquake felt like, but it seemed right.

I glanced around, but the Dakota had disappeared. Maybe the big neon sign advertising KARAOKE TONIGHT had frightened him off. I was sorry I couldn't hitch a ride and leave this little adventure to Joel.

And to Bitsy?

I recognized the silver MINI Cooper as it pulled in behind the Mustang. She got out and scurried toward us.

"What are you doing here?" I asked.

Bitsy grinned. "I love this place. I've always wanted another excuse to come here."

"But you could come here anytime."

"No one ever wants to come with me, and I can't call Rick again. Our breakup was pretty hard on him."

Bitsy was picky about men and had left two ex-husbands in her wake, as well as more boyfriends than I could keep track of.

She was already halfway inside the door, and Joel shrugged at me. I sighed. If Simon and Elise didn't show up here, I didn't know what I'd do. Because it looked like Bitsy was here for the long run.

"So Ace is at the shop?" I asked, uncertain I wanted him running the place. He'd never been there alone, or closed up alone, as long as I'd owned the shop.

Bitsy waved her hand at me as she walked to the bar. "He's fine. Don't worry about it. He used to close up all the time when Flip was here and I was going through my second divorce."

If Bitsy wasn't worried, then I knew I shouldn't be. But it would be a good reason to leave.

"Don't even think about it," Joel whispered, reading my mind. "We're on a mission. *Your* mission."

I wasn't so sure about that anymore.

We walked down a long hallway, and when my eyes
adjusted to the dark interior, I began to notice the decor.
The walls were black, speckled with huge movie posters
for—what else—*Viva Las Vegas*, Elvis and Ann-Margret
cartoony and frozen in a dance step. Black lights illuminated Joel's white shirt, turning him into a beacon moving
toward the bar. I was still wearing the purple top and white
trousers, and I felt like a magician's trick.

When we stepped through a black curtain, the cavernous room spread out in front of us, the lights dim, fading
everyone to a soft sepia. Maybe they thought we'd look
better that way. The red and blue skinny lights hanging
over the long, sleek, black marble bar offered a splash of
color, but it was more like I was in a cave, expecting to feel
the drops from stalactites descending from the ceiling, but
instead only the whoosh of air-conditioning came from an
unseen vent.

A stage with a red curtain was across the room, and
small, round cocktail tables with chairs sat between the bar
and the stage.

Those things didn't worry me. It was the clientele. We
were the only ones there who were not dressed like Elvis.
Even the few women in the room were wearing black wigs,
big Elvis sunglasses—despite the low light—and white se-
quined pantsuits. There must have been fifty Elvises, but a
glance around the room told me Simon Chase and Elise
Lyon were not among them, unless they, too, were in costume. Somehow I couldn't see Simon playing dress-up.
Elise . . . well, I didn't know her, so who knew how she got
her rocks off. She *did* set this meeting up.

But on the whole, it felt like a big bust.

I tugged on Joel's arm; he'd already ordered and handed
me a Corona. Bitsy was seated in front of a pink Cosmo the
size of a Cadillac. She wore a huge smile as she flirted with
the bartender, who seemed captivated. That was the other
thing about Bitsy: She didn't just date little people. She'd

had her share of taller men; the last one looked like Aidan Quinn but his voice was higher.

"Excuse me."

I glanced around into the face of one of the ubiquitous Elvises, leering at me as he leaned one elbow on the bar, his body invading my personal space.

I shook my head. "Not interested," I said.

He straightened up. "Not interested in what?"

"In you." I couldn't be more blunt.

"Excuse me, miss, but I was going to ask if you would like to sign up for karaoke."

So sue me for misunderstanding.

"It's still a no." I turned away from him and took a drink from my bottle.

"I'll sign up!" Bitsy heaved herself off her bar stool and went over to him, telling him her name and saying she'd be up for singing everything.

I rolled my eyes at Joel, who grinned.

"She likes it here," he said.

"We're not here to sing karaoke."

"You may not be, but I think she is."

The bartender had handed Bitsy her drink over the bar and she carried it, sloshing only slightly, as she followed the karaoke Elvis and his clipboard up toward the stage. This was my worst nightmare.

"I don't think I want to stay," I said.

"We can't leave her here alone."

"I should go to the shop and check on Ace," I tried.

"But then you'd miss Simon Chase."

"He's not coming here. I have no clue where he's meeting Elise." I finished off my beer, putting the bottle on the bar. I was about to get up when Joel put his hand on my arm.

"Don't be too sure about that," he said.

Instinctively, I started to turn to look toward the door, but he said, "Don't look."

It wasn't as if Simon Chase wouldn't notice us here, since we stuck out like the proverbial sore thumbs.

"Where is he?" I whispered.

"He's going toward the back, toward the restrooms."

I slid off the stool.

"Where are you going?" he asked.

"To the restroom," I said, seeing Simon's head bobbing up and down among the Elvises.

I wasn't quite sure just what I'd do when I confronted him, but this was a public place, it wasn't his office, and he couldn't kick me out. I would wait until Elise showed up.

When I turned the corner to go down the hall to the restrooms, he was gone. One Elvis brushed past me, but other than him, I didn't see anyone. I paused when I reached the door to the men's room, but I didn't have the guts to push it open. An Elvis walked out, startling me, so I instinctively walked to the ladies' room door and went in, my thoughts scrambling as to how I'd find Simon and Elise.

But the question was answered for me as one of the stall doors opened and Elise Lyon came out.

Chapter 39

She was adjusting her shirt, not paying attention. I leaned against the sink and folded my arms across my chest.

"So, fancy meeting you here."

Her head whipped up and she got that deer-in-the-headlights look, her mouth forming a perfect "O." She was faster than me, and she managed to push me aside as she ran out of the restroom, the door slamming back in my face.

I bounded out into the hall in three strides and crashed right into someone. I stumbled and fell, sprawled on the floor, which was a little sticky and smelled like booze.

A hand reached down, and as it pulled me up, I looked right into Simon Chase's face.

He wasn't smiling.

"I told you not to follow me," he said.

I shrugged, smoothing out my trousers, which now had streaks of dirt on them, and my hands were speckled with whatever was on the floor, tacky against the material. I wanted to go wash up, but I had a feeling that wasn't in his plan.

"I didn't. I'm here for the karaoke," I said more defiantly than I felt at the moment.

I did see a smile then, trying to come out, tugging at the corners of his mouth, but he kept it at bay. "You don't seem the karaoke type."

No kidding, but I had to keep this up now. "My friends and I, well, we're all signed up."

Simon took my arm and began to lead me back down the hall toward the music, which got louder and louder as we approached.

"I'd like to see how you do," he said, not looking at me, which was a good thing because I was in full panic mode.

I hadn't sung since I was forced to be in the choir in high school. And then I'd been kicked out by Sister Mary Eucharista, who proclaimed I had a "tin ear" and I was "ruining the joyful noise."

I was going to be ruining more than that if I got up onstage.

"I have to talk to Elise," I said. "Didn't you see her?"

Simon stopped short, and I bumped into him.

"No. And you didn't, either." His eyes were dark, but instead of scary dark, they were searching mine, seemingly trying to tell me something telepathically.

Sadly, my telepathic powers were lacking. Much like my musical talent.

"What's going on with her? Why is she running?" I asked.

He just shook his head and jerked on my arm, pulling me forward again.

I couldn't tell if Simon Chase was a bad guy or a good guy. Was he helping Elise? Was that why she called him? Or was she calling him to confront him about what was going on?

We stepped back out into the bar, and I glanced over at the stage. Bitsy was singing her heart out, blue suede shoes and all that, accompanied by an Elvis who had to be at least six-four.

"Your friend is good," Simon said thoughtfully.

A thought slammed into my brain. How did he know Bitsy was my friend? He'd met Joel, but not Bitsy. She'd been dissed by the TV people, so he couldn't have seen her during the *20/20* segment. Where else would he have seen her?

I looked around for Joel. Second time in twenty-four hours that a three-hundred-pound man had disappeared. Made me wonder if David Copperfield wasn't in town.

The Elvis with the clipboard was checking with everyone to see if they wanted to sing. He took one look at me and started to pass, but Simon stopped him.

"She wants to sing," he said, his face daring me to contradict him.

The Elvis nodded. "They always come around in the end. How about next?"

One glance at the clipboard told me no one was drunk enough to sign up yet, except for Bitsy. Lucky me.

Simon handed me over, and I didn't even toss a look back at him. I'd have to just get this over with.

"What will you sing?" the Elvis asked.

I shrugged. "I don't care."

"What song do you know?"

I thought a little, and the only Elvis song title I could think of was "Jailhouse Rock," but who knew what it sounded like? I told him the song, and he grinned.

"Great choice."

Bitsy was startled when she stepped off the stage and saw me being escorted up. I shrugged at her. I couldn't think of any way to get out of this.

The Elvis handed me a microphone and showed me the screen where I'd read the words to sing, "just in case you forget them." Just in case.

The music started, and I had no idea where to jump in, so I just started singing, if that's what you could call it. My heart was pounding, and I needed a Xanax in the worst way. Fortunately the lights prevented me from seeing the audience, which started to boo about two lines into the song. I wanted it to be like *The Gong Show*, and someone would hook me around the waist and drag me offstage. But that didn't happen. I got through the whole song, the booing and hissing aside, and when I stopped, applause broke out.

Probably because it was over.

I rushed offstage, tripping over my own feet as I went down the steps, scanning the room for Simon Chase, but he was gone. Great. He made me suffer my worst humiliation and took off on me.

As my eyes adjusted back to the light in the bar, I saw one person who hadn't taken off yet.

Elise was at the end of the bar.

But she wasn't alone.

Matthew, Kelly Masters's brother, was behind her, his hands on her shoulders as they went toward the black curtain.

Chapter 40

When I'd first heard his name, I had wondered if Matthew was Elise's Matthew, but he seemed like too much of a square peg for that round hole. Matt Powell was much more likely, especially since he was close to Chip and, by extension, Elise, and then, of course, there was the little fact that he had that tat on his chest.

But maybe, just maybe, that ink had been done after he'd already been dead. How else to explain the gloves and needle in the bathroom?

I had multiple Matthews, although the Elvises still outnumbered them.

Elise saw me.

She twisted around, her eyes wide with fear. Matthew's head swiveled up toward me, and a grimace crossed his face. He turned his attention back to Elise, pushing her now.

I remembered what Bruce Manning said on CNN when Elise first went missing: He suspected she didn't leave of her own accord, that there might have been another party involved.

This backed up that theory.

I shoved my way through the Elvises and some other ordinarily dressed people who'd come in since we'd arrived for a little karaoke. Behind me, the music started, and another singer—and I use the term loosely—began warbling

"Are You Lonesome Tonight?" Something about the voice made me pause. I stopped to see if I was right.

It was Joel, belting out the song as best he could. Which wasn't saying much. Although I certainly wasn't one to judge.

Our little excursion had brought out the inner Elvis in my staff. Who knew?

I didn't have time to ponder this, however, since Elise and Matthew were already a few minutes ahead of me. I bounded through the black curtain, momentarily distracted by the darkness, but the door opened, letting in a streak of light, and I followed it, like you're supposed to.

The motorcycles still filled most of the parking lot, and one was speeding out toward the main road. Two people. A man and a woman. No helmets. Who had told me Matthew was a biker? They were too far away for me to say for sure whether it was Matthew and Elise.

I saw my Mustang in the lot and considered my options. If I left Joel here with Bitsy, there was no way he'd fit into that little MINI Cooper of hers. He'd give me a lot of crap over that.

As I debated, the motorcycle was getting smaller and smaller, farther and farther away.

There was no way I could catch up to it.

I heard Springsteen.

It took a second for me to realize it was my cell phone in the bottom of my bag. I swung it around and dug around inside until I found the phone, checking the name on the front and flipping the top up.

"Hey, there," I said to my brother.

"You never got back to me."

"About what?"

A heavy sigh. "About the tattoo. Did you get the pictures in your e-mail?"

Oh, yeah, right. "Sorry. I've been a little busy."

"So?"

"Listen, there's something you should know." I paused.

How to approach this? Straight out would be a good idea. "Elise Lyon is alive. I just saw her."

"Where?" I could practically feel his blood pressure go up over the phone.

"Viva Las Vegas. You know the place?"

"You're there? Why on earth would you go there?"

I considered telling him the truth: that I'd gotten locked in Simon Chase's office, heard Elise's message, then high-tailed it over here because Bitsy was on the inside when it came to Elvis. But it sounded a little deranged. So I settled for, "Bitsy wanted to come to karaoke night. I saw Elise in the ladies' room, but she left in a hurry. With Kelly Masters's brother. Matthew."

Silence. So long that I thought I might have lost the connection.

"Hello?"

"I'm here, Brett. He's not bothering you again, is he?"

"No, but he's got Elise Lyon." I tried to keep the frustration out of my voice, but I wasn't too successful.

"And they left?"

"I thought about following them."

"Why?"

Why, indeed? Why would I do that? Because I'd gotten in over my head on this one?

Tim spoke before I could answer. "Don't play hero, Brett. Where did they go?"

"I don't know. I think they left on a bike."

"A bicycle?"

"Motorcycle," I said sarcastically. "There are almost as many bikes here as there are Elvises."

"Which direction?"

"I don't know. Looked like they were heading back downtown, but who knows?"

More silence.

"She looked scared," I offered.

"Did you talk to her?"

"No." But something tugged at my brain. Why had she

run from me? And what was Simon Chase's role in this? He was nowhere to be seen. He'd gotten me up onstage, singing, and then took off. Leaving Elise to Matthew.

Maybe he hadn't seen her.

Or maybe he'd set her up. Maybe he and Matthew were in cahoots together.

Cahoots? What was I, a hundred years old?

My thoughts jumbled around like the letters in Boggle. I'd seen Simon with Matthew, outside Giverny before our lunch date. Maybe I wasn't so far off in my suspicions.

This time Tim thought he'd lost *me*. "What's going on, Brett?"

"Umm, well, you might want to talk to Simon Chase again," I said, throwing caution to the wind and any possible romance out the window.

"Why?"

"He was here, too. I think he was meeting her here."

"How do you know that?"

Uh-oh. How to get out of this one? "He might have said something."

Even more silence. "You know, Brett, I can't bring someone in and question them just because my sister might have suspicions. I need more than that to go on."

I knew that. I also knew that if Tim called Simon in now, Simon would know who'd ratted him out.

Simon Chase emerged from around the far corner of the building. Quickly, I ducked behind a pickup truck that was taller than me, and I watched him scan the parking lot.

Was he looking for Elise and Matthew? Or for me?

"Listen, Tim," I said, "maybe I'm wrong. If I find out anything else, I'll let you know." I started to flip the phone shut but heard him saying, "Brett? Wait."

Lifting the phone back up to my ear and keeping an eye on Chase, I said, "Yeah?"

"That tat. On Matt Powell. What did you think?"

"Professional. Definitely not a scratcher. It looked remarkably like my drawing."

"Remarkably?"

"Almost identical, except for the name. Apparently Powell came in looking for a tat like that and Ace showed it to him by accident. We've got a file on him. On Powell, not Ace. But Ace didn't do the ink. I don't know who did."

Simon Chase was now weaving through the bikes in the lot, getting closer. I ducked a little lower, but not too low, so I still could see him through the window of the truck.

"Do you think Coleman did it?"

"I don't know, Tim," I said, lowering my voice a little so Chase wouldn't hear me. Voices can travel on that still desert air pretty easily. "I have to get going."

"Okay, sure, but, Brett?"

"Yeah?" Chase was getting closer.

"Powell's ink? It was done after he was dead."

Chapter 41

I closed my phone, pondering Tim's words, but not distracted enough to realize I had to duck down farther so I couldn't see Chase, because I didn't want him to see me.

I squatted behind the truck, praying that he'd just go inside and stop trolling the lot.

Sister Mary Eucharista wouldn't be happy with me for making such a selfish prayer, but it was called for at the moment, and I hoped God wouldn't mind. I spent most of my school days hoping God wouldn't mind one thing or another, so it was sort of habit for me.

Footsteps stopped on the other side of the truck. I leaned against the hot metal, holding my breath, realizing that for the second time that day I was hiding from Simon Chase. It pretty much guaranteed that I wouldn't get another one of those kisses.

And sitting there, not breathing, I knew I wanted another kiss. Only this time it could be longer so I'd have more time to enjoy it.

I mentally slapped myself. One moment I was thinking the guy was a possible murderer, the next I was hoping to get to know him better, even in the biblical sense. Especially in the biblical sense.

I was a sucker for a bad boy.

Especially when he was hot.

Like Simon Chase.

I was a lost cause.

I was also moments from being discovered.

Sweat dripped down between my breasts, but I wasn't sure whether it was from the heat or anxiety. Probably both. I was also incredibly uncomfortable in this position. These trousers were definitely done for.

Springsteen started blaring. I hadn't shut off the cell phone. Stupid me. By the time I muted the thing, noting that it was Tim again—he'd just have to wait—Simon Chase was leaning over the hood of the truck, staring down at me with a grin on his face.

"What are you doing down there?" he asked, holding out his hand to help me up.

I took it. What else was I supposed to do?

"Dropped my keys," I said, cleverly having taken them out of my bag as I shut the phone. I dangled the keys in front of his face. "Silly me."

He didn't buy it. Not for a second. But to his credit, he didn't call me on it, just said, "You have a very . . . well, interesting voice."

He was referring to my karaoke attempt inside. My speaking voice was just fine, thank you very much.

"I'll get you back for that someday," I said.

"I certainly hope so."

The flirting was back; the darkness from before had vanished like Elise and Matthew. Which reminded me . . .

"She left."

"Who?"

"Elise. With Matthew. What's going on? Why did she want you to meet her here?"

Simon shrugged. "Talk about old times?"

"How old were those times, really? Didn't seem like they were too old," I said.

He stepped closer and ran a finger along my jawline, his

face close, his eyes smoky. "They're old enough," he whispered and leaned in, this time really kissing me, not like that little peck outside the elevator.

His hands slid around my torso, one landing on the dragon's tail, the other on the lily just under my breast as we each leaned closer, our bodies pressing against each other, neither of us wanting to come up for air. I let my fingers do a little walking under his ever-present suit jacket, outlining the muscles that I'd seen in that picture on my Google search.

Someone shuffled by. "Get a room," he said loudly as he passed.

Proper Catholic embarrassment caused me to pull away, even though I didn't want to. The disappointment in Simon's eyes was obvious.

"I've been wanting to do that since I met you," he said.

I didn't trust myself to say what I'd wanted to do since I met him, because I might just actually tell him.

"Bet you say that to all your girls," I tried lamely.

He took a step back, adjusting his shirt and jacket as he nodded. "All right, I guess I deserve that. But maybe I'm just looking for love in all the wrong places." He ran a hand through his hair and gave me another intense look, one that I felt between my legs.

I caught my breath. I had to change the subject.

"Why did Elise want to meet you here? What's going on with her? Have you known all along where she was?" I asked, not sure what direction to go in.

It was a wrong turn. If I could do a U-ey, I would.

"I don't know why you keep pushing this," he said.

I wasn't sure why, either, but I was like a dog with a bone. I didn't want to let it go. He saw that, too, and sighed.

"I'm going back inside. Maybe you should figure out what you want." He turned and started back for the bar.

I stared after him. He thought I kissed him only because I wanted information about Elise. I opened my mouth to call him back, but I shut it again and watched him go inside without turning around. I still wasn't sure what he was up to, and I didn't want to get in too deep, just in case. There were too many unanswered questions.

I had dropped my bag on the ground when he'd kissed me, so I reached down to pick it up, slung it over my shoulder, and went inside.

Joel had stopped singing and was now sitting at the bar with Bitsy, who had another big, colorful cocktail in front of her. Joel was nursing something that could have been a gin and tonic or just a tonic. I didn't see Simon Chase anywhere.

I slid up on a bar stool next to Joel.

"Where'd you go?" he asked. Before I could answer, he said, "Hey, you got up and sang. Good for you."

"Glad you enjoyed it, because you'll never see it again," I muttered.

The bartender asked if I wanted a drink and I shook my head. "I need to get out of here," I said.

"What about Elise?" Bitsy asked as she slurped her drink through a straw.

"She's gone. Don't know where." I got off the stool.

Joel made a face at me. "I can't go home with Bitsy. I can't fit in that car," he said.

"Well, the Mustang's leaving, so if you want a ride, you have to come with me now."

Joel looked from me to Bitsy and back again. "I want to stay," he whined.

Why anyone would want to stay here baffled me. It had gotten more Elvis-congested since I'd been outside; the music was blaring, the singing atrocious. But Joel and Bitsy did seem like they were having a good time. Go figure.

I pulled a twenty out of my bag and dropped it on the bar in front of Joel. "Cab's on me," I said. "Sorry, but I really do need to go."

Bitsy waggled her fingers at me as she turned her attention to an Elvis who'd come up behind her and started chatting. Joel pocketed the twenty and asked for another drink before leaning over and air-kissing my cheek.

"See you tomorrow, hon," he said cheerily.

I did a quick look to try to find Simon, but when it seemed futile, I wandered back out through the black-lit hall and pushed the door open. The sun had almost set now, streaks of red and yellow dancing across the desert sky, the air almost comfortable.

I climbed into the Mustang and turned the key in the ignition. As I waited a few seconds for the air-conditioning to kick in, movement in the rearview mirror caught my eye.

Simon Chase was coming out of the bar. He hit a button on a key fob and opened the door to his vehicle.

A white Dodge Dakota.

Chapter 42

I watched it ease out of the lot, and I didn't waste any time. While I hadn't followed it before, I certainly wasn't going to miss the opportunity now. Especially since Simon was driving, and even if he were mixed up in something criminal, I didn't think he'd hurt me.

Of course, that's what abused wives always tell themselves, too.

I pushed my concerns away and concentrated on the Dakota in front of me. He was going about ten miles above the speed limit, which was ten miles above my comfort zone, but I wanted to keep up. I also didn't want him to see me behind him, so I kept a couple of cars between us. The Mustang was low enough to the ground and the Dakota high enough off it so maybe I was out of his line of sight.

He turned toward downtown, and soon we were heading along the Strip.

I knew where we were going.

The Dakota pulled into the Versailles entrance, and I parked along the side of the road with my flashers on. Pretty anticlimactic. I shouldn't have assumed he would lead me to Elise and Matthew.

But then a thought crossed my mind.

What if he had?

What if he was hiding them in plain sight?

He was the manager. He could give them a room easily. Granted, Chip and his father were also at Versailles, but the place was enormous. How hard would it be to stay out of someone's way?

I told myself that as I made an executive decision to go back in there. Even though I was banned. But this time I wouldn't go through the lobby. I'd go into the casino, where there were plenty of people to mask my arrival and plenty of slot machines to hide behind if I needed to. Granted, I was taller than most women, and I had tats, short bright red hair, and rows of piercings in my ears, but odder-looking people than me hung out in casinos. It was worth a shot.

The room was buzzing with activity, the cocktail waitresses barely able to keep up and keep their bosoms in their corsets. I thought about Robbin, the girl I'd met in the ladies' room. She had a hot date with the guy who ran the place. Was that why Simon had come back?

A short man with a bad toupee bumped into me.

"Excuse you," he muttered, wandering away.

I weaved around the slot machines, the flashing lights making me blink, the little musical dinging sounds bouncing off the ceiling. Sheryl Crow was singing about leaving Las Vegas, piped in from undisclosed speakers, no one really hearing it—it was background noise to replace that of the coins dropping into metal bins. I was a little dizzy as I approached the blackjack tables, Tim's old stomping ground. He could still count cards, but only if there was a one- or two-deck shoe. It looked like these tables had at least six decks. No way to win, every way to lose.

I didn't like casinos; they had never managed to win me over. I used to like the heavy feel of the plastic cups holding five or ten dollars' worth of quarters or nickels, slipping the coins into the machines. But now that they'd done away with the coins—you just put in a bill and got back a little ticket that you slipped into a machine like an ATM to get your meager winnings—it had lost any magic for me it might have once held. There were other things I'd rather throw my money away on, like Kenneth Cole shoes. While I'd be poor, at least I'd look hot.

Hot like Simon Chase, who was standing about fifty feet away from me as I stumbled around a slot machine that wore a guillotine hat. Quickly, I ducked back behind it, peering over the top. The woman playing it didn't even notice, she was so intent on pushing that little PLAY AGAIN button. Another downside to the new ticket system: Put in a bill and there was no reminder of just how much you were losing.

Matthew approached Simon, who looked like he'd been expecting him. They shook hands, Simon nodding, Matthew's mouth moving. I can't read lips, so I was at a loss. I could read expressions, and Simon's was exasperated as he straightened his shoulders and stood taller. I could see his mouth form the word "no."

So maybe I could read lips a little.

Add it to the résumé.

I scanned the room, looking for Elise. The way Matthew had pushed her out of Viva Las Vegas worried me. Maybe she was in a room upstairs somewhere, locked in, these two guys arguing about her fate. Would she die like Matt Powell? Like Kelly Masters?

As I thought those things, I realized that people didn't just get murdered for nothing. What did Kelly and Matt know that they had to be killed to keep them quiet? Kelly was pregnant; who was the father? Matt was in love with Elise—the tat told the story.

I couldn't see Matthew killing his sister. But he might kill Matt. And he had enough tats so he probably knew how it was done.

But the ink was too good, too well drawn.

As my thoughts spun around like the Scrambler, Simon started walking away from Matthew, who began heading in the opposite direction.

Whom to follow?

"You go after Chase; I'll follow Matthew." The voice

made me jump, and I turned to see Jeff Coleman standing next to me. Some detective I would make; I hadn't even noticed him there.

"Meet you back here in half an hour," Jeff said.

I just stood there, and he frowned at me.

"If you don't go now, Kavanaugh, you'll lose him."

As he spun around the slot machine, the guillotine came crashing down and the bells and whistles rang in my ears.

Chapter 43

Jeff was right: I didn't have time to stand here and contemplate how he'd gotten there and why he'd barked orders at me. Simon's head bobbed among the crowd, and I kept my eye on it as I weaved in and out among the slot machines. Soon I was past the slots and amid the tables: blackjack, roulette, craps. People huddled over them, their eyes wild with hope and despair.

I could get cynical, but I can't lie. Vegas is a great place for a tattoo shop, and I make a lot of money off those dreamers who came here looking to win big but didn't. They wanted to go home with something, and saying, "Hey, I got this tat in Vegas," sort of made up for it.

Sure beat a T-shirt.

I wondered what Simon Chase would look like in a T-shirt. So far I'd only seen him in a suit and tie.

And as I had that thought, I realized now I couldn't see him at all.

I stopped and scanned the room, all the heads looking identical to one another, even the bald ones. They became a blur, and I blinked a few times to get my focus back.

There he was, leaving the casino, going toward the lobby.

Not a good place for me. Not enough places to hide. All those mirrors.

I sped up slightly, because I didn't want to lose him again, even though my heart had started pounding with the possibility of getting caught by Bruce Manning again and, if not, how I would approach Simon about why he was following me around in a Dodge Dakota for the last couple of days.

Somehow I hadn't pictured that as his vehicle of choice. I saw him more as a Ferrari sort of guy, maybe a Maserati. Something cool, like those guys on *Entourage* would have.

He was a little older—sort of like Kevin Dillon but way better-looking. I could so see him in *Entourage. Entourage International*, maybe.

I reached the hallway that led to the lobby, where the mirrors started. I had no choice but to just boldly forge ahead.

Simon Chase was standing by one of the big, lush floral displays, talking to a young woman in a skintight black dress, her dark hair all tousled in that fashionable way, her long legs stretching into those same Kenneth Cole shoes I had my eye on.

I didn't like her.

Simon Chase seemed to, however. He was laughing, leaning toward her, whispering something in her ear. He squeezed Skinny Girl's hand and walked away, whistling. Whistling. Yikes.

Simon began chatting up the concierge, and I saw the futility in this quest. I wasn't going to catch him in anything. I didn't exactly want him to know I'd followed him, either, but he'd put two and two together if I approached him casually and said, "Fancy seeing you here."

"You got the hots for him, Kavanaugh?"

Jeff Coleman sneaked up behind me, making me jump.

"Don't do that," I hissed.

His leer made me squirm.

"He's smooth, but I'd stay away from him."

"Oh, yeah? And who do you think you are, my father?"

Jeff clicked his tongue and shook his head sadly. "He'll break your heart. He's broken others."

"Kelly's, for one," I said before I could stop myself.

But Jeff wasn't exactly waxing sentimental about his ex-wife tonight. "Yeah," he said absently before changing the subject. "Can you find out if your brother's still looking for me?"

"He is," I said. "You should just go talk to him. Tell him the truth."

He snorted. "Like he'd believe me, Kavanaugh. You and I are not the upper end of society, you know. You just got a pass because he's your brother, or you'd be sitting in a holding cell right now for that guy's murder."

"They fingerprinted me," I said.

"They had to. The guy got stuck with a needle. One of ours."

"I remember. You don't have to tell me. I saw him." I shuddered as I pictured it in my head. "You know, he was in my shop. Wanted a devotion tat, like Elise Lyon. He didn't show up at your shop after that, did he?"

Jeff's expression changed, but I couldn't read it. I never liked to look that closely at him anyway.

"Not that I know of," he said. "I can check with my mother. She's been holding down the fort."

"Hey, what about Matthew? Did you see where he went?"

Jeff shook his head. "Lost him."

I wasn't quite sure how you could lose a six-four, bald, heavily tattooed man, even in the casino crowd. But before I could make a snide remark, he surprised me.

"You can't sing."

"What?"

"That karaoke thing, tonight, at Viva Las Vegas."

"You were there?"

"I got a call."

"What? You got a call? A call from who?"

Jeff shrugged. "Someone left a message to meet you there."

"Meet me—" I stopped. Someone had texted me to have

me meet Simon Chase and it was a lie. I told Jeff about that, and added, "Do you think someone's setting us both up?"

Jeff sighed. "I've thought about this, Kavanaugh, and I just don't see why. I mean, I haven't seen Kelly in a long time. I don't know this rich bitch everyone's looking for. I just do my job. What's the motive?"

I was stuck on that, too. Unless it was totally random. Whoever was moving all the pieces had found us and decided we'd be part of the game. The tattoo needle fit into that theory.

"Listen, Jeff, I'm tired. I need to go home and get some sleep and get up and go to work tomorrow. I'm tired of this cat-and-mouse crap. Let's call it a night."

"Don't tell your brother you saw me," he said, just before turning and walking away, back into the casino.

I had to go that way, too, so I could get my car from the lot.

It had cooled down to about eighty degrees, and I felt like I could even use a sweater. Go figure. I put the top down on the Mustang, eager to enjoy the night air, and eased out of the lot, heading the car toward home.

The flashing lights bounced off the rearview mirror. Familiar lights, and not of the neon-sign type.

I pulled over, grabbing my license and registration out of my glove box.

Chapter 44

The flashlight in my eyes blinded me, and I put my hand up to cover them.

"Yes, Officer?" I asked, ready to drop Tim's name so I could get out of here as soon as I could.

"Do you have any idea why I pulled you over?"

I shook my head, the light still keeping me from seeing anything but his silhouette.

He dropped the flashlight to his side, and in the headlights from his cruiser I could make out his shape. He looked remarkably like a fireplug.

Willis?

I flashed a smile. "Fancy seeing you here," I tried. Better here than outside my shop again.

He scowled. "One of your taillights is out," he said matter-of-factly, as if he didn't recognize me.

Not that I wasn't recognizable with the tats. So that was the way he was going to play it.

"I had no idea," I said. "I'll bring it in to get serviced first thing in the morning."

He flipped out a pad. "Have to give you a citation."

"Not just a warning? I mean, I didn't know." I was not above tears in situations like this, so I made my voice go all trembly in anticipation of my next move.

"You have to realize that just because your brother is

a detective we can't give you any special treatment." His voice was still flat, but at least he acknowledged me now.

"I didn't ask for any," I said belligerently, knowing it was not the right tone, but it was late and my emotions were all over the place like Mexican jumping beans.

He scribbled on his pad, then ripped off the page and handed it to me. "You'll have to go to court."

"Court? For a taillight?"

"You were also driving very recklessly. So I've got you down for that, too."

Reckless driving? Me? Give me a break.

"Listen, Willis," I said. "This is a load of crap."

"Do you want me to add any other charges?"

I shut up, took the ticket, and nodded. "Okay, fine."

"Be a little safer on the road next time," he said, his words butting up against a harder edge.

I didn't want to push my luck, so I just nodded again and reached for the stick shift. But before I could put it in gear, he slammed his hand down on the windowsill.

"Next time, when someone asks you a question and you know the answer, you should just be honest," he said, an edge in his voice.

"And maybe when you're asking about something, you might want to give more of an explanation," I said defiantly.

He stared at me a second, and I wondered whether he would give me another ticket for talking back, but then he surprised me by sighing, shaking his head, and turning away.

I watched him in the side-view mirror as he walked back to his cruiser, his shoulders straight despite the heavy chip that obviously sat on them.

I crumpled up the ticket and tossed it in the glove box. I'd give it to Tim when I got home.

Speak of the devil, Tim was making scrambled eggs and toast.

"Breakfast for dinner?" I asked, slinging my bag over the back of a kitchen chair.

"Most important meal of the day," he said.

"In the morning," I reminded him. I threw the ticket I'd gotten from Willis on the counter in front of him. "Met up with that cop who was looking for Elise that first day, and it seems he's making my personal life his own personal business."

Tim uncrumpled the ticket and read it. "Reckless driving? You?"

"Hard to believe, but Willis seems to think that staying within the speed limit is reckless."

Tim shoved it in the pocket of his trousers. "Don't worry about it. I'll take care of it."

"He said I shouldn't rely on you."

Tim grinned.

"He's holding a grudge. Because I didn't answer his questions."

Tim's eyebrows popped up into his forehead. "Don't blame the guy," Tim said, scooping the eggs onto a plate. He cocked his head and frowned. "Speaking of guys, what's up with you and Simon Chase?"

"What do you mean?"

"I called the shop and Bitsy said you were out to lunch with him. What's going on?"

"Don't play big brother with me."

"Hey, who took care of Zack Turner for you?"

I smiled involuntarily. When we were in middle school, Zack Turner grabbed my science report out of my backpack and threw it out the school bus window. The bus driver wouldn't stop. I cried all day, and after school, Tim went to Zack's house, brought him to where my papers were still littering the side of the road, and made him collect them and come and apologize to me. I never knew exactly what Tim said to him, and no one ever mentioned the bruise on Zack's cheek, but after that, Zack Turner left me alone.

I took off my red heels. My feet immediately expanded

and began to throb. I plopped down into a chair at the table. Tim grabbed another plate and gave me some of the eggs. I dug in, giving myself a few minutes to formulate what I was going to say.

"I don't know what's going on with Simon Chase," I said when I finished the eggs. "We had lunch, but then he got a call from Elise to meet her at that bar, and I went over there, and he saw me and made me sing karaoke; then we talked in the parking lot, but then he disappeared. And I saw him get into a Dodge Dakota."

Tim's confusion was clear. "What does his truck have to do with this?"

I told him about the white Dakota following me around.

Tim immediately became concerned. "Have you gotten a plate number?"

I shook my head, biting into a piece of toast. "No."

"Why would Chase be following you?"

Matthew had been following me, too. Or at least watching me. I told him how I'd seen Chase and Matthew talking at Versailles. "Maybe he and Matthew think I know something I don't."

Tim rubbed his chin. "Possibly. Did Elise say anything to you that night she was in the shop, anything at all that they might think would implicate them in something?"

I'd been over it a hundred times, with Bitsy, too. "No. I've got nothing."

"What about that tattoo on Matt Powell?" Tim asked. "Any idea who might have done that?"

"No." I almost told him I'd seen Jeff Coleman, too, but decided to keep that out of this conversation. "Elise looked scared tonight. I don't know where she is, but she's definitely alive. Have you found any other connection between her and Kelly Masters other than that they both dated Simon Chase?"

Tim pursed his lips in a way that told me he very well might have found something. And that he certainly wasn't going to tell me.

But I can be a pit bull when I want to be.

"Come on, Tim. I've got people following me around. Maybe knowing what the connection is might help me figure out why."

He was wavering.

"If you tell me, I might have some information about Jeff Coleman."

That got his attention.

"Do you know where he is?"

"Not at the moment," I said. That was true. I didn't know when or where Jeff might actually show up, either, so I'd be useless on that front as well.

"What do you know?" He could be a pit bull, too. It was in the genes.

"If I tell you, you'll tell me what you've got, too, right?"

Tim sighed. "Okay, fine, but you have to promise to stay out of it."

"As much as I can," I said, crossing my fingers underneath the table so he wouldn't see.

"You first," he instructed.

I didn't think I had a choice. I told him how Jeff showed up at Circus Circus, how I saw him tonight at Versailles, how he was as baffled as I was, that I believed he didn't kill Matt Powell or Kelly Masters.

Tim snorted when I got to that last part.

"What's wrong?" I asked.

"Your friend Jeff Coleman, who tells you he's so innocent? That he hadn't seen his ex-wife in years?" He paused.

"We did a DNA test. Kelly Masters's baby was Jeff Coleman's baby."

Chapter 45

Afffter a second of being stunned by this news, I thought of something else. "How do you have Jeff's DNA?"

"He was a suspect a few years back in a sexual assault case. We took his DNA. He didn't do it. Seems the woman had a grudge against him. He didn't want to marry her."

"But you're sure that this baby is his? He and Kelly couldn't get pregnant; it split them up."

Tim was surprised to hear this. "Really?"

"That's the story I got."

"Well, someone's lying."

And we both knew who that was. Jeff must have seen Kelly in the last few months, otherwise she wouldn't be pregnant with his baby. But that still didn't explain what was up with Elise Lyon and why she was using Kelly's name.

I was really disappointed in Jeff Coleman. While we hadn't ever been on very good terms—all that "Kavanaugh" stuff, and him constantly making references to me thinking I was better than he was just because I didn't have a street shop or flash—I had begun to believe and trust in him on this. He'd seemed genuinely sincere, and genuinely surprised about Kelly being dead.

"Next time you see him, you have to let me know. Keep him wherever you are and call me so we can come get him."

"You really did find his fingerprints on a gun in her car?" I asked. Tim nodded. "So he really is a suspect?" I thought a moment. "Why would Jeff kill her if she was pregnant with his baby?"

Tim sighed. There were way too many questions and not enough answers. "I have no idea," he said. "That's what we're trying to find out."

"So then what's the link between Kelly and Elise? You promised," I said.

"Do you promise to let me know if Coleman contacts you again?"

I nodded. "Okay, sure. No more stalling—what's up?"

"Kelly Masters called Elise Lyon in Philadelphia the day before Elise disappeared."

"Really? What for?"

Tim shrugged, getting up and clearing away our dishes. "We don't know. But something made Elise run, and that's the only thing out of the ordinary that happened in her last few days there. Other than that, it was wedding business as usual."

I helped Tim load the dishwasher, pondering why Kelly would call Elise. The presumption was that they didn't know each other before they met up in Vegas. Or did they?

"Had they met at all?" I asked Tim.

He shook his head. "No clue. We can't find anything else, except Simon Chase, and he swears that they never overlapped in his life."

Tim wiped down the counter, then started for his bedroom. He paused at the hallway. "Remember, any word from Coleman . . ." His voice trailed off.

I nodded. "Yeah, yeah, yeah, I hear you," I said as I went into my own bedroom and changed into my cotton pajama bottoms and a T-shirt. I tossed the white trousers in the hamper, but they seemed to be a lost cause. Too bad. They'd grown on me.

In the middle of brushing my teeth, I heard my cell phone blasting Springsteen. I didn't want it to bother Tim, so I bounded across the bedroom, toothpaste in my mouth, and took the phone out of my bag, flipping up the cover, not recognizing the number.

"Yes?"

"Kavanaugh?"

Jeff Coleman.

"I've got to talk to you," I started.

"No time. But I think I know what's going on."

"I really need to talk to you," I insisted.

"I'll call you tomorrow. We have to meet. It has to do with your friend Simon Chase."

I couldn't help myself. "What about him?"

"Listen, I know you've got the hots for the guy, Kavanaugh, but he's not what he seems."

I paused. "And what's that?"

"He's more than a rich casino manager."

"So what is he?"

Jeff chuckled. "He's the one who made the appointment."

"What appointment?"

"For the tat. The guy at Versailles. The one I asked you to cover."

"How do you know?"

"I've got his cell phone."

"What do you mean, you've got his cell phone?"

"I lifted it at Viva Las Vegas tonight."

He lifted it? "You mean you stole it?"

"For a cause, Kavanaugh. For a cause. I checked his call history. He made that call to me. It's the same number, the same time. Don't trust him. He set me up. And by extension, he set you up, too."

"But how did he get that tat done? How did he get the needles and gloves?"

"Gotta go. Tomorrow, Kavanaugh."

And the call ended.

Chapter 46

I tossed and turned all night. I could've blamed the heat, but the air-conditioning was doing a fine job keeping the house cool. When I did drift off, images of Simon Chase and Jeff Coleman and, oddly, Willis floated through my dreams. At one point I was giving Elise a tat in the shape of a guillotine.

It was a relief when I woke and saw the sun streaming through the miniblinds.

Tim was already gone. I'd promised to tell him when I'd heard from Jeff again, but he wasn't making it easy for me. Sure, I could've told him last night, right after Jeff called me, but everything was running around in my head and I wanted to let it settle a bit first. I toasted a bagel and made some coffee, thinking about Simon Chase's cell phone. I'd had suspicions about him all along, but deep down I'd hoped I was wrong, that it was all a mistake. But if he really did make that appointment for Jeff, he was definitely guilty of something.

I took a shower and threw on my usual uniform of a print cotton skirt and a navy tank top. I debated Sylvia's offer to ink my other arm. But what would I get? I paid homage to the Impressionists on one arm; what about my neoclassicists this time? But I couldn't exactly see *The Oath of the Horatii* or the *Death of Socrates* as appropriate, but David's

Bonaparte Crossing the Alps at the St. Bernard Pass could be pretty cool, with Napoleon on the horse going up the mountain. I would have to make the stencil myself, though. I didn't really trust Sylvia, who worked with flash only, to design something.

I didn't hit any traffic on the way to the Venetian and ended up being the first one there. That was unusual, but Bitsy probably had a late night last night at Viva Las Vegas.

I lifted the gate and let myself in through the glass doors. I walked by the front desk, stopping when I saw that the purple orchids on the desk had fallen over, the flowers out of the pot, like they'd been pulled out. What was this? I glanced around, but nothing appeared out of place. Nevertheless, I was cautious as I went to the back of the shop and opened the door to the staff room.

It was a shambles.

File folders, papers, and stencils were strewn on the floor, the file cabinet drawers yawning wide; boxes of baby wipes were tossed here and there, with wipes loose and wet clinging to the floor and the light table. Packages of disposable razors, needles, and latex gloves were scattered over every surface. The refrigerator door was open—the contents of some Chinese takeout from a couple days ago spilled across the shelves, and soda cans had been opened and upturned to create a sticky brown mess that seeped to the floor. Toilet paper had been unrolled in the bathroom, covering much of the tiny floor space.

I dropped my head into my hands and fought back a sob.

This wasn't supposed to happen here. Not at the Venetian. Not with the security, not with the way these shops were locked up every night. How could this have happened?

Panic rose in my chest. I waded through the mess and stooped down to look under the light table, where we kept a small safe that held all our cash until Bitsy could get to the bank. It was gone. Granted, Bitsy had gone to the bank yesterday, so there wasn't much in there, but it was still a crime.

I couldn't breathe.

I stepped back out into the hall, noticing now that the doors to all the rooms were shut. One by one, I opened them, revealing the same sort of chaos that had been inflicted on the staff room, only this time, ink was smeared everywhere.

By the time I reached my room, I was numb. As I absently began picking up the ink pots, I heard a small sound.

It wasn't out front; it was from somewhere in here.

It sounded sort of like a cat's meow, but how would a cat get in here?

Same way whoever tossed the place did, I guessed.

I picked my way through the mess, following the noise to the waiting area across the hall.

The sofa was askew, away from the wall, more on an angle than usual.

Something was behind it.

It was larger than a cat.

I saw a foot move, and I froze.

I still had my bag slung over my shoulder, and I grabbed at it so I could get my phone.

"Brett?"

The voice was barely above a whisper, and if I'd been breathing I might not have heard it. I dropped my bag and went to the sofa, pulling it back.

Ace rolled out from behind it, landing on his back, his nose crushed, blood smeared across his face and matted in his hair. An arm draped across his chest, and his eyes sought my face.

"Brett?" he whispered again.

I knelt down next to him, touching his face, his shoulder. "What happened? Who did this to you?" My other hand reached for my bag, my phone, to call 911.

"Big guy. Eagle tat. He didn't think I was here. I surprised him."

Matthew. Where I had felt numb just moments before, now the rage began to take over.

My fingers found my phone.

"What did he want?" I asked, my voice trembling with anger. "What was he looking for?"

Ace tried to shake his head, but he moaned again with the movement. "Don't know. Didn't say. Slugged me; I hit my head. Went out awhile, I think."

"Don't say anything else," I said as his voice faded even further. I punched numbers into the phone and told the dispatcher I needed an ambulance.

My next call was to Tim.

"Someone broke into my shop," I said without identifying myself.

"What? Brett?"

"He beat up Ace, left him here, destroyed the place."

"Slow down, Brett. What's going on?" Tim's voice was hurried, full of concern.

I took a couple deep breaths and told him what I'd found here.

"You called an ambulance?" he asked.

"Yeah." Ace had closed his eyes again, his head lolled to one side. "I hope they get here soon. Ace needs help."

"I'll be there as soon as I can. Don't touch anything; don't disturb anything." And he ended the call.

I sat by Ace, watching him struggle to take breaths. My chest was heavy, my stomach in my throat. Guilt took over the anger. I should've been here last night, not gone off on that wild-goose chase to Viva Las Vegas. This was my shop; Ace was paying dearly for my selfishness. I had no business looking for Elise Lyon. What had I been thinking?

The mall outside was waking up, shops opening. I could hear gates being raised, then finally, knocking on the glass. I got up and let in the paramedics and the gurney, leading them to Ace in the back.

When they put the oxygen tube in his nose, Ace audibly

sighed, a smile tugging at his lips. I should've gone over to the oxygen bar and gotten one of those for him.

The paramedics pushed me back, and I just watched from a few feet away, until more heavy footsteps invaded the shop. Two uniformed officers, three mall security guards, a crime scene forensics guy, and Tim came down the hall. I pointed all of the former to the staff room; Tim stayed outside with me.

"Tell me everything, from the time you got in," he instructed, a little pad ready for his notes.

I went through all of my steps until he showed up.

Our backs were to the front door, and I didn't see her until I heard, "What's going on?"

Bitsy's eyes were wide as they took in the paramedics, Ace on the gurney, Tim acting all coplike.

Quickly, I told her what happened before turning to Tim. "Ace described the guy who was here, the guy who beat him up." I paused. "It was Matthew, Kelly Masters's brother."

"How do you know that?"

"He said he had an eagle tat on his neck. He was a big guy. I've seen Matthew. And Matthew's been following me around."

Tim sighed. "Do they think you're hiding a million bucks in here or something? Is that why he broke in?"

His words stopped me for a second, and I frowned. Did someone think there was something in my shop that was worth all this? But what would it be? I had nothing of worth in here. There hadn't been enough cash in that safe to warrant taking it. Of course, he couldn't have known that until he got out of here and opened it.

The phone at the front desk rang, and Bitsy went to answer it. The paramedics were rolling Ace out through the shop. Tim stopped them and started asking Ace some questions.

"Brett?"

I heard my name and realized Bitsy was indicating that the call was for me. I squeezed past the gurney and Tim and took the phone.

"Brett Kavanaugh," I said, trying to sound professional even though my world was falling apart.

"Kavanaugh?"

I didn't have time for this. "Jeff? I can't talk now. My shop got broken into and Ace got beaten up—"

"I need to see you," he interrupted.

"I can't. Didn't you just hear me? My shop is a mess. Ace is a mess. I can't leave."

"Believe me, Kavanaugh, you want to see me, too."

Something in his tone made me pause. "Why?"

"I know why Matthew broke into your shop. Two o'clock, at that little crepe place in Paris. Be there." He hung up.

I stared at the phone.

How did Jeff Coleman know it was Matthew who'd broken into my shop?

Chapter 47

Tim had taken my statement; his forensics people dusted for prints, leaving black dust on top of the mess. It was barely noticeable.

"Sorry about this," Tim said softly, crooking his arm around mine and squeezing my hand. I knew he wasn't just talking about the fingerprint dust.

I leaned my head on his shoulder and closed my eyes.

"He was looking for something," Tim said.

"He took the safe. Maybe he just wanted money."

"But he doesn't know what's in the safe. Maybe he thinks there's more than money in there."

I had a hard time with that. We were a tattoo shop. What would be in our safe? We never even had that much cash around. We usually just took credit cards.

I also had a hard time thinking that Matthew had just been hanging around waiting to break into my shop. What did he expect to find here? Elise's tattoo drawing had already been on national TV; I'd already found the Murder Ink address on the back.

Both Matt Powell and Chip had been here. Chip just whined about Elise; Matt looked at my drawing for Elise and then it was inked on his chest after he was dead.

What did Jeff Coleman know? I thought about how he wanted me to meet him in two hours.

"I know where Coleman is," I told Tim. "He wants to meet me at that crepe place in Paris."

Tim pulled away from me and nodded. "It's about time you were straight with me about him."

"He says he knows why Matthew broke in."

"You can't trust him."

"Yeah, yeah, I know." I tried to sound cynical, but I was just too spent, so it didn't have the effect I'd been going for.

"I'll go meet him. I'll take him in, and we'll get to the bottom of everything."

Tim was making sense, but something tugged at the back of my brain. Even though he seemed convinced that Jeff was the key in all this, I still wasn't. He saw me hesitate.

"What?"

"Why don't I go meet him, talk to him, and then you can show up, say you followed me?" His expression told me he was dubious. "Listen, Tim, if he's innocent in all this, like he says, I'm still going to have to deal with him from time to time. I'd rather it didn't look like I ratted him out completely."

Tim sighed. "I see what you mean, and maybe this can work to our advantage."

I didn't like the way he said that. "What do you mean?"

"You can talk to him, get him to talk to you. He obviously feels like he can trust you."

Slowly, his words penetrated, and I had a sinking feeling in my gut.

"You want me to get him to admit to something."

"Do you think you can?"

"Maybe. He's told me some stuff, but nothing incriminating against him. I mean, he told me someone took the gun from his shop. His mother left the door unlocked." As I said it, again I was struck by how silly that sounded. How guilty it could sound.

"Just get him to talk," Tim said. "Once he starts, it's possible he'll spill everything."

I nodded. "Okay, fine, but how will you know? He's been pulling these disappearing acts, one minute there, the next minute gone."

Tim was quiet for a second, then, "We'll wire you."

"I offer up Jeff Coleman and suddenly you turn me into Sammy the Bull?"

"It's the only way we can get him on tape to incriminate himself. And the only way I'll let you go."

"You're not my mother."

He cracked a smile at that. "I'll tell Mom if you don't play nice. And you know I'm her favorite."

He meant it, too. He'd tell her and I'd catch crap about how I should help my brother, because he was doing the right thing, he should be admired for his public service. Blah, blah, blah.

I had no choice. "Does the tape come off without hurting?" I asked.

Tim laughed out loud. "You stick needles into your skin and you're worried about a little tape?"

Touché.

"So how does this work?"

"When does he want to meet?"

"Two o'clock."

Tim glanced at his watch and panic crossed his face. "Have to move fast." He disappeared into the staff room, where the forensics guys and the uniforms were still doing their thing. When he came out again, he nodded. "I'll be back in an hour. Be here; be ready."

And then he was gone.

The other cops left shortly thereafter, and Bitsy and I stared at the destruction, not quite sure where to start cleaning up. We'd called Joel, who was calling Ace's girlfriend, and he was heading to the hospital. Bitsy had already called our clients who were scheduled for the day and canceled them before locking the doors so no one would see what had happened.

Bitsy sifted through the papers on the floor in the staff room and then began picking up the baby wipes and throwing them into a large trash bag she'd rummaged out of the cabinet. I collected the file folders, putting the scattered papers in piles and then their proper folders. After three-quarters of an hour, it was still a mess, but we were making progress.

"I hate to leave you with this," I said. "But Tim's going to be back soon."

Bitsy shrugged. "It's okay. Just find out why he did this, okay?"

It was the only reason I'd agreed to Tim's plan.

"Did you have fun last night?" I asked, trying to lift our moods a little.

Bitsy smiled for the first time since she'd come in. "You missed a great night." But then both of us realized that because we'd been out playing, Ace had encountered our intruder.

We didn't have time to contemplate it further, though, because Tim was knocking at the door. I let him in, along with another guy wearing jeans, a T-shirt, and a baseball cap. Tim introduced him as Nate. He held a case that looked remarkably like my tattoo case. Which reminded me . . .

"Am I getting my tattoo machine back anytime soon?" I asked as Nate unraveled some wires.

Tim led me to the sofa in the back of the shop, out of sight of anyone passing by the glass doors. "I'll check on that," he said absently. He was concentrating on the wires now. "You have to take off your shirt."

My eyes grew wide and I cocked my head at Nate. "What about him?" I didn't have much of an issue with my brother doing this, but a stranger?

Tim chuckled. "He doesn't care."

But as I slipped my tank top off to reveal my lacy white bra, I could've sworn I saw a leer.

The tats didn't seem to faze him, though. He just started taping the wire to my torso.

"She's going to need a looser shirt," he said to Tim, as if I were just some mannequin that didn't have ears.

"I don't have one," I said. "Not here."

He muttered something I really didn't hear this time.

Bitsy appeared around the corner. "I'll go pick up something for her," she volunteered, and Tim nodded.

"Thanks."

While Bitsy was gone, Tim and Nate tested the equipment. They had some sort of recorder in the case, and they stood at different places throughout the shop, and I had to say something every few seconds so they could make sure everything worked right.

"Where are you going to be?" I asked, still in my bra, but it had been long enough that I wasn't self-conscious about it anymore. Sister Mary Eucharista would've demanded that I cover myself, but she had never had to wear a wire. God forbid.

"Don't worry about us," Tim said.

Nate closed up the case just as Bitsy came back, wielding another Ann Taylor bag. I was going to have to buy stock.

I pulled the blue blouse over my head. It was one of those loose sixties-style shirts with a square neck, and it billowed down to my hips. It had puffy short sleeves that grabbed my biceps with elastic. It totally did not go with the skirt, but Tim and Nate didn't seem to care. They liked that it covered the wire, and even when I leaned over, it didn't show anything but a little cleavage. And the dragon.

"Good to go," Tim said, starting to leave with Nate on his heels.

But at the door, he stopped and turned.

"Remember, get him to tell you as much as possible about that gun and his ex-wife. It was his kid, so he was lying about when he saw her last. Get him to tell you what the real story is."

I nodded and saluted. "Yes, sir," I said, but immediately

pulled my arm down. The movement had tugged on the tape holding the wire, and it hurt.

"And one more thing," Tim said. "Ask him what he and Matt Powell were talking about when he met him at Versailles the day before he asked you to go over there for him."

Chapter 48

I froze. "He was with Matt Powell? How do you know that?"

Tim smiled in a way that told me he wasn't about to tell me anything. "Just ask him, Brett, okay?"

"He's going to wonder how I know that. . . ." My voice trailed off as the door closed behind them and they were gone.

So the cops didn't just want Jeff Coleman in Kelly's murder, but also for Matt Powell's. Suspicion crept into my head again. He'd sent me over to Versailles. Matt Powell had been inked by a tattooist who knew what he was doing. Did Jeff set me up? Had he been playing me all along, and I fell for his sympathy cry?

Bitsy noticed the shirt didn't go with the skirt.

"You might want to get a pair of jeans or something."

I'd spent enough money on clothes the last week. "No, I'm all right." Although a glance in the full-length mirror showed that I needed a little help from those *What Not to Wear* people. Even the dragon looked a little embarrassed. I shrugged, as if to say, *It's not my fault; I'm on a mission,* and left the shop.

Paris was just down the Strip, and I decided to walk to clear my head, get myself into game mode. I was wearing

Tevas, which were good to walk in, although sadly did not add to my appearance.

Most of the people moving down the sidewalk, how-ever, didn't exactly look like they'd just walked off the set of *Sex and the City*, either. It was too hot to do anything but melt anyway; everyone just hurried to get to their next air-conditioned space. I stopped a couple of times to hover in the doorways of casinos, letting the cool air wash over me so I could make it the next few feet without passing out. I should've brought water.

Which made me wonder if sweating would harm the wire. I hadn't thought about that, but it was too late now.

Paris is another illusion, like the Venetian or Versailles; it's got a great shopping area with little Disney-like stores and restaurants and cobblestone streets and trees. A little farther up was the casino that sat underneath a replica of the Eiffel Tower.

La Creperie is a walk-up joint, where for $8.99 you can get an incredibly decadent crepe with any filling you want. I like the fruit ones.

Jeff Coleman wasn't waiting for me. Glancing around, I didn't see him anywhere, but that wasn't a total surprise, since he kept sneaking up on me all over the place. He was probably watching me, just like the cops were watching me—and listening to my stomach growl as I saw someone walk by with a crepe full of ham and cheese.

While the morning had gone in slow motion as I picked up the pieces that were Ace and my shop, now I was liter-ally wired and ready for anything. Food would've given me a real boost, but I didn't want to be shoving crepe into my face when Jeff Coleman jumped out from a corner.

I found a seat at a table in the area next to La Creperie and tapped my fingers as I waited.

And waited.

After fifteen minutes, I said, "I'm not sure he's coming," seemingly to no one—although passersby probably would think I was on my cell phone, even though I didn't have one of those dorky things sticking out of my ear like some sort of *Star Trek* character. I had no idea where Tim and Nate were waiting. I wondered if this was what their job was like, those stakeouts on TV and in movies that made police work seem so glamorous but in actuality were duller than dirt.

Antsy, I got up and went across the little cobblestones to a shop that sold French cheese and wine. As I browsed, I kept an eye on La Creperie, but there was still no sign of Jeff.

Springsteen sang in my bag. I dug around until my fingers touched my cell phone, and I flipped it open.

"Hello?"

"Kavanaugh, you should be arrested for wearing that outfit."

"Where are you?" I asked. "I'm here, but you're not."

"And when you get rid of those cops, I'll meet you."

I hesitated a second. "Cops? What cops?"

"Don't play games, Kavanaugh. I'm not stupid. You never wear shirts like that, although I did like the one you wore on TV."

He was here somewhere.

"You're supposed to tell me why Matthew broke into my shop." I was talking too fast, the words spilling out of my mouth on top of one another. "And why did you meet with Matt Powell at Versailles? What's up with that?"

"No time for chitchat, Kavanaugh. You've got something in your shop they want."

My chest felt heavy as his words sank in. Tim was right. "But my shop was trashed. Matthew probably got whatever it was."

"No. He didn't."

He sounded so sure.

"How do you know this?" Skepticism seeped into my voice. "I mean, really, how do you know? Do you have something to do with this?"

"I've got my ear to the ground, something you should've

thought of instead of traipsing off and becoming a TV star."

"I didn't choose that."

"Fair enough. But really, there's something everyone's looking for, and everyone thinks you've got it."

"What is it?"

Silence for a second, then, "Not sure."

"Okay, so you're getting on my case for not keeping my ear to the ground, but that's all you've got?"

He didn't answer.

"So what about Matt Powell? Why did you meet him? Do you know who did his ink? Was it you?"

"No."

When he didn't say anything more, I said, "You don't know anything, do you? You don't know what it is Matthew was looking for when he tossed my shop. You don't know how Kelly got pregnant with your baby." I was struggling to keep my voice down, but I wasn't entirely successful. I began walking toward the casino.

"I do know," he said softly.

"Do know what?" I barked.

"I know how she got pregnant."

"Well, I think we can figure that out, can't we?"

"It's not what you think. Really." He didn't sound like himself, and I stopped walking, moving out of the line of foot traffic.

"Then what is it?"

"We had embryos."

"What?"

"Embryos. For in vitro fertilization. We never used them; she left me before we could. I went to the doctor's office yesterday. I got one of the nurses to tell me Kelly had three embryos implanted four months ago. One survived.

"The cops were right. She was pregnant with my kid."

Chapter 49

He sounded so sad, so deflated. So I made an executive decision. I let him go.

I hung up and walked back to La Creperie, putting up my hands in a sign of surrender. Tim was already coming toward me.

I told him what Jeff had said, but he wasn't as gullible as I was.

"You should've reeled him in," Tim said. "There are still too many questions."

"He said there's something in my shop," I said. "That's why it got trashed."

"What is it?"

I shrugged. "He said he didn't know."

"He's pretty clever, feeding you bits of information to get your sympathy but not really telling you much more," Tim said bitterly. "You should've gotten him to meet you." He put his hand out, and I frowned, not knowing what he wanted. "Your phone. I want to see the number he called you from."

That was easy enough. I gave it to him, and he gave the number to Nate, who wrote it down.

I knew the number, though. And I knew he wouldn't get anything out of it.

"It's Simon Chase's number," I said flatly.

Tim and Nate stared at me.

"He's got Chase's cell phone," I said cryptically.

"Why?"

I tried to look nonchalant.

"Why does Jeff Coleman have Simon Chase's phone, Brett?" I recognized the big-brother voice, but instead of the good "I'll take care of Zack Turner" big brother, this was the one who always came out before he chased me around the yard threatening to "get" me for something or other.

"He . . . well, he got his hands on it last night at Viva Las Vegas. He said he'd give it back." Had he? I wasn't so sure.

Tim took a deep breath. "You do realize that even if the guy didn't kill anyone, he is a thief?"

"Oh, yeah, I know that," I said. "Believe me, I don't like the guy—never did."

Tim and Nate rolled their eyes at each other.

"Give us the wire," Tim said.

"Right here?"

"Find a ladies' room. We'll wait."

It did hurt pulling the tape off, in a different way from getting inked. In a worse way, really, because it left nothing but a big, red, raw patch of skin. The dragon had gotten caught under it, and he looked uncomfortable.

Almost as uncomfortable as I felt in the ridiculous outfit. I couldn't wait to take off this shirt and change into my tank top.

I handed the wire to Tim as I stepped outside. "I'm done?"

"You weren't much help," he said. "I'm going to catch a lot of crap for using this stuff and not having anything to show for it."

"Sorry," I said, meaning it. "I didn't get the cop genes."

I must have touched a nerve, and it looked for a moment like he wanted to give me a hug, but Nate was hovering. It wouldn't be macho, so he just said, "Let me know if anything else happens."

"Sure." So much had gone on in the last couple days, I wasn't sure I could cram any more in. I needed to get back to the shop and help Bitsy pick up the pieces. I also needed to call the hospital and Joel and see how Ace was doing.

"I'm on my way back," I said when I called Bitsy as I waited in line for a crepe. Might as well have lunch first; who knew when I'd get another chance?

"It's okay. You don't have to hurry. I've got a lot of it done already."

I was incredibly grateful. Bitsy and I had had a hard start when I bought the shop from Flip. She was convinced I was enemy number one and would fire everyone and bring in my own people. She had a chip on her shoulder bigger than she was, which almost made me take her up on her prediction. But she's incredibly efficient and ran Flip's shop like clockwork for ten years. I couldn't let her go. Gradually, we began to grow on each other. Except for that stool.

"Have you heard about Ace?" I asked.

"Joel called a little bit ago. Ace had a concussion, so they're going to keep him overnight. But he's doing okay, keeps asking for oxygen. So how did it go with Coleman?"

"He never showed. He called me with some crazy thing about how Matthew had trashed the shop looking for something, but he was sure he hadn't found it. If you see anything that might warrant someone breaking in and beating up Ace, let me know."

"Nothing here that's not familiar," she said. "But I'll keep an eye out."

I ended the call after telling her I'd be there shortly and was walking out onto the sidewalk, back toward the Venetian, when my cell phone warbled.

Simon Chase's number. I flipped the phone open.

"Now that you've gotten rid of that wire, we can talk, Kavanaugh."

I whirled around, looking for Tim, but seeing nothing but a sea of tourists.

"He's long gone."

"Where are you?"

Jeff Coleman fell into step beside me, his phone to his ear, a grin on his face. We hung up at the same time.

"My brother's not happy you have Simon Chase's phone," I said.

"And he's really not going to be happy when you bring it back to Chase." He dropped the phone into my bag.

"Why am I doing that?" I asked. "I don't want to see him."

"It's your way into Versailles."

"And why do I want to go there? The last time you sent me there, I found a dead guy in a tub." Which reminded me . . . "What did you and Matt Powell talk about?"

"He told me to watch my back."

Chapter 50

I stopped short and a heavyset man slammed into me. He growled and moved past. I grabbed Jeff's arm and pulled him through the door into O'Shea's Casino.

"Watch your back? Why?"

Jeff gave me a wan smile. "Seems he was acquainted with my ex-wife."

"He knew Kelly? How? Why didn't you tell me sooner?"

"You didn't ask. And anyway, if you knew, you might have told your brother, and the cops would have had even more of a reason to nail me."

I studied Jeff's face, which was remarkably free of any emotion, except perhaps a slight tug of amusement at the corner of his mouth.

"You didn't do that tat, did you?"

Disgust replaced the amusement. "Kavanaugh, I don't touch dead people."

"So who did it?"

Jeff shrugged. "Maybe Kelly did it."

Kelly? I didn't get a chance to react, though, because Jeff kept talking.

"All I know is, this guy called me, asked me to meet him in the Bastille Lounge at Versailles, it was about Kelly. I met him—his name was Matt. He said Kelly had been in over her head, that she'd done something she shouldn't have." He bit his lip. "I guess he knew she was pregnant, but he never said exactly what it was she'd done. I figured she'd just screwed the wrong guy one way or another, same old story for her. I told him I hadn't seen her in a long time, but he said I should watch out, that she was up to something."

"Did he know about the embryos?"

Jeff bit his lip and nodded. "Thinking about it now, he had to have known about that."

"But why would he warn you? What was she going to do?"

"I don't know. While we were talking, someone came into the bar, a young guy, maybe thirty, tops. Rich-looking. Matt said he had to go, but he'd call me later. He went over to the other dude, who was pissed about something; his face was all red. They left together."

"Was it Chip Manning?"

Jeff shrugged. "Maybe."

"His face has been all over the news because of Elise," I said.

"I haven't exactly been pinned to the TV, if you haven't noticed, Kavanaugh."

"Yeah, right. Sorry."

We started walking again. The air wrapped itself around us like a fleece blanket. I still hadn't gotten a water. I pondered Jeff's story. It sounded like the truth, and the pieces were starting to fall together.

"What about Matthew, Kelly's brother?" I asked. "Why wouldn't he have contacted you if Kelly was in trouble?"

Jeff chuckled. "Matthew and I aren't exactly on the best of terms."

"How would Matt Powell even know about you, though?"

"If he knew Kelly, she might have told him."

True enough. And if Matt Powell was Elise Lyon's Matthew, and Kelly and Elise knew each other, then it was like one big, happy family. Until Matt and Kelly ended up dead.

Maybe Elise killed them. Nothing would surprise me now.

"So why do you think I'm going to Versailles?" I asked.

"You have to give Simon Chase back his phone."

"Why?"

"You'll look like a hero, Kavanaugh, getting his phone back. Maybe he'll want to suck face with you again." The grimace was probably supposed to be a grin.

I ignored him. "So you have no idea why Matthew trashed my shop?"

He shrugged. "Something's there. Don't know what." He sounded like a broken record. "Listen, I've got to get going. I'll be in touch." And before I could say anything, he was halfway across the street, jogging toward the Bellagio.

I stood there, staring after him for a few seconds, then continued back to the Venetian.

If Matthew thought I had something he wanted, that could explain why he'd been following me around. Maybe he thought I'd lead him to it.

But then, why was Simon Chase following me in that Dodge Dakota?

I'd seen them together. Chase and Matthew. They could be in on it together.

Despite the heat, a chill crept up my spine.

I might have a reason to go to Versailles after all.

Bitsy was right. She had done a lot of work while I was gone, which made me feel guilty. I didn't need Sister Mary Eucharista on my shoulder today. I was doing a pretty good job of giving myself a guilt trip.

While I wiped up the last of the ink off the floor in Joel's room, all the events of the last few days swirled around in my head. What had I gotten mixed up in? Everything that had happened had happened because a woman left her fiancé at the altar. She'd sneaked off in the night, taking someone else's identity, and disappeared.

But I'd seen her. Last night. At Viva Las Vegas. Why was she still in town? If I were her, I'd be long gone by now.

I threw the sponges covered in ink in a bucket and surveyed the floor. It sparkled as if it had never been violated. Bitsy had taken care of the rest of the room, stacking all the ink pots in a row on the shelf, the disposables neat in their boxes, Joel's tattoo machine perched and ready for the next customer.

I had to get Tim to give me my machine back. And the case, which was Ace's.

I wondered if whatever it was Matthew had been looking for was in the case, which was why he didn't find it here last night.

As I took the bucket out to the bathroom off the staff room and tossed the sponges in the sink to be cleaned, a cell phone started ringing. It wasn't a familiar ring, not Springsteen or Bitsy's "Dancing in the Streets." Instead, it was a real ring, an old-fashioned sort of ring. A ring, well, with that low-toned, rough *brrring brrring* that you hear on British television.

Simon Chase's phone.

Curiosity got the better of me. I rummaged around in my bag and pulled the BlackBerry out. I had no idea how something like this worked. My phone wasn't nearly as sophisticated.

I hit the little green phone button and after a second heard, "Chase, where the hell are you?"

Bruce Manning.

I just did a little "mmmm," lowering my voice so he'd think it was Chase.

"Where's the girl? What did you do with her?"

The words made me freeze, my heart in my throat.

He didn't wait for an answer. "I know you've got her, and I want to know where it is. I don't care about her—you can do what you want with her—but I want it back."

Chapter 51

I ended the call. Let him think Chase did. He obviously thought Chase knew where "it" was, whatever "it" was. And Chase had Elise. That was clear. Matthew must be working for him, as I suspected. He must have sent Matthew over here last night.

My staff room was clean, tidy, smelling like Pine-Sol. No thanks to Matthew or Simon Chase. I wanted to go over to Versailles and . . . what? What did I want to do? Yell at him, hurt him, like he'd hurt me?

Like he'd care. Like I meant anything to him. Obviously he'd been using me to try to get whatever it was everyone thought I had.

I wondered if Tim still had that wire handy.

Bitsy came into the staff room.

"You look like you just saw a ghost," she said.

"Did you find anything that shouldn't have been here when you were cleaning up?"

"That again? No, Brett, there's nothing here. I think the guy found it and took it. He took the safe, for Pete's sake."

True enough.

Simon Chase's phone began ringing again. Bitsy frowned.

"Where'd you get that fancy phone?"

I looked at the number of the incoming call, and it wasn't the one Bruce Manning had used. On reflex, I answered it.

"Yes?" I asked, not bothering to disguise my voice now.

"Who is this?" The English accent came through loud and clear.

"Oh, hi, Simon. It's me, Brett." My tone was casual, like I was expecting his call. His call on his phone. What was I—insane?

"The police said Jeff Coleman had my phone."

Okay, I'd spilled the beans on that one; how to explain how I got the phone? Why not try the truth?

"He gave it to me to give to you. I guess he figured we'd see each other, you know, after last night." There it was again, that affected accent. With a distinctively chilly tone around the corners.

He didn't seem to notice. "Oh, well, yes." His own tone had softened. "I would very much like to see you again. And I certainly would like my phone back. Shall we meet? Dinner?"

I didn't want to go back to Versailles. I felt too vulnerable there. I wanted him off his own turf. And I wanted to be on mine.

"Can you come here? There are a couple of nice places to eat at the Venetian," I suggested.

He was quiet a second, probably checking his schedule, then, "That's a splendid idea. Then I can see your shop. How's eight o'clock?" There was an eagerness in his voice. Sure, he wanted to see my shop. Then he could search it, too. I saw this now as a bad idea, but I couldn't go back on it without raising his suspicions. Bitsy would be here, and probably Joel would be back by then. I wouldn't be a sitting duck, like Ace had been last night.

"I'd like that," I said, forcing my voice to sound normal, but it still came out stilted.

"Shall I make reservations somewhere?" he asked.

Wouldn't you know a kidnapper and murderer would be the most chivalrous guy I'd been interested in in a long time. Just my luck. I'd fall for him and he'd end up in the slammer, twenty-five to life, and I'd be signing up for conjugal visits every six months.

Every six months seemed like a good idea, considering it had been longer than that since the last time I got naked with someone.

What was wrong with me? That kiss—oh, that kiss—had just been a ruse to distract me from Elise.

"I'll take care of it," I said, hoping that by doing so I could maintain control over this situation.

"Lovely. See you then." And he hung up.

"You'll take care of what?"

Bitsy's voice made me jump about five feet in the air.

"Don't do that," I said, a little too harshly.

"Sorry." While I was frosty, she was definitely sarcastic. I immediately felt bad.

"No, I'm sorry. I think I'm just freaking out. Too much crap in the past few days."

She nodded. "Know what you mean." She paused. "Would you mind . . . well, if I took the rest of the day off and went home? I'm a little freaked out, too."

But she was supposed to hang around so I could have backup when Simon Chase showed up.

Bitsy's face was showing the strain of the day, and I couldn't keep her here. She'd already done so much.

I nodded. "Go home. Get some rest. Hopefully we'll be back to normal tomorrow. I'll finish up here."

The relief that crossed her face made me feel even worse.

"Thanks, Brett."

She gathered up her purse and went to the door, turning just before she left. "Lock up behind me. Don't let any strangers in."

That was all there were out there—strangers. As I did what she said, I watched the people moving past the door, looking as they passed but not attempting to come in. I went over to the mahogany desk and sat in the leather chair. Joel should be back soon. I'd be a lot less jittery then.

Bitsy had replaced the mess of the purple orchid with the old white one. I wondered where she'd had it stashed so it survived the melee. It still wasn't looking good. I reached over and touched the dirt. It was bone-dry.

I kept pressing down on the dirt around the orchid's stem. My finger penetrated the soil and I pulled it out, my fingernail black. Shaking off the excess, I went to get some water for the flower. I filled a glass in the bathroom, trying not to look in the mirror. I still hadn't changed out of the ill-fitting shirt, and dark circles accentuated my eyes.

I poured the water around the base of the orchid and watched it seep into the dirt. As I turned to take the glass back, something glinted at me.

I stuck my finger into the soil again. It was wet this time, and I knew I was going to have to seriously wash my hands. But my finger caught on something, and I dragged it up.

The largest diamond ring I'd ever seen sparkled brightly as it caught the overhead light, casting a gleam against the wall and Ace's Mona Lisa.

I'd seen this diamond before.

But the last time it had been on Elise Lyon's finger.

Chapter 52

This was what Matthew was looking for. I could bet on it. And I'd win. What are those odds in Vegas?

Elise must have stuck it in the plant when she was here. Why, though? Because it was Chip's ring and she was going to run off and marry Matt? Why wouldn't she just give it back—or keep it? It must be worth something.

Bruce Manning's words on the phone jolted my brain. He'd said he didn't care what Simon Chase did with the girl, but he wanted it back. Must be the ring. So it *was* worth something.

I turned it over in my hand, watching the colors change in it. It was spectacular.

For a second I had a crazy thought.

I didn't have to give it back. While they thought it was here, they'd already trashed the place and hadn't found it. Who would be the wiser?

I would. I couldn't do that. I had to give it back.

But to whom?

Elise was the logical choice. Granted, she'd left it here, abandoned it for anyone to find. But it was hers—and her decision whether she wanted to give it back to her former fiancé or his father.

She wasn't exactly accessible right now, though. Simon Chase and Matthew had her. They must have asked her where the ring was—maybe that was what was going on at Viva Las Vegas last night when I saw Matthew taking her out of there. She must have refused to tell them, since Matthew ended up here and hadn't found it.

Was she going to show up dead now? Or were they still trying to get the ring's hiding place out of her and then they'd do away with her?

Had Kelly Masters known about the ring and refused to say where it was? Was that why she was killed? And Matt. What about Matt?

I was having dinner with Simon Chase in a few hours. Like I would be able to act natural now.

Maybe I could try to get something out of him about Elise. Where she was, what was going on. No. A dinner date wasn't going to soften him up enough for him to spill his guts about his crime. Tim's wire was another idea. It didn't work with Jeff, but I knew Chase would show up. He wasn't on the lam.

I dialed Tim's number but only got voice mail. I left a cryptic message, asking him to call as soon as he could.

I'd been turning the ring over and over in my hand and now slipped it on my finger. It looked good. But how could it not? I remembered that other ring, the one Paul had given me. It was a quarter the size of this, but it had felt bigger. Heavier.

I couldn't wear the ring. I didn't want to leave it behind, either. What if Matthew came back and decided to give it another go?

I stuck the ring in my skirt pocket as I went back to the staff room and into the bathroom, changing into my tank top and throwing the poofy shirt on the light table. As I started to go back out, I heard the front door open. Peeking out, I saw Joel lumbering in, his face drawn and tired like Bitsy's, like mine.

He pulled me into a hug.

"He's okay," he said into my hair.

I nodded, carefully extracting myself. "I know. I'm glad. It could've been worse."

Joel shrugged. "That's the funny thing."

"What's funny?"

"Ace said it was more like an accident."

"Accident how? I mean, his face was all bloody. He had a concussion."

Joel took a deep breath. "Ace said the guy came in, pushed him around a little. Ace told him there wasn't any cash. When the guy went into the staff room, Ace tried to be a freaking hero and jumped him. The guy hit him across the nose, but didn't break it. Ace said he fell then—it wasn't because the guy pushed him—and he slammed his head against the floor and then passed out."

"Sounds like it was convenient," I said.

"Yeah, maybe. But weird. It looked like the guy had beaten Ace to a pulp, but when he got all cleaned up, it had just been a bloody nose, and he'd bitten his tongue when he hit the floor, which bled like crazy."

We pondered that a few seconds, not really knowing the significance.

"But it doesn't mean he didn't mean to hurt him," I finally said. "And he did trash the place. Did the guy tell Ace what he was looking for?" The outline of the diamond was sticking out of my pocket, but no one would notice but me unless it was pointed out.

"No. Ace said it happened really fast." Joel looked around. "Did a good job cleaning up."

"Bitsy did most of it. I was out playing detective with Tim, but I'm not changing jobs anytime soon." I told Joel about my afternoon. "I have to get over to see Ace," I ended.

"They're keeping an eye on him, and your brother was over there, too, asking him all about it." Joel snickered. "Ace is loving the attention."

"Wouldn't have guessed," I said.

"Why don't you go over there now, before visiting hours are over?" Joel said.

I looked anxiously around the shop.

"Why don't we just close up? Put the gate down."

He had a point. The mall security folks knew what had gone down here. I couldn't be held responsible for shutting down early, considering. On the whole, they didn't like that, but these were extenuating circumstances. I nodded.

"Sure. Sounds like a plan."

We went through the motions, locking the front doors, pulling the gate down, locking that, too. Passersby didn't even seem to notice. It was almost suppertime anyway.

Which reminded me . . .

"I have to make reservations for eight across the way," I said, indicating Wolfgang Puck's restaurant. It wasn't nearly as fancy as Giverny, but I wasn't in the mood for fancy.

Joel frowned, and I told him about my date with Simon Chase.

"You like this guy?" he asked.

That was a loaded question if I'd ever heard one. "He knows Matthew, the guy who broke into the shop," I said.

"And you want to know if he knows anything about this," Joel finished for me.

I nodded.

"So you're going to wine and dine him? What else are you going to do?"

I slugged him on the shoulder and made a face at him. "What do you think?"

"I think you like this guy, even if he's mixed up in all this."

"It's complicated."

"Isn't it always?" He put his arm around me. "Want me to sit at the next table and glare at him?"

"No. But I wouldn't mind knowing you're nearby somewhere."

He thought a second, then said, "Okay, I'll come at eight and hang out in the square, have some gelato or something. I'll keep an eye on you. Make sure you sit outside."

The restaurant had tables on the square.

"Sounds good, but you have to try to be discreet." I was

a little worried, because Joel wasn't exactly the type to melt into the background.

"Don't worry about me."

We parted ways at my car, and I watched Joel's frame make its way to his Prius. I looked for more notes on my windshield, but it was clear. Had that drawing been Matthew's way of warning me he'd be coming around?

I pushed the thoughts out of my head and backed out of the space, following the exit signs.

As I turned the corner, my rearview mirror revealed that I wasn't the only one following the signs.

A white Dodge Dakota was gaining ground on me.

Chapter 53

I couldn't stop and get out to confront him. Not that I
didn't want to, but I couldn't because of the way the parking garage was configured and the fact that there were two
cars coming toward us going in the opposite direction and
then it was too late. I'd started down the incline.

The Venetian's garage had steep entrance and exit
inclines—streets-of–San Francisco steep. The ceiling hung
low, so it probably would take off the roof of a Hummer,
but I was disappointed to see that the Dakota, while large,
managed to be barely under the height requirement. I could
hear a sort of scraping sound, and I hoped it scratched the
crap out of the Dakota's roof.

I was going too fast. He was right on my back, nudging
me forward, and while I usually didn't hit the accelerator
going down, I tapped it and the Mustang lurched forward,
tires screeching. I gripped the steering wheel, nudged the
brake, and felt the slight impact of the truck on the back of
the car as we skidded down the concrete path.

The turn came up fast, and I yanked the wheel around,
smelled the rubber, saw the truck looming large in the mirror, sliding along the bumpers of three parked cars.

I didn't stop at the stop sign, barely glancing to the left
as I spun the car to the right, onto Koval Lane.

He didn't stop, either.

He was gaining on me as I turned right, toward the Strip. This might be a mistake, since traffic was abysmal and pedestrians crowded the intersections, but it could slow him down, and if the traffic gods were with me, I'd sail through a light that would turn red, keeping him from pursuit.

The speedometer inched up higher than I was comfortable with, but I didn't have a choice. While I'd toyed with the idea of just pulling over and confronting him in the nanosecond before we started down that incline, I wasn't leaning in that direction now. I just wanted to get away, slow my heartbeat to normal, and then call Simon Chase to find out why, if he was meeting me in a few hours, he felt compelled to show up early and scare the bejesus out of me.

Oh, right. I had the diamond. But he didn't exactly know that right now.

The light was red ahead of me, where I'd turn onto the Strip. A mass of tourists moved like a slow swarm of bees. The light turned green just as the last pedestrian moved out of my way, and I sped to the left, the Dakota hot on my butt.

This wasn't the way it was supposed to work.

I squinted ahead and saw the next light was red. And stayed red, the closer I came. Lights on the Strip were longer than James Cameron's *Titanic*.

A minivan slipped between me and the Dakota. I could see a slip of smoke coming out of the driver's-side window of the truck. Simon Chase smoked? Oh, right. All those Europeans were like chimneys. Another thing I could bolster my resolve with when I met him tonight.

If he didn't manage to get me beforehand.

If he'd wanted to meet earlier, I would've been open to that.

The light changed. Cars ahead of me began to crawl toward the next light, which was, remarkably, still green halfway there. I put a little more pressure on the accelerator, spun around the taxicab in front of me. The light blinked yellow, and I threw caution to the wind, weaving around a tour bus as if every nerve ending weren't on fire, and got through just a second after the light turned red.

A glance in the rearview mirror showed the Dakota stuck behind that minivan.

I resisted the urge to pump my fist and instead took my sunglasses out of the glove box and slipped them on. I went past the Monte Carlo, New York New York, the MGM, and sat at the light at the Tropicana. Where was I going? Home? I was pointed in that direction; I could use a nap.

But the truck was still behind me somewhere. He might figure I'd go home, and I didn't want to go to a place where he'd find me alone.

My options were limited. I should've stayed at the shop with Joel.

A phone rang.

Simon Chase's phone.

I took it out of my bag and hit the button to answer. "Hello?" I asked, this time not bothering to disguise my voice. He knew I had the phone. It might even be him.

"Brett?"

It *was* him.

"Yes?"

"Something's come up. I can't meet you this evening."

Something came up, all right. I just outran him. I smiled. "That's too bad. I was looking forward to it." Considering how fast my heart was pounding, it was amazing my voice didn't vibrate.

"Me, too."

"Listen," I started.

"Yes?"

"Why did Matthew trash my shop, take my safe, beat up one of my tattooists?"

Silence.

I didn't want to let him off the hook. "I saw you talking to him. At Versailles. And you and he and Elise were all at Viva Las Vegas last night. And why are you driving a

Dodge Dakota, and why did you just chase me out of the parking garage?"

He was so quiet, I thought he'd ended the call. Just as I opened my mouth to ask if he was there, he spoke.

"What are you talking about? I'm not driving a Dodge Dakota. I'm in my office, at Versailles. I haven't left all day."

Chapter 54

I looked at the phone number on the BlackBerry. It was his office number.

If Simon Chase hadn't been driving, who was?

"You were driving a Dakota last night," I pointed out, uncertain where to take this, doubts about all my theories crowding my head.

I heard a short intake of breath, then, "We've got a couple here at the hotel for management to use, left over from when it was just a construction site. I took one last night because, to be honest, a place like that isn't a place for a Mercedes."

I could hardly blame him.

"Why the twenty questions, Brett?"

Why, indeed? "Because you met Elise last night, and you know Matthew, and you dated Kelly, and you obviously knew Matt Powell, and you seem to be some sort of link between everything that's going on." I hadn't really meant to let it all out like that, but I was tired of the whole thing.

Surprisingly, I heard him chuckle. "Why don't you leave the detecting to your brother, Brett? I'm sure he'll get to the bottom of all this."

"Do you know where Elise is?"

"Let it go, Brett." It had gotten a little frostier in the car, and the air wasn't even on all that high.

"I just want to find her," I said.

"Why?"

Should I risk telling him I had the diamond? If he was in on it, then it would give him another chance to sic Matthew on me. No, thank you. I'd have to try another tack.

"Someone thinks she left something behind when she came to my shop."

"Did she?"

"Someone thinks so."

"You didn't answer my question."

"And you didn't answer mine."

Silence indicated we were both going to be stubborn about this.

"I'm going to make time to see you," Chase finally said, like it was totally putting him out. "I'll be there at eight, as I said. But I won't have time for dinner. I'll just meet you at your shop."

"Don't go changing plans just for me."

"I think we have some things to clear up. We need to do this in person. I'll see you at eight." And now he really did end the call.

I stared at the BlackBerry, then tossed it on the passenger seat. What exactly had just happened here? The only thing he said for sure was that he wasn't driving that Dakota. It was the only thing he hadn't skirted around.

Speaking of skirts, I touched the outline of the diamond in my pocket. I couldn't drive around with this; I needed to do something with it. Put it in a safe place. But where? My safe was gone, lifted—literally—by Matthew. The safest place for the ring, ironically, had been in that orchid pot. I probably should've just left it there.

The sign for the In-N-Out beckoned just ahead. When in doubt, go for a Double-Double.

I took my burger and lemonade to an empty table and sat down, peeling back the paper on the burger and taking a big bite. I was still chewing when my phone rang. My phone, this time, not Simon Chase's.

"Hello?" I asked after swallowing, wiping my mouth with a napkin.

"Brett?" It was Tim. "What's going on? What do you want?"

"I found something," I said. "I found what they were looking for."

But before I could elaborate, a hand clasped itself over mine, yanking the phone away from my ear. I heard Tim distantly asking, "What?" as another hand twisted my other shoulder.

I wrenched my head back as far as I could to see the eagle wings on his neck.

Matthew.

Chapter 55

His breath was hot against my ear.

"You're coming with me." His voice was deeper than I'd imagined, gravelly, like he smoked three packs a day. But I didn't smell cigarettes on him, just a musky odor mixed with sweat.

His hand shifted underneath my armpit and lifted me up. I still held the burger as he almost carried me out the door. My phone was on the table.

I expected to see the Dodge Dakota, but it wasn't in the parking lot. Instead, Matthew led me to a motorcycle, a Harley.

"We're going for a ride," he said, handing me my bag and taking the burger, throwing it in a trash can.

I slung my bag over my shoulder and shook my head. "Not on that thing."

He nodded. "Yes, on that thing."

I shook my head more violently. "I don't ride bikes. I can't." The tremble in my voice caused him to hesitate, peer into my face. "I really can't," I whispered, memories flashing through my brain like a slide show: motorcycle, asphalt, blood, exposed bone.

My fear must have registered with him, and his face changed slightly.

"Tell me why," he said.

I swallowed hard, but the fear still stuck in my throat.

Finally, he nodded, the veins in his neck pulsating, causing the wings to move. "We'll take your car. But I'm driving."

I looked around to see if anyone was nearby, but the line for the drive-up window was on the other side of the building, and it wasn't exactly lunchtime, so there was a distinct lack of customers. As I pondered screaming—not even sure I could because my mouth was so dry—he shoved me into my car after grabbing my bag and finding my keys.

He'd started the car, and we were peeling out of the lot when I realized he hadn't shown a gun or knife or anything. He was just there. Big and imposing. I found my voice.

"Where are you taking me?"

He glanced at me, then looked back at the road. "Where is it?" he asked.

I forced myself not to touch my pocket. "What?"

"You were saying you found it."

"My keys. I found my keys. I'd lost them."

"You said you'd found what 'they' were looking for. That doesn't sound like your keys."

Give the guy a gold star. He wasn't stupid. Even though he might look it.

"I misspoke." I sounded like one of those politicians making excuses for saying something truly stupid.

"No, no, I don't think you did."

"Where's Elise? What have you done with her?"

"Don't worry about her."

"Why not?"

"What did you do with it?"

Back to the diamond again. This guy was getting a little tiring. I studied the eagle on his neck for a second.

"Coleman does a nice tat," I muttered. "Even if he likes flash."

"It's not flash."

"What?"

"My sister designed it."

"Kelly?"

"She was good."

"I saw she worked at that shop in Malibu."

He gave me a quick glance before looking back at the road again. He didn't speak for a long time as we headed west on 215, and abruptly he got off the highway, turned onto Charleston toward Red Rock Canyon, through Summerlin. The housing developments on our right clashed with the brown desert on the left. Everything was brown here; it was the hardest thing to get used to after the greenness of the East Coast. But after a while, I saw past the brown to the touches of green in the banana yuccas, the Joshua trees, the bright blooms of the desert in the winter, the red rocks that crashed into a bright blue, cloudless sky.

"She loved him at first," Matthew finally spoke, and I took "him" to mean Jeff Coleman. "She was grateful for what he did. I was grateful for what he did. But she got restless. And she was pretty once she got cleaned up, really pretty. Coleman kept her in that shop; she needed to go."

I knew how she felt.

"Who killed her?" I asked.

He slammed on the brakes, the car skidding across the road and over into the breakdown lane. When we stopped, he twisted around in the seat, his left arm draped across the steering wheel, his right looping over the top of my seat. His fingers grabbed my hair and yanked me back.

"Don't worry about that."

There were a lot of things to worry about now, and he was right: Kelly Masters's murder wasn't exactly at the top of the list for me at the moment.

"I was just making conversation," I tried.

He let go of my hair and turned back to the wheel. My fingers found the armrest and crawled over to the door release latch. I had to get out of here. The guy had beat up Ace, trashed my shop, and who knew what else?

I yanked at the release just as the car started to move. My door swung open, and before he could register it, I threw myself out of the car, rolling along the dirt by the side of the road. When I came to a stop, I saw the car was next to me, idling, and Matthew was getting out.

I scrambled to my feet, hoping the Tevas would find purchase in the slick desert sand, happy when they did, and I took off toward a subdivision entrance just a few feet away.

The sign proclaimed it Desert Bloom. A lovely name for rows and rows of red-tiled roofs over caramel-colored stucco. I could hear Matthew's feet pounding the pavement but didn't turn around for fear of losing ground. I dashed around one of the town houses, skidding a little on my Tevas as I rounded the back of it. My chest heaved as I panted, sucking in air as quietly as possible. The dry heat filled my lungs, and I wanted to cough in the worst way.

I peered around the side of the house and saw Matthew almost straight ahead, bent over, his hands on his knees. He was breathing heavily—I could hear him, the air was so still. I was lucky I was just wearing a tank and a light, billowy skirt. He had on jeans, a T-shirt, and the jean jacket with the sleeves cut off. Too much clothing for a run. I didn't wish bad things to happen to most people, but right then, I wanted him to pass out in the worst way.

I had a feeling Sister Mary Eucharista would be okay with that.

I had nothing that could help me except the heat and the sun. No phone. No people around. Too late I realized this development was still under construction, and no one had moved into this section yet.

I was alone out here with Matthew, a sitting duck. He could kill me and either leave me here or dump my body in the desert just across the street, and I wouldn't be found until the next batch of houses were going up.

It was not the most reassuring thought.

Matthew straightened up again, and I ducked behind the house again just as he swiveled his head around, searching for me. I held my breath, waiting to see him pop around the corner, but nothing. I risked peering out and saw him running in the opposite direction.

I had a plan.

He was going away from the road. I would go toward it. I sneaked around the backs of the houses, furtively zigzagging from one to the next. I felt a little like John Belushi in *Animal House* when he's sneaking around the women's sorority house.

When I got to the last house, I didn't even stop. I made a mad dash around the fence and out the entrance and turned the corner. My car sat where I'd left it and Matthew.

He hadn't even turned off the engine.

I didn't have time to think. I had no idea where Matthew was, but I wasn't going to check. I ran to the car, throwing open the driver's door, and jumped in. No time for seat belts; I just slammed my foot on the clutch, threw it in first, and pressed down as hard as I could on the accelerator. The Mustang shot off onto the road like a Bullitt.

Chapter 56

Matthew was in the rearview mirror, getting smaller and smaller as I drove. I'd hung a U-ey and was now going toward downtown on Charleston.

About three miles later, my heart stopped pounding like it was going to come through my chest, and I managed to slip on my seat belt. My bag was on the floor in front of the passenger side, all its contents strewn about. It looked sort of like the way I felt: all discombobulated, shaken up.

He hadn't had a gun. Or a knife. At least not one he'd shown me. His ultimate weapon was his size and how overpowering he was.

I was trembling, holding on to the steering wheel for dear life, because if I let go, I'd come apart.

For a second I thought about going up back to Red Rock, despite the heat, just to get a little of that chi balancing effect that it always managed to give me. I couldn't risk it, though. Matthew was in that direction, and Red Rock would be a worse place to get stuck alone when a murderer was after you.

Asking about Kelly had brought out Matthew's anger even more than when he'd been trying to get the diamond back.

The diamond.

I reached down under the seat belt and patted my pocket,

feeling the rock's sharp edge under the cotton material. At least I hadn't lost it. Although I wasn't quite sure just what to do with it. It seemed everyone was after it. Everyone except Elise, who'd gotten rid of it.

I got a little hostile thinking about that. She caused a lot of problems for me. For Ace. Maybe she didn't deserve to get it back after all.

Thinking about Elise made me think about Kelly again, how she'd designed the eagle ink. She was talented; Jeff and Sylvia had trained her well. Too bad it wasn't enough for her.

Why had she called Elise in Philadelphia? What had she said that lured Elise here?

Again, the link between the two women was Simon Chase. I kept coming back to him. Not that he wasn't a nice place to visit, but it would've been nicer if we'd met under better circumstances.

Or if I didn't have so many questions about him.

Twisting all this around in my head helped calm me slightly, distracting me.

The clock on the dashboard told me it was just after six. The gas gauge showed I needed some fuel, so I pulled into a Terrible's. I also picked up a water while I was there. It was long overdue. As the tank filled, I went through the stuff from my bag. I didn't have my cell phone, but I had Simon Chase's BlackBerry. I punched in Tim's number.

When he answered, I didn't bother identifying myself. I just said, "Matthew Masters is walking along Charleston Boulevard, up near the exit for Red Rock, in Summerlin. He kidnapped me at the In-N-Out and took me up there, but I managed to get away." The words jumbled together, like it was one big sentence.

"What?"

"I was at the In-N-Out burger. Matthew came in, grabbed me, took my car keys, drove up to Summerlin. I jumped out of the car and got away. You have to go get him."

"Did he hurt you? Did he have a weapon?"

"I didn't see one. He just grabbed me, pulled my hair." My heart started its *rat-a-tat-tat* again. I took a couple of deep breaths.

"Are you all right? He didn't hurt you?" The panic rose in Tim's voice.

"I'm okay," I said, trying to reassure myself as much as him. "But he must still be out there. He didn't have a car or anything. I saw him walking as I drove away."

"Tell me exactly what happened."

I did.

"He kidnapped you?"

I didn't want to get into the whole motorcycle thing, so I left that part out. "Yeah."

"I'll send a cruiser out there. Hold on."

I waited a few minutes before he came back on the line.

"Where are you now?" he asked.

"Terrible's. On Charleston. Heading back downtown."

"You said you found something." Tim reminded me that I'd started to tell him what before Matthew took my phone.

"I've got it," I said. "I think it's why he kidnapped me."

"What is it?"

I pulled the ring out of my pocket. The stone flashed white, almost blinding me.

"It's a diamond. Elise Lyon was wearing it when she came into the shop, but for some reason she stuck it in my orchid."

"Excuse me?"

So now I had to explain about the plant. "This is what they're looking for, I think. It's got to be."

He was quiet, then, "Bruce Manning said she stole it."

"What? Wasn't it her engagement ring?"

"There are things about this that the media doesn't know. That you don't know, Brett." He paused. "We've been treating this as a missing persons case, but Manning's convinced she took off with this other guy and planned to hock the ring. It's worth two million."

"Two million dollars?" I'd slipped the ring on my finger,

and I stared at it. It was hypnotic. Even more so now that I knew how much it was worth. I needed to get rid of it before I lost it.

"Where is it now?"

"I've got it," I said.

"With you?"

"Yeah. It was in my pocket. Matthew didn't know I had it." As I said it, I was struck by how stupid this was. I should've brought it to Tim from the get-go. I had another thought. "Is Elise missing because of this ring?" Or maybe she was still alive because she knew where it was and no one else did.

"We still don't know why Kelly Masters called her in Philadelphia."

The words hung between us.

"Or why she was using Kelly's name when she was here," I added. "You have to get Matthew Masters. He had her last night. I hope she's okay."

"He didn't say anything to you?"

"He's not exactly Mr. Sociable."

"We've got a cruiser out now in that area, looking for him. I'll let you know when we get him. In the meantime, bring me the ring."

I bristled at that, not because I was getting comfortable wearing it, but because I had this crazy idea that if I kept it, I could find Elise and give it back to her. But Tim was right. I had to turn it in.

"Where are you?" I asked.

"Come to the station. We can file an official report, get a warrant. Put out a bulletin, find this guy, and arrest him."

Sounded like a plan. But I hesitated.

"What?" he asked.

"I'm meeting Simon Chase at eight. I saw him with Matthew. A couple of times. I think they're in on it together. Maybe you could wire me again, and I could see what I can find out."

"You think Simon Chase wants to steal that ring? Why?"

He had me there. I had no clue. "He knows Matthew," I repeated.

I heard him sigh. "I can't wire you again. My boss wasn't happy that we did that yesterday and nothing came of it. We've got cruisers out looking for Matthew. You come in here, file a report, we'll arrest the guy. Forget about Chase. Stand him up."

"But he—"

"Forget about him."

Easy for him to say. I finished filling up the tank and put the gas hose back, hitting the button for a receipt. Something in his tone made me frown.

"Why? Do you know something I don't?"

"No, no."

He was lying. I grabbed the receipt and climbed into the car, turning over the engine while I still held the Black-Berry to my ear. "I'm going to start driving now. I'll be there as soon as I get there." I'd see what I could get out of him when I saw him. I put my hand on the steering wheel and watched the diamond glisten. I kept waffling between wanting to get rid of it and wanting to spend more time with it. Like a guy you should break up with, but you don't want to end up alone on Saturday night, so you let him stick around.

We ended the call, and even though there were still too many questions, talking to my brother had calmed me down.

Until I saw the white Dodge Dakota behind me.

Chapter 57

This game had gotten so old. I drove slower than the speed limit, and I could see he was trying to force me to go slightly faster. After a few blocks, I couldn't take it anymore. I slammed on the brakes; the Mustang skidded around, wedging itself perpendicular to the Dakota so the truck couldn't move forward. I didn't let myself think as I jumped out of the car.

The driver tried to swerve around me, but I was on top of him before he could, pounding on the window like a crazy person.

The Dakota's window rolled down and a bald head emerged. But it wasn't the bald head I'd been encountering. It was a strange bald head, devoid of any tats. His ears were fringed with salt-and-pepper tufts, his face totally unfamiliar except for the rage I saw there.

"What the hell are you doing?" he demanded.

All of my anger melted away into embarrassment. I swallowed hard. "I'm sorry. I thought you were someone else," I said contritely.

He didn't seem to notice the apology. He reached for the door latch, and the look on his face told me that while I might have escaped Matthew relatively unscathed, I might not be so lucky now.

I hightailed it back to my car and spun it around and

down the street, leaving yet another angry man in my wake. I hoped this wasn't going to be a trend.

The diamond flashed like a white laser across Tim's desk.

"You're *wearing* it?" Tim was doing his hunt-and-peck typing as he wrote up the report of my kidnapping.

"I didn't want to lose it," I said.

"Just give me the ring," he said, holding out his hand.

Reluctantly, I slipped it off my finger. "You realize I'll never wear anything like that ever again."

"It's not all it's cracked up to be," Tim said, turning it over and over, watching the prisms of color that slashed through it as the fluorescent overhead light hit it.

"See?" I asked. "It's got powers."

"But are they good or evil?" he asked, sticking the ring on his desk next to his computer.

"What are you going to do with it?" I asked.

"I'll call Bruce Manning about it."

"What if Manning is lying about it being stolen? I mean, she was engaged to his son; it's an engagement ring. If Chip gave it to her, then it's hers, right? She can't steal what's hers, right?"

Tim looked like he wasn't paying attention to me as he studied the computer screen. After a few seconds, he looked up at me. "Oh, by the way, just thought you'd like to know there was no big, bald, tattooed guy walking around Summerlin. Two cruisers were out looking."

My chest constricted. They hadn't found him? Where had he gone without a vehicle?

"What about the motorcycle? The one at the In-N-Out?"

"Brett, you really have to tell me every detail so I can cover all the bases."

Right. He'd just turned this around so I was at fault. And I'd been the one to get kidnapped.

We went over everything about three times, and he finally got it all typed up.

"You should go straight home," he advised as he walked me to my car. "Don't stop anywhere; just go home and lock the doors, and I'll be there in a couple hours."

My watch told me it was almost time to meet Simon Chase. I told Tim as much. "I didn't cancel," I added.

"Call him and cancel, then," he said.

I made a sort of nodding motion with my head, but it wasn't really a commitment. "I'll go home," I said, giving him a hug and a little wave good-bye.

As I started the engine, I knew Tim was right. I should just go home, even though my head was toying with the idea of meeting Simon Chase anyway. But how stupid was that? He might have been the one to rescue Matthew from Summerlin, and he might decide to bring him to my shop.

I turned down Las Vegas Boulevard. It wasn't the most direct route home, but it was going in the general direction. I saw Goodfellas Bail Bonds on my left, Murder Ink next door. Sylvia was walking down the sidewalk.

The Bright Lights Motel's parking lot beckoned, so I pulled in and parked. I honked the horn just as I climbed out, but Sylvia didn't turn around.

I jogged down the sidewalk, jaywalking when I caught up with her. I reached over and tapped her on the shoulder.

"Hey, Sylvia," I said, panting from the heat, not the jog.

She turned, her smile bright. "It's good to see you, dear. How's your big friend?"

"Fine," I said, figuring she was referring to Joel. "How's Jeff?"

Her face clouded. "He's not happy with me. He said it's my fault things are being stolen from the shop." She leaned toward me, whispering conspiratorially, "I told him he could take the gun. He didn't *steal* it."

I stiffened. "Who?"

"Your big friend."

Dementia rears its ugly head again. I wondered if Jeff had thought about assisted living. This could only get worse.

"Why would Joel want Jeff's gun?" I asked.

Confusion crossed her face. "Oh, dear, I didn't mean your *homo* friend."

Okay, so she had dementia and she was politically incorrect at the same time. I guess when you get old, you can be whatever you want to be. Halfway through that thought, it dawned on me: If it wasn't Joel, who did she think was my "big" friend?

"Sylvia," I said, "who exactly are we talking about?"

Her smile was so pure, her face shining.

"Why, dear, Matthew, of course."

Chapter 58

I felt like someone had punched me in the gut.

"Sylvia, Matthew isn't my friend." It was all I could do to keep my voice from shaking. Post-traumatic stress, and all that. I could end up worse than Pavlov's dogs; just mention the name Matthew and I'd crumble into a million little pieces. At least the dogs got to ring a bell and then forget about it. "When did he take the gun? And why would he set Jeff up for Kelly's murder?"

"Oh, he didn't set Jeff up. He just took the gun."

"But the gun was found in Kelly's car. So how did it end up there?"

Her smile turned a little sad, like she thought I'd become too dim-witted for this conversation. "Why, he gave it to Kelly, of course."

I thought my head would explode.

"What for?"

"She never liked having the gun in the shop, you know."

We were on a carousel, going round and round but heading nowhere except on Sylvia's own little Magical Mystery Tour. I didn't think it would do any good to pound my head against the wall.

"How do you know that Matthew gave the gun to his sister?"

"That's what he told me he wanted to do."

Just when you think there's no logic in anything, something coherent pops up.

"Any reason why?"

She patted my forearm. "He said Kelly had gotten into a little trouble."

That coincided with what Matt Powell had told Jeff. But if her brother gave her a gun, that might indicate something a little worse than just deciding to be a single parent and not bothering to tell Jeff that she was confiscating their embryos for her own use.

We'd walked all the way down to the courthouse, and Sylvia abruptly turned on her heel and started walking back.

"Where are we going?" I asked.

"Oh, I just like to walk now and then." She hooked her arm around mine, patting my hand. She was so little; I towered over her. But her hand was warm, comforting. After the day I had, I didn't mind having a little TLC, even if Sylvia was a little nuts.

"You should let me ink your arm," she said after a two-block silence as we approached Murder Ink.

I thought about Napoleon. "I'm going to do a stencil," I said. "I'd love it if you could do it." I told her what I planned.

She snorted. "Dear, you're a six-foot-tall woman. You don't want a five-foot-two man on your arm. Let me do something more appropriate."

I didn't want to argue the issue. I wasn't in the mood. I let her reel off the possibilities as I wondered why Kelly Masters would need a gun.

"I'm going to close up the shop now, dear," Sylvia was saying as we stood in front of Murder Ink. She unhooked her arm. "Thank you for walking with me. You're a nice girl."

"How's Jeff?"

"He's fine. I'm sure you'll hear from him soon."

I was sure of it, too. He'd become my new best friend. Well, except for Sylvia.

I gave her a quick kiss on the cheek, her skin thin and transparent, her wrinkles rippling across her cheeks. Her face was the only place that wasn't inked.

I glanced back at the shop when I reached my car and watched Sylvia pull open the door.

I was concentrating so much on her that I didn't see it until it swerved into the Bright Lights Motel lot. The Dakota spun around my car faster than I could move, blocking me from the door so I was trapped.

Chapter 59

I just couldn't deal with road rage right now. If it was that guy I'd stopped earlier, I might as well just throw my hands up and surrender.

"Brett Kavanaugh?"

I didn't think that guy knew my name. And, anyway, it wasn't a guy. It was a woman's voice that came out of the truck.

I walked around the massive hood, noticing the scratches on the roof. This was the Dakota that had chased me in the Versailles garage.

The window was rolled down, and she stuck her head out.

Elise Lyon. Elise? She was the one driving the Dakota?

Her eyes skipped all around me before landing on my face.

"Get in," she said.

I sighed. "Listen, Elise, if it's all the same to you, I'd rather not. Why don't you get out and we can talk here?"

A gun barrel peeked out beneath her face.

"It's not an option."

Kidnapped twice in one day. Go figure.

I walked back around the truck and opened the door, climbing up inside. A blast of cold air hit me in the face and

I shivered, welcoming it. I'd been outside long enough so I'd almost gotten used to the heat.

I shut the door after me and turned in my seat to see Elise Lyon still holding the gun on me.

"You know, people have been looking for you. Where have you been?" I asked.

"There are a lot of places to stay in Vegas, and not just on the Strip." Her expression changed slightly. "We're going to your shop," she said, although she seemed perplexed as to how she'd drive and still manage the gun.

I shook my head. "It's too late."

The gun whipped up and the barrel rested on my forehead. My heart missed a couple of beats.

"What do you mean?" she demanded.

"I found it. The ring. And I gave it to my brother."

"Your brother?" She was confused a second, then, "The cop?"

I nodded. "I didn't want it. He said Manning said you stole it."

The gun moved off my forehead and circled up toward the ceiling. "What? I can't believe it. Chip gave it to me. It was my *engagement* ring. It was mine."

"That's what I said." I hoped that by offering some sort of support she'd feel kindly toward me and stop waving that gun around. "But he wanted it anyway. He's my brother. What was I supposed to do?" I had no idea whether she had siblings, but I took a shot that she'd know what I was talking about.

She lowered the gun and put it on the console between us. I felt my heartbeat going back to normal.

I was about to ask her why she was following me around when suddenly she floored the accelerator and we were flying out of the parking lot, going down Las Vegas Boulevard toward the Strip.

"We're going to your shop," she said again.

"But it's not there."

"I don't care. You're going to give me that tattoo."

"Huh?"

"If the ring's gone, well, there's nothing I can do about it. I'll figure out something. But I want that tattoo. I need it. I need it to get me through this. To give me courage." She was babbling, but I understood the basics of what she was saying. I'd do the ink and she'd leave town, leave everything behind and move on. It was her rite of passage.

I nodded. "Okay. I can do that. But just tell me: Are you the one who's been chasing me all over town?"

"You didn't have to go so fast in that garage."

"Why have you been chasing me?"

"I needed to know if you found the ring. Or if it was still at your shop."

"Why couldn't you just call and be straight with me? Then we wouldn't have gone through all this."

"I couldn't risk that. Everyone's looking for me. Bruce Manning thinks I'm a thief and would throw me in jail, and it's my word against his."

I remembered how Manning had treated me at Versailles, gripping me so hard but making it look like we were just having a casual conversation. Elise and I were in the same boat: Who would believe *us* when one of the richest men in the world gave his version of reality?

Elise was still talking. "I couldn't risk going to your shop; someone might see me. Simon said he'd get it tonight, when he saw you."

"You told him about it?" So that was why he wanted to meet me at The Painted Lady. He wanted to feel up my orchid.

Elise's eyes left the road for a second as she gave me a long look. "Of course. He and Mattie are the only two people I can trust."

I didn't want to remind her that Matt Powell was dead. That she was talking about him in the present tense.

"Simon lent me the truck," Elise said.

Nice of him, I thought. Chivalrous as usual. I wondered if he knew she used it to follow me.

"How did you know Kelly Masters?" I asked, changing the subject.

Again with a look, then she was staring straight at the road, her jaw tense. "Chip. Chip was having an affair with her. She called me. She wanted to meet me, and when I came out here, she told me she was pregnant."

I let that digest a little as we stopped at the light next to the World's Largest Gift Shop. I'd never been in there. I'd never needed any Large Gifts.

I took a shot. "Chip said you had an affair, and you told him it was over."

She snorted. It was not attractive. "He thought Simon and I hooked up again. He was so wrong." The light turned green. "Simon likes the chase, you know, but he's not a long-term sort of guy." She glanced at me as she pressed down on the gas. "Be careful."

"I think I can take care of myself." I bristled.

Elise chuckled. "Every woman thinks she can change him."

I didn't want to change him. I wasn't sure what I wanted.

She kept talking. "He thinks you're exotic, you know, all those tattoos. Like Kelly."

I didn't much like being compared to Kelly. And he'd talked about me with Elise? This was just getting stranger and stranger.

We were quiet a few minutes, and finally she reached the Venetian, pulling into the valet parking lane.

"I hate that garage," she tossed at me as she scrambled out of the truck.

I was close on her heels, realizing I had absolutely no idea what was going on except that I had an unexpected client. Before long I was leading the way, since I could get around the Venetian with my eyes closed. We followed the canal to the shop, a gondola just ahead of us.

The Painted Lady had been imprisoned behind the gate. I unlocked the glass doors, leaned down and unlocked the gate, and lifted it up, letting it rise over our heads, disappearing into the ceiling.

I led Elise into my room, where I set up my inks. I took a disposable razor out of a package and wet a washcloth.

"Where do you want it?" I asked automatically, although I already knew.

Without any ceremony, Elise pulled her shirt over her head to reveal a lacy pink bra that barely covered her nipples. She pointed to a spot just above her left breast. "Here."

The hair on her skin was fine, but I'd still have to shave it. My hands were shaking slightly, though; the day's events and an ever-lowering blood sugar level weren't good for tattooing. I still had the stencil I'd made in the staff room, so I told Elise to wait in the chair while I got it, stalling for a few minutes.

I found half a meatball sub in the fridge, and I picked out one of the meatballs and chewed it whole as I rummaged through the files, finally finding the stencil in a folder marked *Kelly Masters*.

While I wasn't keen on devotion tats, this was a memorial. Not unlike the kid who had Jesus on his back.

I grabbed a handful of disposable needles, still in their packages, from a box in the closet. The meatball had erased my shakes. I was running through the whole process in my head, my own little ritual, so when I finally started back to my room, it didn't register for a moment.

But when I heard him say, "Trust me," and I heard the whirring of the tattoo machine, my first thought was that I should've put that gate down and locked it after us.

Chapter 60

My second thought was, How did Chip Manning learn how to use a tattoo machine? Because, as I peered around the corner into my room, I saw he was drawing a heart on Elise Lyon's bared breast.

His back was to me, and the machine was loud enough so he didn't hear me approach. Elise saw me, though, since she was facing the door, and she opened her mouth, but I put my finger over my lips to silence her. She shut her mouth and looked at Chip's hands. He hadn't even put on a pair of gloves.

Scratcher.

"Did you really believe that I would love her more than you?" Chip was asking. "Did you think I'd marry that slut instead of you? You should've just stayed home, and we would've been married right now."

"I couldn't marry you."

"Oh, that's right. Matt was the love of your life. I thought he was being a good friend, offering to come out here to find you, and the next thing I know you're getting a tattoo with his name on it."

"That's—"

I crinkled the needle package in my hand by mistake. The machine stopped.

"Is she coming back?"

I couldn't risk peering around the door again.

"Maybe she's in the bathroom," Elise suggested.

The machine started again.

"Owwww. Watch it."

"Did you think it wouldn't hurt, Elise?" I wondered if he was talking about the tat or about Matt Powell. "Finding out that my best friend was my fiancée's secret lover?" Okay, question answered. "What did you think I was going to do? Sit around and watch him take you from me?"

"You had Kelly." Her voice was barely above a whisper.

"She meant nothing. That's why I did what I did, to show you that she was nothing. She was to me what Chase was to you. We had it all, Elise, and you destroyed it."

"I didn't kill Simon, though. But you killed her. I was glad she told me about you, how you met in L.A. and couldn't keep your hands off each other. She was pregnant, Chip." Desperation laced Elise's voice.

He didn't seem to notice. "With her out of the way, you and I can get married. Anyway, I found out it wasn't my baby. It was her ex-husband's. I got lucky that she had his gun. Now everyone thinks he killed her."

"But without Kelly, I wouldn't—" She stopped suddenly. "What are you doing?"

"I'm going to put my name in this heart. That way you'll never forget your promises to me."

"It's too late, Chip."

"My father will fix it. He fixes everything."

"Did he fix Matt? Was that him, or was that you?" I heard a catch in her voice. "Matt was innocent, Chip."

I didn't wait around to hear his answer, figuring that the machine's noise would mask my footsteps. I heard more talking, but I couldn't make out what they were saying.

Simon Chase's phone was in my bag on the light table. I took it out and saw that the screen was blank. Uh-oh. Guess it hadn't been charged in a while. We didn't have a landline extension back here, since someone, usually Bitsy, was always in the front of the shop to answer the phone.

It might not be that hard getting out of the shop. Chip was one guy. He wasn't nearly as big as Matthew, and I'd managed to slip past *him*—well, it wasn't easy, but I did it.

I opened one of the packages I'd set down, sliding the long, silver needle out of its casing. While I hoped I didn't have any use for it, I had to have something, and Elise had left that gun in the truck.

I walked as quietly as I could, stopping just outside the room again.

"Tell me where the diamond is," Chip was saying.

"The police have it." Elise's voice was stronger now, anger weaving through her words.

I peeked around the door to see Chip finishing up the heart; it was rough around the edges. Elise's voice had been firm, but her eyes were laced with tears. It was possible she'd been too jittery, moving too much.

Elise caught my eye, shaking her head slightly.

Before I could duck back, the machine cut off and Chip swung around in the chair. I turned to get away, but he was fast. He grabbed the back of my shirt and yanked me into the room as he held the machine over my face.

"Have you ever tattooed someone's eyeballs?" he hissed.

He fell onto me then and I twisted my head slightly, the needle in the machine raking me just behind my ear, sliding on my hair. After a second, I realized what had happened: Elise had lunged toward him, and they both ended up on the floor, the impact knocking the machine out of Chip's hand.

I stood over them, hesitating for a second.

It was too long. Chip threw Elise off him, grabbed the machine again, and plunged it into my thigh, but its design kept it from going in too deep.

The needle in my hand, however, had no restrictions. I swung it around and stabbed Chip's shoulder. The needle went in the front and stuck out the back. Sort of like a live shish kebab.

He made a yowling sound, dropping the tattoo machine—but not before it slid across my calf, drawing a crooked black line—his hand reaching around to pull the needle out of his shoulder. He screamed as blood spurted across his chest.

I grabbed Elise's hand and pulled her out the door, to the front of the shop, toward the doors. I glanced back to see Chip holding the needle, chasing us.

I reached for the front door handle when everything got dark.

Matthew Masters stood on the other side of the glass, glowering with anger. He pulled the door open and stepped inside. But to my surprise, he pushed us aside and went after Chip, who'd stopped suddenly. Matthew grabbed the shoulder I'd stabbed, causing Chip to scream again and drop the needle.

Matthew turned and looked at me, studying my face for a second before his eyes moved to Elise. I saw what he saw: Elise's bare torso, the bra hanging open, exposing her breasts, the beads of blood slipping down over the black outline of the heart and the start of the "C" that Chip had drawn.

"Are you okay?"

His voice wasn't what I remembered from our earlier encounter. While it still had its gravelly tone, the roughness was replaced with a gentleness. His eyes matched his voice as he gazed at her, and Elise began to sob, reaching her arms out to him.

He shook his head, but I saw a glint in his eye, too, a tear in the corner that he blinked away as he yanked harder on Chip's shoulder.

"You," he said loudly to me. "You—call the cops."

Before I could move, though, the door swung open and Simon Chase came into the shop.

Chapter 61

He took one look at Matthew and Chip and muttered, "I may have to find another job." He then looked at me, at Elise and put his arm around her. She clung to him, the sobs more audible now. "Brett, can you call the police?" he asked, his eyes again moving to mine.

Everything started falling into place. I'd seen it in Matthew's expression when he looked at Elise, when she reached out to him.

He was her Matthew.

When I'd seen her with him at Viva Las Vegas, she wasn't afraid of *him*—she was afraid of me finding her. It all made sense now.

I went to the phone on the desk and dialed Tim's number.

"You have to come to my shop," I said when he answered.

"Why aren't you at home?" he demanded.

"Let's just say I got sidetracked." I paused, looking at Matthew, who was still clutching Chip's shoulder. "Your murderer is here, if you want him."

"What?"

"It's Chip. Chip Manning. He killed Kelly Masters. He might have killed Matt Powell, too."

I told Tim the rest as quickly as I could, and he finally interrupted me to tell me he'd be right over with the cavalry. I hung up and looked at Matthew Masters.

"Who killed Matt Powell?"

"Kelly did," he said quietly.

Everyone stared at him. It was possible no one else had known this until just now, from their expressions.

Matthew sighed. "He threatened to tell Chip about the baby. How it wasn't Chip's. Kelly couldn't let him do that. Her plan was to tell Elise about her and Chip, the baby."

"And she thought Chip would marry her?" I looked at Elise.

"She thought that if I knew, I would break it off. And then she would get Chip because she was pregnant."

Seemed like a simple plan, but what went wrong?

"I wanted to meet her, see if she really was pregnant. Kelly was all for it; she even sent me her ID so I could get an airline ticket under her name, because I didn't want anyone knowing where I was going. I figured I'd be back the next day. I went to D.C., because I didn't want to run the risk of anyone seeing me in Philly at the airport. Matthew picked me up here at McCarran, and we got to talking. He told me everything Kelly said was true. By the time we got to the hotel and met up with Kelly, I was so done with Chip."

"What hotel?" I asked.

She shrugged. "We've been staying off the Strip." She gave Matthew a sidelong look that told us what they'd been doing when they weren't following me around.

Elise didn't seem to have a problem jumping from one man to the next.

"Kelly went to Matt Powell's room to try to talk him out of telling Chip about the baby," Matthew said, taking over. "She ended up killing him while they were fighting about it. She said it was self-defense."

"But she had a tattoo needle on her?" I asked.

Matthew sighed. "She had a case with her. She was going to give Elise her tattoo after she met with Matt. But when she realized Matt was dead, she figured she could protect Elise and me, and she gave him that tat."

"How did he get to Chip's suite, though? He wasn't found there until the next day."

Matthew nodded. "I moved him. Made it look like I was helping a drunk friend to his room, so anyone watching the cameras wouldn't catch on."

"And who had the brilliant idea of setting up Jeff Coleman?"

Matthew actually looked embarrassed. "Never liked the guy," he admitted.

Well, who did? Except for Sylvia, of course. But that wasn't a reason to frame a guy for murder. Two murders.

"I knew about that client of his," Matthew continued. "And I knew he'd been in town. Kelly told me. She'd inked him, too. It was easy to arrange." He looked apologetically at Simon. "I used Simon's phone."

"So you set Jeff up to be in that room, but instead of Jeff, *I* ended up there," I mulled out loud before having another thought. I looked at Elise. "Why didn't you just have Kelly do your devotion ink in the first place, instead of coming here?"

Elise gave Matthew a small smile before answering. "I told you; I wanted to surprise him. If I had Kelly do it, he'd know. But someone had seen me here, and then the cops were all over the place, and I couldn't come back."

Seemed reasonable. But one thing didn't. "Why did you kidnap me today? Why didn't you just tell me you were with Elise?" I asked Matthew.

"I was going to try to scare you into telling me where the diamond was."

He'd scared me, all right, but he hadn't had a chance for negotiations after I jumped out of the car.

"Who left me that drawing on my car?"

Elise and Matthew exchanged a look, both of them shrugging.

"You were sticking your nose in where you shouldn't." Chip, the peanut gallery, had spoken.

"Did Matt Powell show you that sketch I did for Elise?" I asked.

Chip made a face. "He wanted to prove to me that he wasn't her lover. He showed it to me—out of loyalty, he said. I didn't believe him. I mean, it said Matthew. What did he expect?"

Matt Powell had been playing all angles, it seemed. He knew about Kelly and her pregnancy, he knew about Elise and Matthew, he knew about Jeff Coleman. But what he'd known ended up being his own death sentence.

Matthew was still holding on to Chip's shoulder. Chip was slumped over now, sort of like a rag doll, his eyes glazed and unblinking. Without waiting for an answer, I went into the staff room and found a roll of paper towels and brought it out, wadding some up and pressing them to Chip's wound. He blinked at me a couple times.

"Don't thank me or anything," I said curtly, then looked at Matthew. "Take him to the couch and sit him down."

Simon was still holding Elise, and gently I took her arm, nodding at Simon, who released her. I brought her into my room, shutting the door and sitting her in my chair, reclining it.

"What are you doing?" she asked through her tears.

I had to do something about the tat. It wasn't done right, and she'd have trouble with it if I didn't take care of it. I pulled on a pair of latex gloves and took a baby wipe, moving it across the ink. The blood smeared over her skin.

"I'm going to fix this up for you," I said. "It'll get infected if I don't."

She nodded and closed her eyes. "I saw him kill her," she said softly.

My hand froze a second before I resumed wiping down the tat. "Is that why your driver's license was found in the car? You were with her?" The tattoo was clean now, the outline a little rough. I slid a clean needle into my machine and dipped it in red ink.

She tensed when she heard the machine start.

"It's okay, Elise. Trust me."

She relaxed a little. "I was with her. Kelly was taking me to the airport. I was going to go home, tell everyone I wasn't going to marry Chip, and that would be the end of it. I would go back and meet Matthew after I took care of everything." She paused and gave me a sad smile. "Kelly wasn't a very nice person. She told Chip we were going to be there. He showed up, but she didn't realize that he would choose me over her, even though she was pregnant.

"When Chip told her he still wanted to marry me, she pulled a gun on him. He got it away from her, and I tried to stop him. I fell and cut myself. He threw me into the backseat, told me to stay there, but I didn't. I heard the shot as I was running away. I called nine-one-one after I called Matthew to come get me."

I filled in the heart with the red ink and drew a black arrow through it, turning the start of the "C" into feathers.

I heard a knock at the door, and Simon Chase stuck his head inside. For a second he didn't say anything, just looked at my handiwork.

"It looks good," he said. "Your brother's here."

That was fast.

"We'll be out in a few minutes," I said, and he closed the door after himself.

"Why didn't you just come back for the diamond?" I asked Elise as I touched up the scraggly lines of the heart. "Why did Matthew have to break in?"

"He looked in the orchid first, but it wasn't there. He thought you'd found it and put it somewhere else."

It was the wrong orchid.

"He felt bad about hitting your friend."

I wasn't sure that was going to really comfort Ace, knowing Matthew "felt bad."

"Why didn't you just ask me for it?"

"We knew everyone thought Matt Powell was my lover. We didn't want anyone to suspect about Matthew. We were going to just disappear."

"With a two-million-dollar diamond," I said flatly, wiping the tat and assessing the work. It wasn't the best I'd ever done, but it was a satisfactory cover-up. I took a hand mirror off the shelf and handed it to Elise, who studied the heart.

She smiled shyly. "It's nice," she said, handing me back the mirror. "But I really did want Matthew's name."

I could remind her that she'd been engaged to Simon Chase once. That she'd been engaged to Chip. That love sometimes doesn't last, but the devotion ink would.

I just nodded, wrapped the tat in Saran Wrap, and told her how to take care of it. She adjusted her bra and buttoned up the blouse as well as she could. The corner of the Saran Wrap peeked out from behind it.

Tim hadn't waited for me. A paramedic was dressing Chip's wound as Tim read him his rights. Matthew saw Elise and drew her to him, his big arms surrounding her. Simon Chase raised his eyebrows at me, and I nodded to indicate everything was all right.

But it wasn't all right. Tim saw me, and looked up at Matthew.

"This was the guy who kidnapped you today, right?"

Description fit to a T. I thought about Jeff's warning about Matthew, how he was "bad news." So maybe he was trying to turn over a new leaf or something with Elise, but he still had a long way to go in the social skills area. He obviously hadn't had a Sister Mary Eucharista to keep him in line.

"He also fits Ace's description of the guy who broke in here," Tim said, nodding at the uniformed cop, who now gripped Matthew's arm, pulling it to his back, taking out his handcuffs.

For a nanosecond, I felt a little bad, thinking about Elise. But he did trash my place; he did kidnap me. He'd been following me around, scaring me for the last few days.

"You're not arresting him, are you?" Elise's eyes were

wide as she confronted Tim. She swung around to me. "Tell him to stop. You know he didn't mean it."

"It's okay." Matthew's voice resonated through the room as he smiled sadly at Elise. He looked a little too comfortable in those cuffs. Obviously, he'd been here before. I had about as much confidence that this relationship would work as I did in that devotion tat. Sure, he looked at her with some softness in his eyes, but I couldn't forget that the diamond was what he was after all along. Two million dollars was nothing to sneeze at.

"Don't worry. Simon'll take care of you until I get out," Matthew was saying.

Oh, yeah, Simon. "Why were you helping them?" I asked him.

"Because I still care about Elise and want her to be happy." Simon cocked his head at Chip. "And because I couldn't stand what he'd done to her. He was making dates with cocktail waitresses even while she was considered missing."

I thought about Robbin, the woman in the restroom at Versailles who'd fixed my makeup. So her date was with Chip, not with Simon. I'd jumped to the wrong conclusion.

"And I found out that Chip was the one who lured you to my office with that text message. Your number was queued in. He's also the one who locked you in. He wanted his father to find you there," Simon said.

I mulled that over for a second. It made me less sorry I'd skewered Chip's shoulder. But I had another question for Simon Chase.

"I overheard Manning asking you to take care of something, saying you could 'let him come back' after 'it all died down.' What was that all about?"

Simon shrugged. "One of our employees is facing a deportation issue, despite our sponsorship. We agreed to continue to help him get his visa, but he has to go home for a short while. That's all."

Made sense, now that he explained it.

"You might want to just ask for what you want the next time," I told Matthew, then turned back to Simon. "And you, too. I mean, you just made that date with me so you'd get the diamond for them."

A twinkle flashed in his eye. "That's not the only reason." And his gaze made me catch my breath.

Chapter 62

"**Y**ou could've called and told us what was going on," Bitsy scolded.

"I thought you'd had enough excitement yesterday," I said. I'd just gotten back from bringing Ace home from the hospital. Somehow he'd managed to bribe a nurse into giving him his own private oxygen tank. Never underestimate the power of a handsome face. Even after its nose gets crushed.

Joel handed me a doughnut and a cup of coffee. "Our lives are boring," he teased. "We can always use a little more excitement."

"Do you think Elise really loves him?" Bitsy asked. "I mean, that guy's definitely not in her league."

"I think she *thinks* she does," I said. "She finds out her fiancé is having a baby with another woman, a guy who's so totally not what her family would want for her pays attention, offers her a shoulder—and a lot more than that—and she thinks she's in love. It's happened before."

"What about the blood you saw on Chip's shirt?" Bitsy asked.

"It was red ink."

"Tattoo ink?" Joel asked.

"No, from a pen." The ink splatter made me think of something else. I showed them my leg, where Chip inadvertently had drawn the black line. "What should I do here?" I asked Joel. "I've got to cover it up somehow."

Joel studied the short line, nodding. "How about a quote? Isn't *Macbeth* about murder? 'Out, out damned spot,' or something like that?"

I shook my head, but couldn't help smiling. "Oh, by the way, we need to talk about Charlotte Sampson. How she wants to train here. I almost forgot all about her."

"She's coming in day after tomorrow for an interview," Bitsy said.

"Sounds a little formal," I said, looking at Joel. "What do you think?"

He shrugged. "She's a nice kid. Can she draw?"

Bitsy was one step ahead of him, pulling some sketches out of a file folder. "She dropped these off."

They were good. Really good. Bold use of lines and color, geometric shapes, butterflies, flowers, even a portrait. She must have taken some art classes in between all that math. Seemed like a no-brainer to me, and from the way Joel was nodding, it could be unanimous.

I sipped my coffee and heard the front door open. I stepped out into the hall. Jeff Coleman stood awkwardly next to the front desk, staring at Ace's paintings. He grinned when he saw me.

"So, Kavanaugh, this is your shop."

He'd never been here before.

"That's right," I said.

He walked toward me, sticking his head into a couple of the rooms. "Swanky. Just like I expected. No self-respecting tattooist works like this."

"Want some ink as a souvenir?" I teased.

He grinned. "I just wanted to thank you for talking to your brother, clearing everything up."

"Well, it all sort of cleared itself up," I said. "I'm sorry about Kelly."

His face softened for a second. "Thanks, Kavanaugh." He spotted the box of doughnuts and Bitsy and Joel in the staff room. "Doughnuts? Really? I don't think I can deal with this. It's way too clean-cut for me." He started backing up. "Oh, by the way, my mother wants you to come by. Said something about a date with Napoleon." He frowned. "Sometimes I just can't figure out what she's talking about anymore, but she swears you know what it means."

I laughed. "Yeah, I do. And tell her I'll call her next week. But she's going to have to come here."

"She won't like that. And you won't be able to change her mind."

Maybe not. But maybe if I promised her a ride in a gondola she might.

Jeff gave me a little punch on the arm. "It's been real. Later, Kavanaugh."

I watched through the glass doors as he walked along the canal and across the footbridge and out of sight.

Napoleon. Now that would be a nice leg tat.

Read on for an excerpt
from Karen E. Olson's next
Tattoo Shop Mystery,

Pretty in Ink

Coming from Obsidian in April 2010.

If your name is Britney Brassieres, going down in a tsunami of champagne might seem only fitting.

One minute she was belting out "Oops! . . . I Did It Again," the next she was on the floor, her arms flailing as the Moët—not the really expensive kind, but that White Star kind you can get at a discount if you look hard enough—showered her.

I know it was Moët because I saw the guy with the bottle. As Britney was singing, he'd come up to the edge of the stage near my table, shook the bottle, and popped the cork. The sound was as loud as a gunshot as the cork went airborne and slammed right into Britney's chest.

Bull's-eye.

It wasn't an accident, either. He'd aimed at her.

I jumped up on a gut reflex and impulsively shouted at the guy. "Hey!"

After successfully hitting his target, he turned the bottle on me—confirming that he'd actually heard me—and everyone else in my vicinity.

Unfortunately it still had some oomph left, and liquid splashed across my face, getting into my eyes and dripping down my face onto my chest. I tried to blink, but it hurt, so I kept my eyes closed, hearing the pandemonium around me: chairs scraping as people scrabbled to their feet, glass shattering. The vibration moved through my legs as the floor shook with the weight, the hurry to escape. I wanted to shout out that it was just champagne, but that cork explosion freaked everyone out, and when they saw Britney fall, they figured the worst.

Bodies shoved past me, jostling me, and I struggled to keep my balance, holding out my arms like a trapeze walker and hitting someone who grunted but didn't stop.

"Joel?" I shouted above the din. "Joel?"

An arm snaked around my waist. "I'm here, Brett. You okay?" His voice was soothing as his big belly pressed into my side, and for a second I relaxed before tensing up again.

"Yeah, just got some champagne in my eyes. Is Britney okay?" I asked, trying to open my eyes, but they still stung and I shut them again.

"She's moving," Joel said. "I think she's okay. What happened?"

"Guy with a champagne bottle. Where'd he go?" This time I forced my eyes open, blinking quickly a few times, clearing the fog. I scanned the dimly lit nightclub. There had been about a hundred people here for the show. Most of them were now pushing one another toward the door; someone was screaming; someone else was wailing.

The scene on the stage looked like something from a Shakespearean tragedy: Britney, her blue and white schoolgirl outfit complementing her long blond tresses, was splayed across the floor as her fellow performers hovered over her, clucking like the mother hens they were. I spotted Charlotte with them, kneeling and stroking Britney's forehead. Britney's lips were moving, and her eyes were open.

MissTique, who ran all the shows here at Chez Tango, flailed her arms as she teetered on six-inch clear plastic stilettos on the edge of the stage—not to stop herself from falling, but because she was trying to calm everyone down. I could hear her shouting, "All right," "Everything's fine," and "Get me a cocktail." The last was said to a young man with a remarkable physique who'd been dancing shirtless behind Britney before the champagne attack.

"Where's Bitsy?" I had to lean in toward Joel so he'd hear me as we took a couple of steps toward the stage.

Bitsy is a little person, and it is easy to lose her in a crowd.

Or bump into her.

"Watch it!" I heard her say, and looked down to see her rubbing her arm where I'd collided with her.

I was about to apologize when it grew darker, sort of like a solar eclipse. But instead of the electricity going out, it was merely Miranda Rites, blocking the light behind her. She looked like someone had dumped a bottle of Pepto-Bismol on her: a vision in pink sequins and a high bouffant of pink-accented orange hair, the multicolored butterfly ink I'd given her a few weeks ago stretched between her shoulders above her ample bosom. It was fake, of course. The bosom, I mean, not the tat.

"She's okay, right?" I asked Miranda, shouting, cocking my head toward the stage.

The dark concrete walls didn't swallow the din; it just bounced off them into my ears with a sort of echo effect.

"I think she's in shock." To compensate for the noise, Miranda's voice had reverted back to its husky tenor, giving her that Sybil split-personality thing: Is she a woman? Is she a man? Can she be both? "I saw it from backstage."

"Did you call an ambulance?"

"They're on their way. Cops, too."

I thought about my brother, Detective Tim Kavanaugh. I wondered if he'd show up. He might be a little surprised to find me here at Chez Tango.

It was opening night of MissTique's new Nylons and Tattoos show, featuring Britney, Miranda, Lola LaTuche, and Marva Luss.

Drag queens.

They'd chosen The Painted Lady, my tattoo shop, as the one they'd entrusted with designing their new ink because

Charlotte Sampson, our trainee, knew Britney, who was Trevor McKay when he wasn't dolled up. In Charlotte's other life as an accountant, she'd done Trevor's taxes the past couple of years. When Trevor found out Charlotte had ditched her former career choice to be a tattoo artist, he said it must be karma.

Because of our contribution to the show, Charlotte, my shop manager Bitsy Hendricks, my friend and tattooist Joel Sloane, and I had been given the VIP treatment: free drinks, a great table, a backstage tour. The only one in our shop who had chosen not to come was Ace van Nes, who had issues with the idea of a drag show—but he had issues with a lot of things. I'd been a little leery at first, too, for different reasons than Ace, but I easily caved to peer pressure when Charlotte, Bitsy, and Joel said we just *had* to be there.

So that's how we ended up covered in champagne, the music blasting, a strobe light cutting across Britney's body as she lay sprawled on the stage, her red platform heels pointing toward the ceiling and looking oddly like the Wicked Witch of the West's just after the house fell on her.

My eyes were still smarting from the bubbly, and I closed them again for a second. When I did, my memory kicked back to the guy who'd sprayed me. I hadn't seen his face. The strobe had created a cutout image, his outline flashing light, then dark too fast for me to remember many details, especially with the oversized hooded sweatshirt and baggy jeans that hung precariously from his hips with bunched-up boxers protruding from the top, in the style of an urban kid.

But he'd had his sleeves pushed up to his elbows. Maybe he didn't want to get any of the Moët on himself. By doing that, however, he'd given me something I could share with my brother the detective. Something I would never miss.

He had a tattoo on the inside of his right forearm. A rather distinctive one.

It was a Queen of Hearts playing card.

Also Available from

Karen E. Olson

DEAD OF THE DAY

An Annie Seymour Mystery

A soggy April has hit New Haven,
Connecticut—along with an unidentified body in
the harbor. The strange fact that there were bee
stings on the body gives *New Haven Herald*
police reporter Annie Seymour an intriguing
excuse to put off her profile of the new police
chief—a piece that becomes a lot more
interesting when the subject is gunned down.

But this is only the beginning of a killer
exposé—because as she connects the dots
between the John Doe, the police chief, and the
city's struggling immigrant population, Annie's
drawing a line between herself and someone
who doesn't want her to learn the truth—
or live to report it...

**Available wherever books arc sold or at
penguin.com**

Also Available from

Karen E. Olson

SHOT GIRL

An Annie Seymour Mystery

New Haven police reporter Annie Seymour
has a talent for running into trouble. So it
should come as no surprise when her
co-worker's bachelorette party at a local
club quickly turns into a crime scene.
What is surprising is that the dead club
manager in the parking lot happens to be
Annie's ex-husband—and the bullet shells
around his body match the gun she has
in her car…

**Available wherever books are sold or at
penguin.com**

Penguin Group (USA) Online

What will you be reading tomorrow?

Tom Clancy, Patricia Cornwell, W.E.B. Griffin,
Nora Roberts, William Gibson, Robin Cook,
Brian Jacques, Catherine Coulter, Stephen King,
Dean Koontz, Ken Follett, Clive Cussler,
Eric Jerome Dickey, John Sandford,
Terry McMillan, Sue Monk Kidd, Amy Tan,
J. R. Ward, Laurell K. Hamilton…

You'll find them all at
penguin.com

*Read excerpts and newsletters,
find tour schedules and reading group guides,
and enter contests.*

Subscribe to Penguin Group (USA) newsletters
and get an exclusive inside look
at exciting new titles and the authors you love
long before everyone else does.

PENGUIN GROUP (USA)
us.penguingroup.com